Aruna Nambiar is a Bengaluru-based writer and editor who grew up in Mumbai, where she studied engineering and management. She started her career with an international bank before pursuing her passion for writing. She has been writing and editing for over a decade now. Her debut novel, *Mango Cheeks, Metal Teeth*, a tongue-in-cheek coming-of-age story and social satire set in small-town Kerala of the 1980s, was published in late 2013. *The Monsters Still Lurk* is her second novel.

She has also written for the coffee table book *Portrait: Kerala*, contributed short fiction and non-fiction pieces to the anthologies *Jest Like That*, *The Itinerant Indian*, *Curtains* and *Winners, Volume-1*, written articles for national newspapers and magazines, and edited non-fiction and fiction for a number of publishing houses.

THE MONSTERS STILL LURK

ARUNA NAMBIAR

RUPA

Published by
Rupa Publications India Pvt. Ltd 2019
7/16, Ansari Road, Daryaganj
New Delhi 110002

Sales centres:
Allahabad Bengaluru Chennai
Hyderabad Jaipur Kathmandu
Kolkata Mumbai

ISBN: 978-93-5333-513-7

First impression 2019

10 9 8 7 6 5 4 3 2 1

Printed at HT Media Ltd, Gr. Noida

To my parents,
who embody what it is to grow old gracefully,
and to Raghu,
with whom I hope to grow old disgracefully.

Contents

PART ONE: SHINING MORNING FACE

1. A Single Bolt of Cloth   3
2. The World's Cheapest Drug Peddler   13
3. Someone in Mind   22
4. Bookended by Disaster   35

PART TWO: LEAN AND SLIPPERED PANTALOON

5. Low-Priority File   51
6. Spectacles for Twelve Rupees   61
7. Gunfire at the Border   72
8. Paper Catching Fire   85
9. Out of the Box   100
10. Black Friday   119

PART THREE: TOWARDS CHILDISH TREBLE

11. Big Fat Monster   135
12. Three Score and Ten   151
13. All He Has   159
14. Bedlam   176
15. Milk of Human Kindness   185

PART FOUR: SANS EVERYTHING

16. Knife in the Wound   197

17. Lab Rat   208

18. Little Left Unsaid   224

19: Flotsam   244

Acknowledgements   251

Part One

. . . .

Shining Morning Face

A Single Bolt of Cloth

Memories. Creatures of whimsy they are; fickle, mercurial creatures, inclined towards intrigue and deception; coy and elusive when you try to pursue them, officious and intrusive when you want to hold them at bay. Sudha claims that her earliest memory is of having her finger caught in Mum's Usha sewing machine at the age of three—of the pain of the needle and the powder blue of the thread, and of Mum's face, tear-streaked, panic-stricken; the ride to the doctor and the one and a half days of maternal lenience thereafter. Govind maintains that he has no early memories at all. As for me, when I scratch at the surface of my first recollection, there are no fossils of childhood accidents or parental indulgence, no well-preserved relics of a particular incident or a favourite toy. Instead, a jumble of images floods my mind, of us meandering around the neighbourhood—in the crook of my father's arm, being led, jelly-footed, by my mother, jostling and racing and laughing with Sudha and Govind.

My parents were habitual walkers. Not the arm-pumping, regulated-breathing kind of walkers you see today, who stride with hands balled into fists, frowns on their faces and gazes fixed on an imaginary finishing tape. No, my parents were long and leisurely ramblers, who ambled immersed in conversation or in companionable silence, while the three of us ran ahead, always falling back at a bark from my father when we were in danger of disappearing out of sight. They paused frequently to look into shops or buy something from a street seller, and never, ever bothered with the paraphernalia of the modern walker. No track pants and T-shirts, no pedometer or Fitbit, not even a good pair of shoes.

We always set out in the evenings after we had finished our homework, after Dad had returned from office, had had his tea and snacks, and lain down, plank-straight on his back, for a fifteen-minute nap. This was in the nine-to-five era, you see, when you could do all this and still set out for an evening walk well before sundown. My mother would be draped in her sari, and she would never have thought to wear anything other than her sandals, completely impractical with their flimsy straps and two-inch kitten heels. My father would have changed from his office wear of shirt and pants and polished leather shoes to his casual wear of shirt and pants and polished leather sandals. The three of us—Govind, Sudha and I—would be in the clothes my mother had stitched for us, usually from a single bolt of cloth. When they were new, they were several sizes too large, so as to accommodate our future spurts of growth. For a very short period, they would fit just right, and finally, when our shorts were clutching our crotches and our shirts baring our midriffs, when Sudha's skirts were showing just a little too much thigh, my mother would buy another bolt of cloth, on sale from Binny's or Mafatlal's on Colaba Causeway, and the cycle would start once more. You would think that we would be embarrassed by our ill-fitting matching attire, but this was the lot of many of our generation, and mortification was a luxury we could not afford.

We followed one of two routes. The first was the longer of the two, and started from our home in Colaba and wound down past Paradise, the tiny restaurant that was ironically as popular

for its Scotch broth as it was for its dhansak[1] and sali murgh[2].
We passed by the lottery shop where Dad bought pink and blue
lottery tickets for years with great hope but no luck, and made
our way towards the Mahadeva temple where, many years later,
the idol of Ganesha would draw mass consternation and surging
crowds by 'drinking' milk. If it were a Tuesday or a Saturday,
Mum would stop to break coconuts for Lord Ganesha and Lord
Hanuman, and we would emerge with a slash of vermilion on our
foreheads and prasad folded into squares of newspaper—a handful
of coconut pieces and sweet orange-coloured boondi. We would
cross the road at the little Parsi shop that sold frankies plump
with chicken and mutton, and wafers thin and crisp and oily as
wafers are born to be; none of those perfectly round, preserved
monstrosities of today that taste like cardboard. We walked down
Colaba Causeway, past Cusrow Baug, the Parsi colony of low-rise
buildings and wide avenues, and at Electric House we followed
the shaded avenue that curved past a colony of schools and the
Cooperage grounds, and meandered past the miniature traffic
lights and pedestrian crossings of the Children's Traffic Park, to
the Bandstand, where once military bands used to play. In the lot
outside the gardens of the Bandstand, aged horses tottered around
with screaming little children on their backs—Sudha had insisted
on a ride once, and had been assigned an uncharacteristically
energetic horse that had cantered around at a lively pace. Sudha
had dismounted white-faced but defiantly dry-eyed, and there had
ended any equestrian ambitions she might have nursed.

From the Bandstand, we would amble towards Marine Drive,
occasionally cutting short our walk at the park in front of the

---

[1] A Parsi dish of meat, rice, dal and vegetables
[2] A Parsi chicken dish

imposing arc-shaped LIC building—playing in the sandpit, on the swings and slides, or, when we were older, sitting slumped and resentful on one of the stone benches, wishing we were back home instead.

But on most days, we carried on towards Marine Drive. At the Aarey Milk kiosk near the Air India building, I would invariably feel faint and thirsty. Although I was far too scared of my mother's brand of discipline to insist that I needed an Energee, that iconic brand of Aarey flavoured milk, to revive, as a child I was sufficiently skinny and pathetic for my parents to buy me—and Sudha and Govind—a bottle of flavoured milk each. We would stand at the stall, slurping our flavoured milk through striped straws, surrounded by Gujju aunties in their synthetic saris and straggling office-goers from Nariman Point, the wind from the ocean skirting past the Air India building and swirling around us, messing up our hair and playing flirtatiously with hemlines.

Stomachs full and 'energee' restored, we would continue towards Marine Drive. Sometimes we would cut across past the foyer of the Oberoi Towers, pausing to gape at the revolving glass doors, the tall turbaned doorman, the fleet of imported cars and the perfumed white men and women who flitted in and out. But most of the time we wanted to scoot past the Air India building and crane our necks to see what the Maharajah had to say that month. The Maharajah was, of course, Air India's mascot, who always featured on their hoarding outside the building—a cute, dumpy, turbaned and moustached cartoon gent with shoes that curled up like cresting waves at the toes. Every now and then, the hoarding was changed, and it was always a thrill to see what witty slogan or topical observation the Maharajah had come up with this time—well, we thought it was witty at the time, anyway.

From the Air India building, we would dash across the road

to the Marine Drive promenade, taking care not to be run over by one of those plodding horse carriages that gave joy rides to sheepish-looking tourists along the waterfront. Once we were on the promenade, we were allowed to run ahead, past the vans (Hungry Dragon? Red Dragon? I cannot recall the names) that used to sell questionable Chinese food to fat ravenous children, past the NCPA, right up till the southern tip of Marine Drive, from where you could see the skyscrapers of Cuffe Parade across the bay.

In later years, when my father bought a car, a lumbersome second-hand Ambassador that my mother insisted on getting painted an arresting apple-green at a time when blacks and whites were the norm, we would drive to Marine Drive and take a longer walk along the seafront, up north towards Chowpatty, past the art deco buildings mottled with years of monsoon moisture, and couples canoodling along the sea wall. When I was older and came here with my college friends, we would stroll on to Chowpatty to risk our lives having pani puri and kulfi on the beach. (You food adventurers who like to brag about eating fugu, or whatever that fat-faced Japanese fish is: Chowpatty chaat, made by a snot-nosed vendor with filthy nails and served in metal plates washed in a bucket of dirty water—go on, I dare you to eat that.) But when we were young, we would cut short our walk at Natraj hotel and on our return, Sudha and I would climb on to the bonnet of the car and sit there bickering or arm-wrestling or playing Chinese bangles, while our parents walked towards the Cuffe Parade end and Govind skulked inside the car hoping that none of his friends would spot him in the apple-green Ambassador.

In the rains, the wind blowing in from the Arabian Sea would be so fierce that it would make us stagger backwards, and even the sturdiest of umbrellas would turn inside-out in a trice. Part of the fun of monsoon walks on Marine Drive was to dodge the tall waves that would leap over the sea wall from time to time and drench us. Despite this, some of the more macho of the roadside Romeos, and some of the more foolhardy of teenagers, would insist on walking or sitting on the sea wall or climbing down to the concrete tetrapods, and not a year would pass without news reports of somebody being washed out to sea.

The monsoons also brought out the bhutta sellers, who would stand grilling cobs of corn over coal. We would teeter on tiptoe peering at the blackening corn, the heat from the coals welcome against the cool breeze, our anticipation heightening as we watched the bhuttawallah fan the coals with a straw mat that made the embers and hot ash fly everywhere. By the time he had grilled the corn, taken half a lime, dipped it in a mixture of salt and chilli powder and smeared it over the corn, and handed the cob over to us in its husk, we would be ready to fall on it as though we had not eaten in days.

When I was older, I would resent the short walk from my bus stop to my office during the rains—the slush on the roads, the squelch of my ruined leather shoes, the unpleasant feeling of wet clothes drying painstakingly on my person in an air-conditioned office. But in childhood, the monsoon walks were my favourite— jumping into the rainbows of oil-slicked puddles, putting out my tongue to catch the taste of unsullied raindrops, wading with bated breath into a knee-deep puddle, hoping I wouldn't be sucked into an open manhole but also kind of hoping I would.

∽

If Marine Drive was flavoured milk and bhutta, the Gateway of India was multicoloured balloons at the end of a stick or string, and seeng-channa[3] served warm in paper cones. The Gateway of India walk was reserved for lazy evenings, or time-straitened ones. It was to be taken only in the presence of adults, for we had to pass the seedy hotels behind the Gateway, which were frequented by drug-addled hippies in the kind of unwashed ganjis[4] you wouldn't wear even at home, and disreputable Arabs in flowing robes and headgear who were on the lookout to do unspeakable things, so we were told, to luscious young boys and girls. As we grew older, we developed a scepticism towards such threats, just like we did towards Mum's ridiculous warnings to never be alone with the Fathers and Brothers of our school. But sure enough, when fourteen-year-old Govind had stridden ahead once, he had been propositioned by an unshaven blond gent from the doorway of a lodge, making him tear back to where he had left us behind. And when Sudha and her college friends had stopped for a soft drink at one of the dingy little cafés on Colaba Causeway, a group of handsome Middle Eastern men at the next table had leered at them and tried to pick up their tab. The girls had left hastily, not even waiting to collect the change for their bill, giggling and shrieking 'So cheap, ya!' as soon as they were safely out of earshot.

From Radio Club, where some of my classmates would go to swim and spend evenings eating golden-fried prawns and other such exotica, we would walk by the ocean towards the Gateway of India. This sliver of water is calmer than the one at Marine Drive, for it rests in a little inlet that curves into the mainland. Although it lacks some of the raw beauty of the unfettered Arabian Sea at Marine Drive, it is prettified by seagulls wheeling overhead

---

[3]Dry roasted peanuts and chickpeas
[4]Sleeveless vests

and boats bobbing in the water and the majestic Gateway at the end of the promenade. Sometimes a ship would anchor in the harbour—the QE2 docked here a couple of times. Despite such attractions, most of the people who leaned against the sea wall would have their backs turned to the water, spending their time gawking at the passers-by instead.

At the bend in the promenade, there was a break in the sea wall leading down to the rocks, where all the leering masses of Colaba seemed to congregate. Here, we—well, not Mum and Dad—would break out into a run to startle the flocks of pigeons pecking grains off the square ahead. They would take flight in a clatter of wings, *kata-kata-kata-kata*, and, mission accomplished, we would run pell-mell all the way to the Gateway, where we would wait, panting, for our parents to catch up. Occasionally we would wander up to gawp at the street seller who sailed tiny plastic boats in a basin of water, or to the man selling toy sunglasses in bright frames. When our parents caught up, we would circumambulate the Gateway, completely impervious to its history, its architecture, its discreet grandiosity, and stop at the steps to watch the boats take off for joy rides in the sea. Our pleas to be allowed to go on the boats would fall on deaf ears, but sometimes, just sometimes, Dad would shell out a coin for the telescope-man so that we could look up close at the boats and ships in the harbour, the mainland in the distance, and the tops of the enormous waste-gas flames belching from the refineries across the sea at Trombay.

Then we would pass through the Gateway, we siblings craning our necks and daring each other to stand open-mouthed below the pigeons nesting in the high recesses of the dome. When the gardens came up outside the Gateway, we would linger there for a while, in the company of stringy young men, their arms platonically around each others' shoulders, burkha-clad ladies with their broods, and the occasional couple sitting on the grass. Then we would cross the road to return home on the footpath outside the Taj, peering inquisitively into every doorway of the hotel as we did, getting glimpses of immaculately painted ladies stepping out of the lobby and florid American men buying medicines at the pharmacy; and at the gratings outside La Patisserie, the cake shop, warm air suffused with the heavenly aroma of baking would swirl up our legs—here, I suspect Sudha might have had some Marilyn-Monroe-in-*The-Seven-Year-Itch* delusions in her teenage years, although to look at her now, you wouldn't think she was ever given to such whimsy, even as a teen. Then we would take one of the lanes back to the Causeway, and thread our way past the stalls and shops and restaurants and tourists, occasionally stopping to buy a cheap belt or bag.

Soon enough, when jogging became a fad, and men in shorts and sweatbands, and Walkman-toting girls in leggings became a common sight, my parents continued to saunter along in their usual leisurely fashion. Older now, we often had to be coaxed out of our indolence, our teenage sulks and our adolescent reluctance to be seen with our parents, before we would agree to walk with them. Later still, we siblings hopped into cars and taxis to bridge a short distance, to outrun time, to avoid sweat and exertion. But my parents continued to walk everywhere—in hot summer weather, sweat pasting my father's shirt on to his back, wetting my mother's elegant sideburn into a curl around her cheek; in the monsoon, wearing plastic slippers and carrying useless umbrellas that barely kept their heads dry; to finish errands; occasionally for their health; sometimes for recreation; but often out of sheer routine, seeking paths and bylanes and the road well trodden. It seems fitting, then, that they both died while out on a walk—my father on his way to the electricity office to pay a bill, my mother while having her evening constitutional in our very own garden.

2

The World's Cheapest Drug Peddler

It is difficult to imagine your parents as ever having been young, although dog-eared albums of black-and-white studio portraits might suggest otherwise. Those were the days when every roll of film was treated with the utmost respect and every picture taken only after a great deal of forethought and planning—it was not unusual for a roll of thirty-odd photographs to last an entire summer vacation. There were no candid photographs, no question of being captured in anything other than your very best clothes and make-up. Here is a photograph of a young boy in long flapping shorts worn almost at the chest, standing ruler-straight in front of a velvet curtain with a doleful expression on his face. There is a skinny girl with knobbly knees in a shapeless dress, plaits slung across the back of her head and tied with satin bows, hand resting artfully on a table dressed with a vase of flowers. Here is one of Dad on his graduation, thin as a strand of hair, in thick-framed spectacles and a David Niven moustache. There is Mum in her first sari, copious hair tied back into a luxuriant bun, eyes lined at a rakish slant beyond the eyelids to make them seem doe-like. Them together—Dad suited and bow-tied like some old-time crooner, Mum bejewelled and beflowered, hair in a bouffant of epic proportions, on their wedding day. Then the less-formal photographs—Mum, windblown, her sari billowing around her on a beach, them on the balcony of our house or posing on the blue Rexine sofa which broke a couple of years later after I jumped on it in an extraordinary fit of boisterousness.

My parents grew up in villages not far from each other, in those rambling Kerala houses with high ceilings, infinite rooms and backyards with cows and poultry, with long-suffering retainers and parents who were somewhat distracted and sporadically affectionate. Their childhood stories seemed to be full of adventure—my father getting chased for several blocks by a neighbour's dog and having to jump into a pond to escape; my mother as a toddler falling asleep in the trough of hay for the cows; a maternal cousin getting vivid flashbacks of a previous life after a bad bout of typhoid; my father's sister almost falling from the roof of their house where she had climbed on a dare.

To us, in our tiny Bombay flat, their childhood seemed terribly glamorous, compared to our mundane one: school and homework and tuitions, half an hour of cricket in the open parking lot of our building which doubled as a play area for the children, an evening dose of *Chitrahaar* or *Phool Khile Hain Gulshan Gulshan* before dinner and bed. The height of adventure was to drink sugarcane juice from the stand on Colaba Causeway, which we had been told would give us typhoid, cholera and, strangely, malaria. Or to eat raw mangoes laced with chilli powder, salt and, according to one school rumour, drugs, from the hawker outside the school gate. (At 50 paise a pop, he might have won a Guinness record as the cheapest drug peddler in the history of the world.)

They met on a summery Sixties afternoon, surrounded by relatives from both families. As Mum tells it, she had her head bent throughout the rendezvous, although not out of coyness as my father insists, but to conceal the giggles welling up inside her at the sight of Dad's unfortunate sideburns which he was growing in a misguided attempt to be trendy. Since my grandparents were broad-minded people, my parents were allowed a fifteen-minute walk in the garden to talk, no doubt being watched all the time through chinks in the flowered curtains and from shadows against the wall. Here, my father insisted, Mum broke out into a high-pitched version of *Teri Pyari Pyari Surat Ko* to entice him. This would always elicit sniggers from us, at the very thought of Mum ever being girlish enough to do such a thing. At this, my mother would threaten to show us Dad's early love letters to her, a threat she used quite regularly when she felt our father had our ear, and Dad would immediately lapse into a thoughtful silence. We would look at his greying head, his veined hands, the hair growing from his nose, his steel-rimmed square glasses, his staid trousers and shirt, and our minds would boggle at the thought of him ever writing love letters, or being serenaded by a girl, even if the girl was Mum.

In any case, they married within a few months and quickly produced the three of us. There are no photographs of my pregnant mother, for it was considered to be something of a condition in those days and not to be talked about until well into the 'confinement'—it seems unthinkable now when expectant mothers think nothing of baring their swelling bellies in tight tank tops. But there are photographs of us babies in the signature pose of the time—on the belly, head raised towards the camera, goofy grin on the face, butt-naked but for a gold chain around the neck.

My mother, like most ladies of her time, immersed herself in marriage and motherhood. A few extra kilos settled around her slender frame and the plait of her girlhood gave way to a bun at the nape of her neck, secured by bobby pins and, during one regrettable period, kept neat in a hairnet. There was a false-hair phase as well, to make the bun look fuller, but she tired of it soon enough, and the coarse, squirrel-tailesque hairpiece found a starring role in our childhood games instead. Whoever was lucky enough to be playing the villain/Pran/Prem Chopra/ Gabbar would be given the hairpiece and some Scotch tape to fashion it into a handlebar moustache, or perhaps into the other hirsute feature deemed to be gravely villainous at the time—the male ponytail.

Mum took to domesticity with ease. She learnt to cook with speed and skill. She took a cooking class and mastered 'fancy' recipes like caramel custard and baked vegetables. She enrolled for stitching classes, bought the Usha sewing machine on which she produced blouses for herself and the matching clothes of our childhood. She tried to knit but never managed to finish the sweater she started, and looked on embroidery as the frivolous pastime of the idle. But she did hem skirts and sew in missing buttons, even repaired a collar or two by turning them inside out and reattaching them to the shirt. For, like all mothers of her time, she was a great economizer, exchanging newspapers and old bottles for cash and old saris for vessels, using old biscuit tins for storage and our beyond-repair clothes as rags, coaxing the last bits of toothpaste out of its tube by rolling it out with a glass bottle.

My father earned well enough to lead a comfortable middle-class life, but no more. He did, however, buy a tiny flat in South Bombay—something of a feat, even in those times. The building was called Dove's Nest, although Pig Sty might have been a more appropriate name. It was tucked in a dodgy little corner off Colaba market and to get to our gate we had to make our way past a lady selling onions, two vegetable stalls, a pile of garbage, a couple of mongrels and a chicken stall. When the wind blew a certain way, the smells from the chicken stall floated into the house, but really, after a while, we hardly noticed it at all. The ground floor of the building was occupied partly by a stationery store, where we bought all our notebooks, the brown paper and plastic to cover them, pens and pencils, colour pencils and paints, crayons and felt pens. The owner, Dineshbhai, always had a pencil behind his ear and kept his right thumbnail an inch long to riffle easily through his cash bundles. Because it was always beautifully manicured and sometimes even decorated with a coat of maroon nail polish, we nicknamed him Flo-Jo, after the runner of that era with the dreadful long nails.

When Dad had bought the flat, Dove's Nest had been the only building in the area and land had been cheap. But as the city had grown, the locality had also started developing, and the market area had grown around the building. Innumerable trips to the municipal office to complain about the garbage, the unauthorized stalls and the hygiene issues posed by the chicken stall had proved fruitless, no doubt because of the hands already greased by the vendors. So Dad resigned himself to either putting up or moving out.

Being of the 'finding the silver lining in every cloud' school of thought, Mum listed the many advantages of living in the area, usually to her sister, my aunt Vimala, who was of the 'put others down' denomination: maids available on tap (all one had to do was tell a vendor in the area and one of their wives or daughters would appear at the doorstep in a trice), the shortest grocery-shopping commute ever, good working-class, salt-of-the-earth-type neighbours who didn't mind if you borrowed a cup of dal and who would feed your children if you found yourself locked out and had to wait until your husband came home from work to be let in.

Nevertheless, all through our childhood, my parents scoured for flats to move to, and every time they would find something somewhat suitable, we would burst into tears en masse at the thought of leaving our familiar neighbourhood. Because we kids loved every inch of it—the fat flower lady who would give a marigold to Sudha every day as she came home from school, the vegetable vendor who practised his entertaining brand of English on us and never minded if an errant cricket ball landed among his brinjals, the stray dogs and cats who appeared at the gate at all hours of the day to be fed and warily petted.

We played cricket with tennis balls in the corridors of the building, inciting the spinster in Flat 4 whenever the ball bounced against her door. We learnt to cycle in the stingy little patch of concrete that separated our building from our compound wall and served as a parking lot-cum-play area. We lit phuljhadis[5] and chakras[6] on Diwali and set a curtain on fire once with a misguided rocket. On Holi, we joined the two other children, and the one overenthusiastic uncle in our building to self-consciously smear each other with gulal[7]. During Ganesh Chaturthi, all the vegetable vendors would pool in to buy a humongous idol of Ganesha with a face the colour of onions, and when it was time to immerse it, the fat flower lady and the English-practising vegetable vendor would dance lustily in front of the procession, with hip-shaking moves that really did not belong outside a cabaret.

But Gokulashtami was our favourite festival, because we could lurk on our balcony to hurl water balloons at unsuspecting passers-by, ducking low before they could look up furiously and

---

[5]Sparklers, a kind of hand-held firecracker
[6]Coiled firecrackers that rotate along the ground
[7]Coloured powder smeared on others on Holi

spot us. There would be two matkas[8] strung up within sight of our building and we would wait all day for the Govindas[9] to come to claim their prize. They were young, thin-limbed men bursting with machismo, strutting down the lane unmindful of, soliciting even, the buckets of water being rained down on them. We would hang over the balcony wall in excitement, our parents holding on to our clothes and limbs, as the Govindas scrambled over each other to form a four- or five-storey human pyramid. They would always fail a couple of times—otherwise, a poor spectacle it would be—and gasps and gleeful cheers would rend the air as the men tumbled down to the road. And then, on the third or fourth attempt, the pyramid would hold and the topmost Govinda would reach for the matka, break it with his hand to the cries of 'Govinda ala!'[10] and spray the curd and ghee and money on to the masses huddled below. Finally, he would haul himself on to the wire and drink the dregs of the matka's contents before releasing the rope and dropping, with full faith, into the waiting hands of his comrades—much as we prayed, the comrades never let him fall with a splat to the ground. Cirque du Soleil be damned, with all its choreographed precision, give me the colour and noise and chaos of Gokulashtami in Bombay any day.

Luckily for us, my father's budget, although increasing with time, always fell short of the escalating real estate prices, thwarting any real plans to move out. So we continued to live with the smells from the chicken stall, the mangy, potentially rabid dog

---

[8]Clay pots, which, during Gokulashtami, are filled with goodies and strung up at a height

[9]Men who enact the butter-stealing scene from Lord Krishna's life on Gokulashtami

[10]'Govinda (Lord Krishna) has come!', a customary chant on Gokulashtami

that roamed up and down the stairs of the building at dawn, the filthy toilet of the stationery stores on the ground floor. Dad's spare money was diverted to buy a few luxuries instead: a Racold oven which Mum would use all her life to bake her fancy cooking-class recipes in and a clothes dryer which was state of the art at the time but wobbled alarmingly during the spin cycle, emptied the wrung-out water through a rudimentary spout into a bucket and came to a stop only with the aid of a foot-pedal brake and Mum's steadying hands wrapped tightly around it so it wouldn't topple over in its dying moments.

It is difficult to explain to my children, with their tae kwon do classes and music lessons, their Xboxes and iPads, what it was like to grow up in that place, in that time. When I recount my childhood stories, they look at me pityingly, trying to decide whether my youth was one of plain deprivation or borderline abuse, and I find that, for a while, they roll their eyes a little less and hold back their sarcasm.

But it was the typical middle-class existence of the time: Dad, the breadwinner, Mum the housewife. The three of us, the archetypal middle-class kids, taking the bus to school in the mornings, coming home with bedraggled uniforms and stains on our shoes. We begged our mother to buy Forhans instead of Binaca so that we could collect the plastic animals that came with the toothpaste, drank Rasna in the summers and spent hours trying to figure out the Rubik's cube. Later, we rocked to Deep Purple and Dire Straits, and fell in love with Sadhana Srivastava on Doordarshan and Brooke Shields in *Blue Lagoon*. (Although, in Sudha's case, it was Kumar Gaurav in *Love Story* and Imran Khan in tight white pants.)

Let me say this: Our lives were far from uneventful, but whatever happened until then changed our lives only in ways we expected. Govind, who was always the achiever of the three of us, got into the prestigious IIT Bombay; Sudha got married, to a doctor no less, and quickly produced two children—twins, a boy and a girl, a feat of gynaecological symmetry that made her quite envied in the extended family; I, contrary to all expectations, managed to get an engineering seat without having to shell out a small fortune in capitation fees. Even when Govind sailed through IIT and got admission for further studies in a reputed university in the United States, it was certainly a milestone for the family but only in a way that was hoped for and cautiously expected. There was a touch of sadness, yes, a feeling of a chapter being closed, a new era dawning, but only in a circle-of-life kind of way. He left draped in a maroon velvet jacket that Mum and Dad had deemed appropriate for formal wear ('I stood outside a hotel and they thought I was a bell boy,' Govind would complain quietly to me later), and armed with a suitcase full of sweaters and thermal underwear, six-months' worth of murukku, mixture, chilli powder, turmeric powder and hand-ground garam masala, and an unused diary from 1978 in a brown plastic jacket filled with recipes of all his favourite dishes.

We were an ordinary family, with conventional lives. We were mostly happy, but always cautious of too much happiness. We were hardly religious, just pious enough to keep us on the straight and narrow. We bickered a little but would never have thought to be estranged. We feared illness and anticipated eventual death, but we expected life to follow a certain path, a particular schedule.

Until...

3

Someone in Mind

It was the summer of 1991. I was at the tail end of a Civil Engineering course that I had survived through a prodigious amount of bunking, big dollops of luck and friends who lent me their assignments to copy. Sudha was in Chennai, struggling with her four-year-old twins, Prakash and Preetha. And my mother was in a spring-cleaning, microplanning tizzy, in preparation for her long-lost son.

It had been two years since Govind had been able to come home, and as always, Mum had started planning the menu for the approaching fortnight the moment Govind had booked his tickets. All Govind's favourites would be made over his stay: dosas—which would be made soft, thick and limp as he liked them, like old blankets, despite my complaints that I wanted them crisp and thin; Alleppey fish curry, all tangy from the chunks of raw mango Mum chucked into it; Malabar chicken fry, laden with pepper and slowly fried over a low fire until the onions were jammy and coated the chicken like a second skin; palada[11], thick with milk and sugar; and badam halva, sickly sweet and marigold-hued with colouring, but delicious nonetheless. 'You only make nice things when Govind comes,' I complained often, mostly in the hope of winding her up, but usually she just brushed me off

---

[11]A type of sweet made with milk and bits of boiled rice flour

with an, 'Oh-ho! Poda[12]!'

Rubbing salt into the wound, she would evict me from my glorified bedroom, which was really not much more than an enclosed balcony too precious in Bombay to waste on plants or garden furniture—the glorified bedroom that I once shared with Govind—on to the sofa-cum-bed in the living room. The sheets would be changed and the flat pillow that Govind favoured over the overstuffed ones that I used would be pulled out from the storage under the sofa-cum-bed.

I was long-suffering but ultimately cooperative. My mother always denied it when we levelled this accusation at her, but in our minds, there was no doubt that Govind was her favourite child. This is not to say that she gave Sudha or me any less of herself. But Govind was mild-mannered, diligent, willing to heed parental advice, and never likely to create a ripple on the surface of our well-ordered lives—what more could a parent ask for? Sudha, on the other hand, could be high-strung and resentful. And I? I was far too laid-back, not ambitious in any way, too inclined to laugh off troubles and always in danger of stepping off the beaten path.

There are few things more treacherous in a middle-class family than stepping off the beaten path.

Govind, on the other hand, had achieved everything that my parents had wished for him (but never forced upon him, Mum was quick to point out): the engineering degree from IIT, the MS and PhD from the States (which he had completed in record time), the teaching and research job he had just landed at MIT in a new-fangled field called Nanotechnology that Mum didn't quite understand but paid quite well, she had learnt.

---

[12]Malayalam word meaning 'get lost, boy!'

There was one last wish Mum harboured for him. 'It is a parent's duty,' she said. And everyone knew that all she had to do was suggest it to Govind and he would comply.

The marriage proposals had flowed in, especially once Mum had let it be known that Govind's employer had recently sponsored his application for a green card. Although Mum secretly wished that Govind would return to India sooner or later, she couldn't help but be proud of the fact that he had been sponsored for permanent resident status in the States within a year of being confirmed at his new job. 'Most employers defer the sponsorship of the green card for many years,' she boasted to Vimala Aunty, who looked as though she had just bit into a lemon. 'But for Govind, they applied almost immediately. Under the "persons with advanced degrees" category.'

After sifting through the proposals Mum deemed mediocre (all coincidentally suggested by Dear Aunt Vimala) my parents shortlisted four: a couple of highly qualified engineers like Govind, both capable of earning as well as he did, a girl who had just completed her BSc in what Mum referred to as 'something called Biotech', which she had verified was a sought-after field in the States, and a BCom graduate, very pretty, who came recommended by one of our relatives—Govind would find her underqualified, Mum said, but her lineage could not be ignored. Of course, the horoscopes had already been scrutinized by the astrologer and only those that matched perfectly with his had even been considered.

Govind had simpered when my mother had broached the subject with him, at the top of her voice over the static during the fortnightly call across continents. Mum and Dad had decided to wait until Govind came home to broach the topic of proposals, but with her usual mix of impatience and eagerness, Mum had blurted out the details to Govind over the phone. Govind had giggled self-consciously but been non-committal, and for Mum, this was further proof of his perfection. 'Poor thing, couldn't even talk to a girl during his college days,' she said.

But things can change in an instant. If my mother had a mantra, this was it. It was bandied around often, to console during bad times, to caution against arrogance in good. She had voiced it darkly when Vimala Aunty's second son had lost the job his parents had been boasting about; she had intoned it motivationally when Sudha's husband Ramu was going through a difficult phase at work.

And yet, she had not been prepared when everything changed.

It was a sweltering afternoon in May when my uncle Shivan, Mum's younger brother, called and broke the news, hesitantly, after cautioning Mum not to overreact. I remember a monosyllabic conversation—Mum agape and speechless, Dad and I exchanging worried looks at her open-mouthed astonishment. The unthinkable had happened: Govind 'had someone in mind'. He was bringing her over with him. I remember my mother laughing uncertainly at this unlikely scenario—Govind was too shy, too proper, too immersed in his work to have anything other than nanotechnology on his mind, let alone 'someone'.

Shivan Mama continued in a nervous torrent. Govind, too embarrassed to tell my parents directly, had routed the news through him and asked him to prepare the ground, smoothen the ruffled feathers. This was not entirely surprising, because Shivan Mama was the resident 'cool uncle'. He had never married and had left an office job a couple of decades ago to open a small music store in a corner of Calcutta. He made very little money, but knew his Wagner from his Vivaldi, his Chaurasia from his

Subbalakshmi, his Led Zep from his Scorpions, and it was fabled that a lesser Beatle had once visited his store. He could always be counted on to give us parental ammunition by feeding us stories about Mum failing at Maths in Standard V or Dad fainting at seeing the dentist's drill, and he always took our side when Dad yelled at us or Mum admonished us for trying to steal a sip from his whisky.

Nevertheless, Mum was not pleased that it was Shivan Mama who was breaking the news to her, but before she could fully develop her sense of outrage at Govind's treachery, or work through her bafflement at shy, awkward Govind 'having someone in mind', Shivan Mama had continued, 'Don't go completely crazy, Latha, but she's an American girl.'

Mum listened on with a dazed look—later she said that she supposed that's how a person felt when they were hit on the head with a frying pan. Finally, she let out a strangled 'I'll call you back' and turned to us to pour out the terrible details: Her name was Maggie, she worked in the university where Govind taught and she was two years older than Govind!

'Maggi? Like the noodles?' asked my father. 'What kind of name is that?' And my mother frothed like a white-water rapid.

'Maggie, with an "e",' she snapped, 'It's short for Margaret.'

What did her name matter? She was not Hindu, not even Indian, but American! And leave alone an engineer, she wasn't even a post-graduate. She worked in the university cafeteria!

'She's a lunch lady? Like Miss Beazly?' I asked tactlessly, and fell about laughing.

'Heh? Who is Miss Beastly?' asked Dad, wearing that slightly mystified look which would only deepen over the years.

'Not Beastly, Dad, Beazly!' I clarified. 'She's that stubbly-faced lunch lady with the hairnet in the *Archie* comics.'

I could have sworn my father's lips twitched, but he took one look at Mum's livid face and murmured, 'This is not the time to joke, Vivek—go and study.'

So off I went to pore over my books for my Drawing exam the next day, while they paced around discussing the unexpected turn of events. Mum kept making sorties to the fridge to drink glasses of water, a sure sign that she was distressed. Was Maggie Catholic or Protestant? Neither of them really knew the difference. Would she convert? What about the grandchildren that would come along? What faith would they be brought up in? Would she look after Govind the way an Indian girl would? Would she make him the food he wanted? Would Govind ever return to India? And—horror—had they been living together?

Dad pitched back and forth on the rocking chair, nodding absently to all of Mum's worries and adding a few of his own: Would Govind be able to maintain a foreign woman—they with their frequent hair treatments and manicures and pedicures, their hard drinking and visits to discos? Had Govind thought about the alimony that there was a good chance he would inevitably have to shell out?

They were still agonizing when I packed up my books and retired to bed, after reminding them to wake me at 5 a.m. sharp so that I could fit in a last-minute swot before my Drawing exam. If you are imagining Drawing to be one of those useless electives that aim to hone your creativity and make you a more well-rounded person, a course with plastic palettes and colourful paints, you couldn't be further from the truth. For this was Engineering Drawing, that branch of Civil Engineering in which you had to design structural elements and then draw them in precise detail—every steel reinforcement had to be marked out, each step on every staircase carefully reproduced to scale. It was the very last examination of my engineering course—at least, I hoped so, because I was woefully underprepared. For four years, I had been getting by Drawing assignments by copying from the class topper, who, although a unidimensional mugpot, was also a sucker for approval and therefore happy to share his assignments with the rest of his classmates. My basics were shaky to start with and poorly revised that year, even more so than usual, given the diversions of the GRE and GMAT exams, in both of which I had done poorly, earning not a single scholarship for further studies abroad. Add to this the anxiety of campus recruitments, during which I had managed to secure only a mediocre and poorly paid job on the very last day of placements, a job that was likely to send me to remote parts of the country to supervise roadworks and inspect construction material, tasks I was absolutely unequipped to do. Given these distractions, I was quite certain I would fail.

So I slept fitfully and dreamt that I had studied for the wrong exam. I woke up sweating and disoriented, stumbling along that bridge between sleep and wakefulness for a while, before the mists of drowsiness lifted. I rolled on to my back. Light was streaming in through the curtained windows of my glorified bedroom. It is at least 7.30 a.m., I thought in panic, judging from the brightness of the sunlight. I was about to bolt up, ready to berate Mum for not waking me up early as instructed. But in some corner of my mind, a niggling voice insisted that it was too quiet to be 7.30— there was not a honk of a car from the road outside, no sound of moving traffic, no pressure cookers hissing, no *Suprabhatam* wafting from Flat 6, no Shrill Woman calling to her husband and kids from the apartment opposite ours, and no deafening rattle of the Sumeet mixer as Mum ground the chutney for our morning idlis and dosas.

I remained in bed, confused, contemplating the ceiling fan

whirring above. Finally, I stirred and made to get up, but a hand on my shoulder restrained me.

It was Mum, and despite my confusion, I noticed that she was without her usual morning air of impatience as she tried to rouse the house and get the cooking done before the maid stormed in to clean.

'What time is it?' I asked.

'Quarter to eight,' she replied.

'What?' I shot up. 'Why didn't you wake me up? I told you so many times to...' I wrestled a bit with the sheets.

'There will be no exam today,' she said quietly. 'It's been postponed for two weeks.'

'What? Why?'

'Rajiv Gandhi has been assassinated. We heard the news soon after you went to bed.'

I gaped. It was unthinkable. And yet, it had happened before, not very long ago. The memories of Indira Gandhi's assassination—shot dead by her bodyguards as she walked in her garden—resurfaced. I had been just a child then, but I remembered the same deathly silence, the same sombre faces, the same feeling of incredulity. It couldn't be; just yesterday, Mum and Dad had been arguing about whether Rajiv Gandhi deserved to come back to power—he was campaigning furiously for the upcoming election, and he had anti-incumbency going for him this time. Dad had carped about the Bofors deal but failed to make a dent against my mother's staunch defence of Rajiv, based mainly, it appeared, on his pink-faced handsomeness, his starched white kurta-pyjamas and stylish bandhgalas, his impossibly sweet smile, his polished manners, his stylish Italian wife and his thoroughbred lineage. For Mum was a patsy for all these things: good looks, good taste, good manners and good family.

In fact, a few years before, when Sonia and Rajiv had been passing through Colaba, Mum had dragged Dad to the Causeway to watch them go by. As the car had rolled by, she had cheered and waved vigorously, and even Dad had got excited enough to raise his hand in a self-conscious wave. 'Sonia looked right at me!' swore Mum. 'Must be my Chanderi sari—she has an eye for a good sari, that Italian woman.' Sometimes Mum could be quite deluded.

I scrambled out of bed to find out the details. Dad was hogging the newspaper but the television was on and the news was gory. That woman who was said to have done it—'such an evil thing, a cussed Surpanakha[13],' said Mum—was also dead. The final images showed her smiling, palms together, then bending down as if to touch Rajiv's feet. He, so unsuspecting, smiling back at her. And then, the aftermath. His body in several pieces, they said. Blasted to smithereens. Body parts everywhere. On the news, former minister P. Chidambaram, so stern usually, like an income tax officer grilling a defaulting businessman, cried like a child.

'Oh my god,' I said. And then I remembered that my exam had been postponed, giving me a reprieve from certain failure, a chance to prepare some more. 'But YAY!!!'

Mum watched, subdued and quiet. If it had been another day, Dad would have been glued to the TV, Mum analysing the terrible events with friends and family over the phone, pausing only to admire Prannoy Roy, who made her quite girlish with admiration. 'I don't like beards, usually, but he carries it off so well!' she would gush.

∽

---

[13]A demoness in Hindu mythology

It's remarkable what sleep can do, even a few fitful hours. Mum had regained her composure somewhat and lost the air of bewilderment she had displayed on getting the news. She had been taken by surprise, that's all, she said. Govind had never let on that he even spoke to girls, let alone 'had someone in mind'.

'I think I understand what happened. Govind is handsome,' she said, ignoring my snigger at this complete misapprehension. 'Qualified, eligible. It was only a matter of time before some girl found a way to break through his reserve, worm her way into his affections. He is far from home, obviously lonely. He has lost his head a bit, that's all. Who wouldn't? The meek boys are always the first to be seduced.'

I rolled my eyes at this, certain that if it had been me bringing an American girl home, she wouldn't have been quite so understanding.

Despite this, Mum declared, she would not call Govind; the fact that Govind had called Shivan Mama and not her to confide had rankled, and she had to show her disapproval. Silence was the best tool. Govind would be waiting nervously for her reaction, she expected.

But Govind didn't call and Mum's calm ebbed with every passing day, reaching a new low when Dear Aunt Vimala called from Hyderabad. 'Aiyye[14], Shivan told me! What is happening to this world? First Rajiv, now Govind and that girl,' she said, neatly encapsulating the level of doom she equated with the match.

Mum started to protest, but Vimala Aunty cut in, 'Are you telling me that you're alright with having a daughter-in-law who prays to Jesus and cleans her bottom with paper? You tell him to call me, I will din some sense into that silly boy.'

---

[14]A Malayalam expression of dismay

'Who is Vimala to din some sense into my son?' Mum said, crossly. It was she who would talk to him when he called. She had no doubt that he would listen to her and come around.

But Govind didn't call, nor did he answer calls from other members of the family—Shivan Mama, my grandmother— who braved ISD call rates to contribute their two-paisa to the situation. Mum hovered around the telephone, picking it up from time to time to see if it was still working, and as she watched repeat telecasts of Sonia Gandhi at the funeral, tearful behind her fashionable sunglasses, deflating against her pretty daughter during the rites, Mum looked as though she would follow suit.

Finally, she could wait no longer. She composed a letter, which she had Dad transcribe painstakingly on to an aerogramme. 'It must come from you,' she insisted. She emphasized how they understood Govind's wish to marry somebody of his own choice, but how they thought that perhaps he was not thinking things through. 'Looks fade, fleeting attractions dissolve, but common cultures, common family backgrounds, common religions, common race—no scratch that last one,' Mum told Dad, 'will last forever.' And what if he had lived with her? I watched Mum and Dad wrestle with whether they should acknowledge this part of his life at all, but they decided that it was something that had to be said. 'There must be educated Indian girls who are broad-minded enough nowadays to look past that,' said Mum. Or perhaps they needn't mention it at all until the nadaswaram[15] stopped playing. Mum was a diligent writer of letters, and I expect this was one of her best works, partly beseeching, partly disapproving, showing the right mix of understanding and concern, with the slightest

---

[15] A wind instrument commonly played at Malayali Hindu weddings

hint of dark consequences, just enough to plant doubt in Govind's wavering mind.

Govind sent no reply and, for the first time since he had left India, missed his fortnightly call home.

Mum turned on me: 'Did you know about this Maggie business? Are you also planning to pull such a stunt of your own?' I thought of my very active love life, which so far had consisted largely of ogling the girls in a friend's *Debonair* magazine and sniggering at the explicit graffiti on the walls by the college urinals, and said, 'Yes, imminently.' She clicked her tongue irritably and called up Sudha to dissect the issue at hand, but if she had expected commiseration from her daughter, she was mistaken. 'Yes, this is what happens when you send your blue-eyed boy abroad. When I wanted to go to study, you wouldn't let me. All kinds of silly excuses—you'll get on drugs, you'll never find a good match back home, you'll run away with a white boy. Who's running away with a white girl now?'

Finally, Govind called, unusually on a weekday, from what was clearly his office, his tone hushed but a bit hysterical. Didn't Mum have any sense, he asked. Maggie had read the letter, and they had had a blistering row. I suppose Mum's heart lifted at this unexpected bonus, until Govind said, 'Why are you doing this to me, Mum—sending letters, asking Sudha to call me? Please, I can't take all this pressure any more, can't you understand? Don't you trust my judgement? She's a lovely person—just like an Indian girl, you'll see.'

Mum, whose heart could soften like ice cream in a Bombay summer when Govind displayed his vulnerabilities, melted immediately, and called up Shivan Mama to pre-empt the admonishing letter she had asked him to send Govind. 'I wasn't going to send it anyway,' Shivan Mama confessed.

So an invitation was extended to Maggie, who, by now I had started calling Noodles. ('Shavam[16]', Mum chided me. 'Don't let that slip out when they're here.') But Mum was still hopeful. How would Maggie put up with this Bombay stink, she said—the dust, the pollution, the garbage and faeces on the streets, the disease-ridden beggars touching insistently at her sleeve? She would take one look at the rambling slums of Dharavi as they landed and would book her return flight home. She would forget Govind's advanced degree, his cerebral job, his exotic good looks…and she would flee like a bystander from a riotous mob.

And Govind? Govind, who had obviously been swayed by the ways of the West, would come back to India and remember—his family, his heritage, the familiarity of the language, the taste of long-known spices… And he would come to his senses.

My father nodded uncertainly, clearly not convinced, as she voiced such thoughts.

---

[16]A mild Malayalam expletive, literally meaning 'corpse'

4

Bookended by Disaster

Maggie turned out to be a petite, fork-thin girl with lank hair of an insipid brown, dressed in pyjama pants and a flimsy spaghetti top. She was determinedly cheerful, squealing with excitement to see us—'Oh my Gaad! The brother!'—greeting us with expansive embraces, even Dad, who stood rigidly with his hands by his side as she enveloped him. She spoke in that rising American inflexion which made even the most certain of declarations sound like a question, and she was a smiler, prefixing and suffixing every conversation with a radiant beam that cracked open her little face and made my jaw hurt in empathy.

She tried hard to endear herself to us. She gave up the spaghetti top for the salwar-kameez that Mum gifted her. She listened patiently to Dad as he held forth on how Narasimha Rao, a quiet enigma of a man with a pout like a supermodel, had, by the manipulations of fate, gone from becoming an almost retired politician to the prime minister of the country. She accepted second and third helpings of everything Mum made, even a fiery curry which made her eyes water like a leaking tap. She repeated everything she said, twice, thrice, slowly, loudly, so that Mum and Dad could part the fogs of her accent and decipher the gist of what she was saying. She did whatever she could to make us like her.

We didn't, of course. Dad was awkward around her,

uncomprehending of her twang, unable to hold her frank, bold gaze. He tried hard to make her comfortable, but I know he found her a little ditsy and way too extravagant. Dad would probably have felt the same way about any American girl, but Maggie just proved his point by making Govind fritter away money on staying with her in Fariyas hotel instead of at home. As for Mum, well, she disapproved of Maggie for multiple reasons, but most of all she held Maggie responsible for changing what was once perfect: Govind. For Govind was discernibly different now: thinner definitely, his shirt, which once stretched tight over a slightly rotund tummy that Mum deemed healthy, now hung loosely from his shoulders. He had developed the slightest of accents that made him say 'ant' for 'aunt' and 'whateverr' for 'whatever'. He had exchanged his reassuringly square attire of dull trousers and polycot shirts for jeans that were fashionably baggy and eye-catching fluorescent T-shirts. He let Maggie stroke his cheek in public and link fingers with his even in front of our gaping maid, Shantabai, and although he had the good sense to blush and lower his voice when he said it, he was prone to address her as Angel. Or Bunny. She reciprocated with Shnookums or Honey, which made me stick my finger in my throat and pretend to barf behind their backs, prompting warning looks from Mum and a small smile from Dad.

As for me, I was a little resentful that Govind—serious, nerdy Govind—was calling into question my self-bestowed title of the coolest sibling in the family—with Govind being the smartest and Sudha the most capable, it was the only title I could aspire to. It was like waking up one morning and finding out that Grandpa was really Batman.

But I was too busy with the changes in my own life to worry too much about Maggie. The postponement of my Drawing exam had granted me the reprieve I so wanted, and I had managed to pass my exams and graduate from engineering college. I had started my mediocre job, which was in a mid-size engineering firm that occupied an entire floor of a cheerless building located in the suburbs. Three walls were lined by cabins for the managers, one by a reception and a boardroom, while the large central space was given over to an open-plan office honeycombed with cubicles. Here sat middle-aged men in a uniform of terrycot pants and shirts, slicked-down hair and neat moustaches, all busy poring over blueprints or drafting plans or going through work orders and structural calculations. Phones rang intermittently, a dot matrix printer scraped and screeched in a corner. The trainees, three boys apart from me, all looking half starved, were ushered into the boardroom and given a pile of books and training material to go through. Over the next few months, we had to familiarize ourselves with a running project we were each assigned to. Mine was a roadwork being built in Rajasthan, and as I sat looking uncomprehendingly at survey calculations and various proposals for concrete mixes, I wondered helplessly if my employers were really stupid enough to put me in charge of any aspect of this project—I could barely figure out the workings of the photocopier, a gigantic thing with multiple functions, capable of photocopying large blueprints and spitting out multiple copies in seconds. I imagined the road caving in at some point, fifty-car pileups and thousands dead, and me being taken away in handcuffs for my role in the construction. My fellow trainees appeared to have no such qualms and spoke excitedly of being able to put their education into practice, and other such blather. I sedated my rising panic with copious amounts of cutting chai[17] from the tea

---

[17]A half glass of tea

stall around the corner and with inane conversations with the receptionist, a middle-aged Catholic lady with orange hair who stayed in Mahim (which she pronounced 'Maim'), wore short skirts and startling purple lipstick and seemed to have the inside scoop on everybody in the office. ('Borkar?' she said, jerking her head towards a bovine man with nicotine-stained teeth. 'His wife's a sex addict, men. Wants to do it everywhere—in the kitchen, in the bathroom, everywhere. Why you laughing, men? I'm not joking!' 'Patil?' she whispered. 'Takes a kickback from every supplier. When the boss catches him, khalaas, finished!')

∽

By the time I was given the order to pack my bags for Rajasthan, it was clear that Govind and Maggie were officially an item, and Mum threw the last log on the pyre of all her marriage dreams for her first-born, and the inevitable arrangements for the wedding began.

On our weekly phone calls, Mum updated me on the endless negotiations for the wedding, for Maggie had her own ideas, she grumbled. Vases of lilies and roses instead of garlands of jasmine and marigold to decorate the wedding hall. Hymns following the Hindu ritual. Chocolate mousse instead of payasam as a sweet in the sadya[18]. A gown instead of a sari for the reception, a reception that Govind quietly suggested be held in a five-star hotel instead of the 'nice hall in Matunga' my parents had decided on for the wedding. Dad's eyebrows shot up like the Sensex during Harshad Mehta's reign until Govind hastily said that he would be picking up the tab, of course. Maggie suggested a wedding rehearsal and Dad wilted like a forget-me-not at the thought of

---

[18]Kerala feast served on banana leaves, especially on special occasions

the added expense, but Govind managed to convince her that Indian weddings didn't need rehearsals, that spontaneity was favoured over meticulous perfection.

I had completed a year in Rajasthan by the time the wedding came around. I was posted in a village ten kilometres from the nearest town, and sand in my mouth and camels on my commute had become my lot in life. The guest house where I was put up was large but rudimentary. The capacious bedroom was indifferently tended to, and I often woke up to a large cockroach on my pillow or lizard droppings on my sheet. The rank common bathroom had only an Indian toilet. A cook, a middle-aged man with shifty eyes who I knew only as Chotu, attended to my meals, and although he was a dab hand with the rotis, he had a limited repertoire of about seven dishes, four of which were permutations of potato, peas and cauliflower. I had not eaten rice for months and my dreams at night were invariably about Mum's mutton stew, her chicken fry, her fish curry, her bread pudding.

Every morning I got into a dusty jeep and rattled to the job site, a highway linking two important towns. It was at a crucial stage of construction, an underbridge being built below a railway line. I was technically the most qualified on the site, and also the most inexperienced. Luckily, the supervisor, a slight man with a moustache that would have put Rajput kings to shame, a quick, loud laugh and an explosive temper if he found any of the labourers shirking, was a laissez-faire kind who did not take advantage of my cluelessness and took me under his wing instead. In actuality, he was supposed to be reporting to me, the engineer. A lesser man would have been indignant, scornful even, but I guess he was used to fuzz-faced engineers from the city flying in and telling him how to do his job. If he was ever scornful, as he had every right to be, he never let on. When he taught me things, he did it with an air of apology, as though he was being forward by advising an intellectual superior. And yet, the little I learnt about building a road, I learnt from him.

In his absence, the workers would often pretend not to hear my instructions, even stare at me, unresponsive and insolent, as I asked them a question or ventured a command. But if he was around, they were as obedient as foot soldiers, scurrying to obey my instructions, not even daring to meet my eye as I nervously instructed them about the day's activities. Even now, over a year into the job, not quite as clueless as I used to be, I dreaded the supervisor's absence and kept a sharp eye out for a mutinous pickaxe or a rebellious boulder heading my way.

I complained long and rather hyperbolically to my parents about the awful accommodation, the terrible pay, the murderous co-workers.

'Pickaxes, hmm? Come home,' said Dad, worriedly. 'We'll find you something here.'

'Try it out a little longer, monay[19],' said Mum, who was more inured to my hissy fits. 'You never know, you may grow to like it. Things can change…'

'In an instant?' I asked, my voice thick with sarcasm and thwarted self-pity.

I returned to Bombay baked to a rich burnt sienna from the hours spent in the scorching sun, seven kilos lighter and with a suitcase full of dirty laundry and clothes with missing buttons and fraying collars that desperately needed Mum's ministrations. I was meant to return to the site immediately after Govind's wedding, but events were to dictate otherwise.

The house was already full with Sudha, her husband Ramu

---

[19]Malayalam endearment meaning 'son'

and the five-year-old twins, Prakash and Preetha. Govind and Maggie were staying at The President, and other guests had been put up in a clean, no-frills three-star hotel in Dadar not far from the wedding hall. I was deputed to meet guests at the railway station. Mum and Dad were haunting the airport to receive Maggie's friends and family, while Sudha was in charge of ensuring that arrangements were going according to plan at the wedding hall and guests were being tended to at the hotel. Sudha was particularly well equipped for this job. Marriage and motherhood had bestowed upon her several extra kilos and an air of authority rarely seen outside army regiments. I felt a fleeting pity for the hotel manager, the caterer and the decorator.

After meeting our respective obligations, we congregated back in our tiny Colaba flat. I remember Sudha was trying to shovel food down Preetha's throat—Prakash ate ravenously and imprudently at any time of the day and didn't require any such coaxing. Mum was tidying up, and Dad, Ramu and I had slumped in front of the television.

We had quite forgotten that there was a big political rally in the north that day, even Dad, who usually absorbed news like blotting paper absorbed ink. It was in faraway Ayodhya at the site of a contentious mosque called the Babri Masjid. Hindu leaders claimed that the mosque had been built at the site of the birthplace of Lord Rama, where a Hindu temple once stood. There had been sporadic tension and riots between Hindus and Muslims over the years, with occasional demands that a temple be built at the site, demands that often coincided with election time. Lately, the mosque had been in the news again. Right-wing leaders were staging a procession to the mosque that day to perform a symbolic puja for a temple. The mosque was to be guarded and cordoned off, and in faraway Bombay, it appeared to be just another politically motivated rally, one which would make headlines for a couple of days and then be forgotten for another decade or so. But things can change in an...

We watched it unfold on TV. The boisterous crowd surging towards the mosque. The Hindu leaders making speeches from a temporary stage. And then, a slight young man, breaking the cordon and scrambling to the dome of the mosque. Slogans being shouted around him. More men scrambling atop the dome. Then the camera zoomed in on one with a pickaxe, just as he brought it down on the dome. Others followed suit, with hammers, with hooks. The leaders, authoritative and pedagogic until then, fell silent, horrified. More men, more axes. Pieces of the building, crumbling. And the aftermath—the mosque flattened, the men jubilant. The images were startling, intense and repeated over and over again all through the evening.

The news anchors were sombre. They were expecting trouble the next day, and bandhs were being called for across the country. Mum and Dad fretted about the implications on the wedding, but decided that we could go ahead. The muhurtam[20] was early—7 a.m.; Maggie had grumbled a bit about the early hour, but there was no arguing with the position of the planets. The guests would arrive long before the professional bandh enforcers would be on the roads, threatening the shops that had dared to remain open, roughing up a bystander or two. We could be done with the wedding and the subsequent celebratory breakfast and be back at home before 10 o'clock. The reception at night, after the enforcers had wound up for the day, would, with a little bit of luck, also go ahead.

As we drove down to the wedding hall the next morning,

---

[20]An astrologically auspicious time

the roads were deserted—not even a milkman or dabbawalla in sight. I felt the hostile eyes of strangers on us as we got out of the car, Mum and Sudha in their Kanjeevaram saris and gold jewellery, we in our zari-tipped mundus[21]. The hall looked quite lovely, bedecked in flowers, but even before the guests could filter in, a couple of policemen appeared at the entrance and asked us to take down the decorations, keep the celebrations muted. So, in the end, there were neither lilies and roses, nor jasmine and marigold; and neither nadaswaram nor hymns. Vimala Aunty said unkindly that it seemed fitting, the entire episode of Govind marrying Maggie being bookended by disaster.

Little did we know that as Govind and Maggie got married— Maggie, her sari draped so as to show a very flat midriff, Govind desperately trying to tame the mundu that was held up by a naada[22]—Bombay was slowly coming to a boil. Mum flitted around, greeting guests, making introductions, ensuring people were not being ignored, that everyone had partaken of the wedding breakfast. Dad, still unable to understand much of what Noodles or her family said, skulked into an anteroom hoping to catch an update on the bandh and the consequences of the demolition. My grandmother, Dad's mum, sat rigidly on the edge of her seat, her face pinched as though the sewage smell from Mahim creek had wafted all the way down to the hall in Matunga, her expression pure martyr, as if she was Mahatma Gandhi on a hunger strike to lift salt taxes; all this because nobody had formally invited her to go and partake of the wedding breakfast. Prakash, after looking intently into Vimala Aunty's mouth as she chewed a vada, turned to his father, Ramu, and asked in a

---

[21]South Indian lungis

[22]A string usually used to secure sari petticoats, etc

carrying voice if he would buy him new teeth for his birthday, like the ones she had. 'Please, Papa, please.' Rajan Uncle, Vimala Aunty's husband, a prize bore who could have been employed by the government to clear unruly crowds and protesting masses by the very threat of his stultifying presence, was reciting a garbled version of William Wordsworth to Maggie's perplexed father—*I wondered lonely as a crowd, That floats on high ore bales and hills, When all at once I saw a cloud, Of golden daffydills.*

We scattered quickly after the wedding, anxious to get back before the bandh turned violent. Reports of stone-throwing and clashes with the police, and rumours of the defacing of temples and mosques, were coming in from across the city. Colaba was peaceful but unusually quiet, shutters down on the restaurants, roadside stalls padlocked and abandoned, the Causeway empty of tourists and shoppers. By evening, it was clear that the violence would not be short-lived. The reception was cancelled—my mother was flushed with unshed tears, my father quiet at the thought of the money that Govind would lose. That night, a curfew was announced—nobody was going anywhere soon. Frantic calls were made back and forth—to cancel tickets for out-of-town relatives who wouldn't be able to get home, to the hotel to extend stays, to the resort in Goa where Govind and Maggie were to honeymoon but could no longer do so.

For days, we sat cooped up in our flat, listening to reports of policemen being attacked with swords, people being locked into their homes and burnt, women and children being mutilated and killed. A friend from Dadar called to tell me he could see a mob with swords and sticks walking down their street. In Thane, my father's colleague counted the number of fires they could spot from their terrace. By the third day, the army was deployed; in a show of might, tanks rolled down streets where cars usually plied. And yet they couldn't reach the rioters, lurking in the alleyways, disappearing into bylanes, only to start rioting afresh when the tanks had gone.

In a week's time, the fires seemed to have been doused, the rioters had been brought under control and the city started limping back to normal. The wedding guests were finally able to make their way back to their homes. Sudha and her family returned to Chennai; Govind and Maggie, and the Noodle Contingent, went back to the States. In Rajasthan, things were still simmering, so I was asked to stay in Bombay until the all-clear was given. I celebrated New Year in a muted metropolis with a few friends from college, and returned to the local office until things settled down in Rajasthan.

But even in Bombay, there were fresh outbursts of violence through the first month of 1993, following an attack on a Hindu family in a chawl in Dongri. A block from our house, a mob did the rounds of the neighbourhood buildings, demanding to be given the names of Muslim residents—to our lasting credit, they went back empty-handed. At last, the rioting subsided, but at the end of it, hundreds were dead across the country, thousands of crores worth of property destroyed. For us, there was a greater loss still—the innocent vision of the Bombay we grew up in, a cosmopolitan, capitalist Bombay which usually stopped for nothing, least of all religion. For, even in those days, Bombay was just a teeming mass of people trying to get by or get ahead. Rich jostled with poor, the honest with the dishonest, the law-abiding with the most hardened of criminals. The poor were as dehumanized as their counterparts in any other part of the country, as illiterate, abused and deprived of basic necessities, but there were unwritten laws of the city that made us middle-class citizens feel safe—that there may be mafia wars going on under our noses, but an ordinary citizen would never get drawn into that world, that the largest and sleaziest red-light area may be in the middle of the metropolis but a woman could walk safe on the street at night as long as she was sensible enough to avoid certain neighbourhoods, that occasionally clashes might break out between Hindu and Muslim, or trade union and employer, but more often than not, they would be in the poorer corners of some far-off suburb and would never really inconvenience the ordinary man, never threaten the relentless forward momentum of the city.

But in the aftermath of the riots, there were maha aartis being conducted at temples, complete with bhajans blaring from loudspeakers and temple bells being rung incessantly, ostensibly to eclipse the long namaz sessions being held in mosques. Each of us, even the most progressive of our lot, for the first time, it seemed, became conscious of our religion, and felt reason to be uneasy of those of another faith. Those few bloody weeks in winter changed Bombay in a way that foreign kings and marauding intruders had not been able to, for it struck at the heart of what we believed—that nothing was important in Bombay other than talent and success, and the colour of money.

∽

It was partly the colour of money that made me decide I wouldn't be returning to Rajasthan. I had never been one of those purposeful types who knew what they wanted to do at the age of fifteen and aimed to be a CEO by thirty-five, but if there was anything I was certain about, it was this: I didn't want to see another concrete mix or steel reinforcement again, nor a cross-section of a road or a blueprint of a dam, and I certainly didn't want to return to the murderous looks of the workers in

Rajasthan. A few weeks in Bombay had reminded me of the luxuries of city-living—the cafés, the movie theatres, the toilets that didn't need the rigorous employment of quadriceps and hamstrings to use, and a complete absence of sand.

'But what are you going to do?' Mum asked.

'I don't know, an MBA perhaps, maybe sit for the GRE again. All I know is I can't go back to Rajasthan, Mum, and slog all day for a pittance!'

'Don't exaggerate, Vivek...'

'I'm telling you! My friends who have gone abroad are earning more in stipend than I am in salary. And those who have done management...'

'But...'

'Let him be,' said Dad, and that was that.

And so it was that as bombs ripped through the stock exchange, the Air India building, the Sea Rock Hotel and ten other locations in Bombay in March 1993, I was preparing for further studies, not quite sure where it was all leading, but making a break from the past. I had just given sample question papers for photocopying at a shop on Dalal Street that offered discounted rates to students, and seeing the queue, had decided not to wait but to return the next day to collect the photocopies. Later, we would analyse that decision repeatedly, whether it was a divine protective hand that had steered me away from the stock exchange, or just blind luck. I had reached the Prince of Wales Museum when I heard it, a loud noise that sounded like metal sheets falling from a height, which made me start and turn around, but I continued walking soon enough, with that relentless rushing, scurrying forward momentum of the born Bombayite, little knowing that I had probably escaped death.

Mum fell on me hysterically when I reached home. 'Thank

god you're safe! Your father called, there are bombs going off all over the city.'

The next day, as though by collective consensus, Bombayites everywhere roused themselves and stepped out—to work, to the market, to school. Mum, too, did not protest when Dad said he was going to work, when I said I wanted to go and check on the boy at the Xerox shop (he was shaken and bruised but alive), although I imagine she nervously drank multiple glasses of water throughout the day and waited by the window to watch us return.

Overnight, the city that never sleeps was back on its feet. There was reason again to be proud of my hometown, and I was very glad that I had returned.

Part Two

....

Lean and Slippered Pantaloon

5

Low-Priority File

My father was very good with his hands. No, he was extraordinarily good. He drew skilfully—charcoal sketches of my mother in various moods, little cartoons scribbled on the postcards he sent us when he had to be away from home, detailed building plans when they were constructing a home, drawn freehand with a steadiness of hand I could never muster despite the years of Engineering Drawing I had suffered. He painted—an eye-catching portrait of a weather-beaten lady with a bunch of grapes that looked so succulent, so real, that it attracted wasps in summer; a reproduction of an M.F. Husain that he gifted Sudha when she got married—the horses fluid, their muscles taut and manes windblown; the walls and ceiling of our house during a misguided attempt at economy, which admittedly resulted in bubbling surfaces and a severe crick in the neck—talented he was, but he was no Michelangelo. He sculpted an unfinished nude which I feared was my mother in her younger days and which I rushed to hide when I had friends over; he crafted a jewellery box with some spare wood and a swatch of pink satin, and gifted it to my mother who admired it dutifully but cast it aside in some forgotten recess of her cupboard. During our engineering days, he completed workshop projects for Govind and me—miraculously correcting, with just a few strokes of the plane, the levelling of a plank of wood that I had almost destroyed, finishing Govind's smithy-class 'girl' and 'boy' parts that fit into each other and made us teenage boys blush (Govind) or break into hastily concealed sniggers (me). He rewired electrical fittings and unclogged drains, sewed covers for sofa cushions and even restored old furniture with Fevicol and a handful of nails. When my mother made the fancy dishes that she had learnt in her cooking class, it was he who fashioned the dough into delicate croissants, he who rolled out the pastry for her quiche Lorraines.

In the early years of our marriage, my wife was fascinated by his multifarious skills. 'You've learnt nothing from him, have you?' she said, with some regret but mostly resignation.

Today, he could have been an artist, or perhaps an architect; a better engineer than any I've known, or maybe a craftsman. But my father grew up in a time when art could never be more than a childhood hobby, a male interest in stitching was regarded with alarm, and investments in anything other than food, clothing and shelter never entertained. I suppose it was because he grew up in a small village in Kerala that he never became an engineer. Dad did what was next best at the time, a BSc in Mathematics. Soon after, he took the usual series of examinations in the hope that one of them would lead to a career—IAS, IFS, IPS, the all-India banking exams. He fared well enough at the banking exams to receive a job offer in a large nationalized bank in Bombay. He worked there for a couple of years before moving to his second and last employer, one of the first foreign banks in India.

Despite working there for most of his life, he never made it to the top rung of management. I doubt he aspired for more; in those days the highest echelons were reserved for those already wealthy and connected, those with friends in high places and a penchant for golf. A white man always sat at the top of the pyramid—today a florid Swiss gentleman, who, rumour had it, still stumbled over the difference between a lakh and a crore, tomorrow a hearty Australian bloke who couldn't understand why Indian women were so fond of their lockers.

So, for the most part, my father was content with his mid-level management position, with his comfortable wage and modest benefits. And then came the early Nineties, and with it, the liberalization policies of the Narasimha Rao government.

∽

Children of pre-liberalization India will remember the era of stifling regulation before 1991, a legacy of the nation's first planners. Post-Independence India was an impoverished nation— British rule had discouraged Indian industry and Partition had emptied the coffers—so the early five-year plans of the country had focused on socialist policies which were expected to build up the economy and alleviate poverty. At the time, it was thought that the indigenous market should be protected from international competition, so stiff import tariffs were levied and restrictive foreign-investment regulations were passed. It seems implausible now, but those of us who grew up in pre-liberalization times remember the awe with which we looked at the most basic of foreign goods: Faber-Castell felt pens, fragrant erasers, scratch 'n' sniff stickers, pencil sharpeners that came with a handle you rotated to sharpen the pencils and a built-in box to collect the shavings, pencil boxes with Hello Kitty or Spiderman covers and magnetic lids, umbrellas that flew open at the touch of a button and could be folded to fit into your bag—only fortunate classmates whose fathers travelled internationally on work or those with relatives abroad could ever hope to possess such wonders. Even then, with stringent foreign-exchange regulations, they were hardly easy to come by.

But even domestic industry was not spared by the planners—you required a licence to start a new business, expand an existing one or even change a product. There were multiple agencies—up to eighty!—that had to be satisfied with your intentions, your skills and your credibility before you could get a licence. And it came with caveats—everything from how much you manufactured to the price at which you could sell your products was dictated by the government. You couldn't lay off workers or close factories without a government nod, which could take years and reams of paperwork. In this climate, innovation got strangled in coils of red tape, and pre-liberalization India was one of glacial growth, inefficient workforces and frugal consumption.

The economy wheezed along for decades, but by the time Narasimha Rao's coalition government took over in 1991, in the aftermath of Rajiv Gandhi's assassination, India was bankrupt, barely having enough dollars in reserve to buy three weeks' worth of imports. To benefit from a bailout from the International Monetary Fund, the nation had to pledge gold and commit to sweeping economic reforms. In a phased manner, the stifling restrictions of the first four decades of Independence were done away with. The number of licences required to start a business was reduced, import tariffs were slashed, the rupee was deregulated, capital markets were liberalized, tax rates were cut and the door to foreign investment was opened. Among the sectors that received immediate benefit from these reforms was the banking industry.

Until then, the banking sector had been a slow, plodding beast. Nationalized banks accounted for over 90 per cent of the fixed deposits in the country, large parts of a bank's funds were reserved for lending to priority sectors like agriculture and small industries, and there was very little discretion in the hands of the banker, so enterprise or effort was considered unnecessary.

Banking was described as a 4-6-4 business—borrow at 4 per cent, lend at 6 per cent and go home at 4 o'clock.

The reforms stood traditional banking on its head, and in the last few years of his career, my father saw more changes in his workplace than he had in the rest of his working life. The bank quickly rolled out plans for new branches and complete computerization, extended working hours and introduced a slew of products from ATMs and credit cards to retail loans. ('People didn't have credit cards?' my daughter asks incredulously. 'How did you buy things?')

To cope with the longer working hours, the greater workload, the need for new skills and the demands of competition, of actually selling products to consumers instead of waiting for them to come to you and practically beg you to open an account or, god forbid, extend a loan, the bank started recruiting heavily—young, energetic things fresh out of business school, who thought nothing of working till 10 p.m. and trawling the city looking for new business. Promotion policies were changed so that experience and seniority counted for little and the young management trainees could climb up the corporate ladder faster than the old hands. When my father joined the bank, your grey hair, your bifocals, the hair growing from your nose and ears were badges of your experience and ability. They qualified you for positions of influence. But the powers that be didn't seem to think so, not any more.

The branch managers got increasingly infantile, and youth and beauty seemed to be the order of the day, as though the bank was recruiting for a Miss India pageant instead of an organization that handled thousands of people's money. To the astonishment of the old-timers, who referred to their bosses as Sir—or if you were on excellent terms, Mr X—now you were encouraged to call these suckling managers by their first names, or even by diminutives such as Sid and D.P. Within a couple of years, Dad was reporting to a mere tadpole of a girl who was not much older than Govind. She had been promoted over her levels of comfort and skill, and spent most of her time cowering inside her cabin pretending to be occupied with important calls. 'Most of the time she is talking to her mother, probably for advice and solace,' said Dad. She did this often: when the crustier of the older employees, for example, was being obdurate, or soon after an irate customer broke through the security cordon of relationship and customer-service managers and stormed into her cabin to berate her for some blunder that was really not her fault, or when a Reserve Bank of India auditor appeared for a surprise inspection—they came often in the wake of the Harshad Mehta scam.

My father, to his credit, felt sorry for her. 'She is probably quite clever, what with her management degree and all,' he said.

But managing a branch took more than that: it took the weight of experience, the gravitas that grey hair lent, the awe that a few bulges and folds inspired. It took the cunning that was required to inveigle auditors, the equanimity to sit calmly through a customer rant, the diplomacy to handle a disgruntled employee and the authority to quell a recalcitrant one.

Old hands like my father, who could reconcile accounts in a trice, recall the account numbers of customers and find the correct ledgers in a matter of moments, and tot up numbers at a glance, were no longer prized. They were yesterday's skills, not required in this age of automation. Their grey hair and slow hands, their reserve and old-world lack of marketing zeal deemed them unsuitable for the front office, and certainly unfit for the more glamorous jobs like handling premium accounts, which required a glibness and sophistication that had passed my father's generation by. Until the bank could find some way to ease the old hands out, they were shunted around from department to department like low-priority files in a government office.

Dad, too, was shunted from branch to branch, and job to job, like the rest of his peers. As cash officer, he wrestled with the ATM, trying to fathom how to load the cash or how to retrieve lost ATM cards. In the front office, he struggled with the new-found demands of computer input, and customers sat sighing heavily or tapped impatiently on the desk while he peered through his bifocals to see where the A was on the keyboard or if he had input the account number correctly on the screen. Dad confessed that many who got to know him well avoided his table and waited an extra few minutes for the quicker, younger front-office girls to become available. In Loans, he butted heads with the direct sales agents who promised dozens of customers that their loan applications would be processed within a couple of days and then expected Dad to not only stay back after hours to finish reviewing the files but also be a little creative with the lending norms so that they could meet their ever-burgeoning sales targets.

Finally, he landed in Internal Audit, the graveyard where all the redundant were sent if it was too expensive to ease them out somehow. It involved travelling to various branches to check their books and processes. It was a vital process, really, to ensure that the bank ran according to rules, so that the house would be in order when the RBI auditors came around to do the real thing. The RBI auditors could literally shut your business down—take away your licence, perhaps even get you jailed for severe trespasses. This was, after all, the era of the draconian Foreign Exchange Regulation Act—when having a few extra dollars in your possession could put you behind bars for a very, very long time.

The internal auditors, on the other hand, were treated with scant respect. If an internal auditor found mistakes, he could merely point them out to be corrected later, and at the most, the branch manager would get a slap on the wrist from the boss. You had no real power but you were definitely a nuisance, because no branch manager wanted to spend time poring over records or digging out ledgers for audit when there were customers to be served, new accounts to be marketed, targets to be met. In the hustle and bustle of the new world, you were more likely to be overlooked for promotion or be dismissed for not reaching your sales targets than for cutting a few corners with due diligence.

So Dad had to endure basilisk stares from busy branch managers when he asked for records or pointed out discrepancies, and often he would be relegated to a desk in an airless basement, just outside the cash safe, or if he was lucky, to a ventilated corner of a back office.

It was far from ideal, but it could have been worse. There had been several rounds of downsizing to make the bank more efficient, and many of Dad's contemporaries had disappeared like the beautiful lady in the magician's trick. Dad had held out hope for a voluntary retirement scheme, which would provide him with a little nest egg on which he could retire early, but when it was announced, the scheme was so unattractive that only those who had been discreetly warned of imminent dismissal felt compelled to take it.

∽

Finally, after thirty-odd years of service, Dad retired, and Mum and I were invited for the farewell party, this at the latest branch he was auditing. I had just completed a management course, two years of balance sheets and Kotler, and looking down on the local minority of BCom and BA students. To everyone's astonishment, I had landed a Day Zero job as a management trainee in an international consulting firm. A similar consulting firm had been hired by Dad's bank to explore avenues to cut costs and thus enhance profits, and after eighteen months of hard work, it had submitted its recommendations—the removal of indoor plants from all the branches, the discontinuation of the practice of serving two biscuits along with the morning tea for staff, and the cancelling of Christmas parties and Diwali hampers for the employees. Like Dad's young bosses, I, too, now wore the uniform of management trainees everywhere—branded shirts and expensive cologne and Ray-Ban Aviator sunglasses—and I had acquired a Rolodex for my desk and a Filofax to remember my appointments by. Dad was unreasonably proud of me, while cursing the slick glibness of the young bank managers and the consultant-firm gasbags in the same breath.

The entire branch gathered around a chocolate cake adorned with a flowery 'Farewell' made with pink icing, but they were edgy, you could tell. The clerical staff were restless, resentful at having to stay back beyond their union-prescribed working hours for the farewell function. They had already said their goodbyes to Dad during the day, and several of them had their bags slung around their shoulders and empty tiffin boxes at the ready, so that they could bolt through the door the moment the cake and wafers had made the rounds, and try to catch at least the 5.32 back home. The relationship managers—mere children, just out of business school—were surreptitiously checking their watches—shiny new things that they had no doubt bought with their first salaries—and longing to get back to their desks, to catch up perhaps on sales calls and weekly reports, or that one premium banking customer whose cheque had inadvertently bounced and who required a twenty-something management graduate to grovel at his feet for half an hour before his anger would dissipate, before his ruffled feathers would be smoothed back into shape.

Dad was presented with the standard tokens of gratitude, the emblems of lengthy service: a Quartz clock with the bank's name emblazoned on it, a Parker pen, a moderately large bouquet of red and white roses, and a silver medal slung on a blue ribbon that Mum got excited about until she learnt it was not made of real silver. I suppose that the sight of these was meant to fill Dad with pride in the winter of his life, remind him of his long-gone glory. His soon-to-be-former colleagues broke into scattered, distracted applause as Dad accepted his farewell gifts from the branch manager, a young man of not yet forty, who made a touching speech that outlined Dad's career, his stints in various branches and departments, making it seem like a story of success rather than the tale of survival it actually was.

'Fool!' said Dad on our way home, scratching his neck with the silver medal. 'Ha, at least I will no longer have to grovel to any customer, nor any barely-out-of-his-shell bank manager, for the rest of my days. I think I will spend my retirement haunting my own bankers, what do you say? Throw my weight around, take out my frustrations on the front-office staff, threaten to close my account and transfer my money elsewhere for the smallest mistake.' And then he laughed ruefully, because we all knew that his modest life savings, even then, marginally bloated with a retirement corpus, would not be coveted by any self-respecting banker—no, not even in the smallest branch of a rural co-operative bank.

6

Spectacles for Twelve Rupees

In the winter of his life, Dad's favourite topic of conversation was the escalating cost of living. Although he often forgot where he had left his keys and never remembered anyone's birthday or anniversary, he had an unfailing memory when it came to the cost of everyday expenses at various stages of his life. Because of this, I can tell you with authority that the minimum taxi fare in the 1960s was 50 paise and that you could travel from Colaba to the airport for just a little over ₹10. A buffet lunch at the Sea Lounge of the Taj cost just ₹12, and the room tariff ₹50. A car would set you back by about ₹15,000. One rupee could buy your daily groceries, a litre of petrol, a haircut, or a movie ticket along with a few snacks and a handful of cigarettes to bide your time. A premium shirt cost ₹25, spectacles could be made for as little as ₹12 and the best Bata shoes were less than ₹50. Starting salaries were a few hundred rupees a month, and a four-figure salary made you the most eligible bachelor in town. A bumper lottery prize was ₹1 lakh, a sum so large that Dad had promised himself that he would kick up his job and live a life of leisure if he ever won it.

Most of that generation were equally aware of the cost of living. Every purchase was scrutinized for necessity, every price tag studied before cash changed hands. Given their circumstances, it was not surprising. For a large part of my father's working life, most of his salary went to the government in taxes; at one time as high as 90 per cent on the highest slab—90 per cent! Even for those with a comfortable job in a multinational firm, life was about making ends meet. Although inflation was a sluggish bovine as compared to the galloping stallion it is today, even the necessities burnt a sizeable hole in your rather slender pocket. Your salary had to stretch to meet the month's expenses, and the dying creature would often require a transfusion at the very end of the month—a loan from a less encumbered friend, perhaps, or a money order from a worried parent.

Every extra rupee was salted away for an emergency, of which there were many. Fixed deposits were the investment of choice, followed by post office accounts, government bonds and the public provident fund. Few dared to invest in the stock market, although you would have probably invested in some UTI mutual funds, under the mistaken impression that they were some kind of government bond. If anything was left over from your Diwali bonus after funding the annual holiday to the ancestral home and the post-monsoon paint job on your second-hand car, you tried to buy a few grams of gold. Not more than a hundred rupees was ever to be left idling away in a low-interest savings account—in later years, I hid from Dad the fact that tens of thousands of rupees were just lying around in mine, out of sheer laziness to do anything about it, really. Detailed calculations were made to figure out how to maximize your interest income, and a large amount of time was spent in outwitting the taxman. Most of that generation had multiple accounts over various banks and branches, so that the interest in any one bank or branch never exceeded the tax-free limit. Those blessed with slightly higher incomes opened accounts in the names of their wives and children as well. They would then just forget to declare the interest income in the tax returns, and in those days, when banking and taxation were still largely manual industries, there was very little chance of the taxman ever finding out. The amount of time spent monitoring multiple accounts was not considered to be anything other than a minor inconvenience, for this was the era in which you stood in line for half a day to book airline tickets, waited a week for a cheque to clear, a month for a letter to reach home from overseas and years to get the telephone connection you had applied for.

Post-retirement was considered the final stage of your life, and it was accepted to be a time of declining health and limited resources. You lived on the interest from the lumpsum that you received as retirement benefits after a lifetime of work, rarely dipping into the capital, in the hope that you could leave a little nest egg for your children after you were gone. And you never really expected to live for much more than a decade after retirement, so you didn't worry about inflation ever eroding the value of your lumpsum. There were no wealth managers who encouraged you to save for retirement, no pension-fund salesmen who tried to sweet-talk you into an insidiously unattractive scheme.

∽

For years, my parents quibbled about where to stay after retirement. Mum wanted to continue living in Bombay, the city she had loved from the moment she had come here as a young bride—although, to us, the Bombay of her initial acquaintance seemed ludicrously simple. Reclamation was still years away, so Nariman Point and Cuffe Parade did not exist and the sea lapped up to the still-to-be-built Air India building. A hotel called Greens stood where the new Taj building is and the gardens outside the Gateway of India were not yet seedlings in some gardener's hand. Bandra was a remote suburb and Vashi not even a dot on the city map. But for Mum, who had never been out of Kerala, Bombay was like some exotic international destination. It had glamorous cafés like Napoli, where a jukebox belched out international hits. Live bands and jazz pianists played at restaurants that served dishes like steak with creamed spinach, and baked Alaska. There were cafés with coffee machines dispensing espresso and cappuccino, shops with trendy clothes and sophisticated handbags, and tailors who knew how to cut a blouse. And occasionally you could spot an actual Bollywood superstar—many a time have I been subjected to the story of how they had seen Amitabh Bachchan towering over a mob of fans outside the Gateway of India, and Hema Malini, doe-eyed and more beautiful than on screen, coming out of the Taj.

'Such a country bumpkin she was,' my father teased. 'Spent the first few years open-mouthed with awe.'

'It's true,' Mum agreed grudgingly, 'I even thought your Dad was glamorous, can you imagine?' And we all guffawed at the absurdity of this notion.

But the city had never won Dad over. He had got inured to the smell of the burgeoning metropolis—that putrid stench of drying fish and garbage, sewage and squalor, decadence and decay. He tolerated the commute—standing sandwiched between other commuters on the local, averting his face from the blistered beggar who plucked at his trousers, and the bare bottoms that squatted by the tracks. Every year, he gritted his teeth and sweated through summer and waded through stagnant monsoon puddles on the way to work. Every day, as he looked up at the mushrooming skyscrapers, as he was carried with the surging crowds on and off the train, as he was stuck in a snaking line of traffic that seemed to extend from one end of the city to the other, he fought a hemmed-in, claustrophobic feeling—the feeling that the city had reached its brim and would overflow at any minute, taking a sea of humanity with it.

Bombay was a young man's city, with its neon-lit glamour and its hungry, questing ambition, its manic, unforgiving pace and its aloof, nonchalant inhumanity. Nobody in their right senses would stay here after retirement, he kept telling Mum.

Dad wanted to go back to Kerala. To him it was the natural choice. 'Our relatives will be close by to help and support us,' he cajoled Mum. 'We can build a little house with a garden. We could visit the temple in the morning and walk by the backwaters in the evenings. Everything is familiar—the language, the food, the culture. And tell me, wouldn't it be nice to leave the world from the very place that you entered it?'

For long, Mum resisted Dad's overtures, but as uncertainty crept into Dad's workplace and the whispers of downsizing grew louder, doubts began to creep into Mum's impenetrable stand too. How could she insist on subjecting themselves to the higher costs of Bombay when it was uncertain if Dad would even be employed till retirement age? So as Bombay was being rechristened Mumbai, a name it would take me years to get my tongue around, my mother started reconsidering her antipathy towards a retirement home in Kerala. She didn't argue when Dad said that a large plot of land could be bought there for less than what it cost to buy a room in the most far-flung of suburbs in Bombay, that it would mean they could build a house in Kerala, sell our house in Bombay and still have some money left to tide over the uncertainties of retirement. 'Our very own golden handshake,' she even agreed.

Eventually, they decided that after Dad retired, they would shift to my mother's hometown, an unremarkable village whose only claim to fame was its proximity to the famous Guruvayur

Sree Krishna temple a few railway stations away. My grandparents had lived there until their demise, but with years of disuse, the ancestral house had atrophied like a paralysed limb. The ancestral land had been inherited in equal shares by my mother and her two siblings, Vimala Aunty and Shivan Mama, and the siblings decided to demolish the house and partition the property into three separate plots.

Each of the plots had a separate entrance, although the driveway was common. Shivan Mama was the first to build, a small functional cottage with one bedroom. At first, Mum worried about having to spend her retirement years in the company of Vimala Aunty. Even as a child, Vimala Aunty had been a bit of a blight, constantly playing the seniority card, always insisting on the first choice of gifts, the largest share of fireworks, the best clothes. Although no longer shaded by the umbrella of sibling hierarchy, she was still competitive with her adult siblings. When Shivan Mama bought a fridge, she bought a bigger and better one. When Mum made a particularly delicious biryani, she made a poor, insipid version which she forced upon us and insisted we admire. When Govind went abroad, she pushed and prodded her sons to do the same. When I got into consulting, she boasted that her youngest son, a well-known good-for-nothing, was the managing director of his firm, a tiny franchise which had salesmen going door to door selling rat poison.

Her husband, our Rajan Uncle, was a good sort, although 'a bit empty upstairs', Dad said, and Shivan Mama asked, 'A bit?' By the sheer force of Vimala Aunty's personality, Rajan Uncle had got a reasonably good job that even afforded them a few stints abroad. Rajan Uncle had been deeply influenced by one such stint, a six-month stay in England in the 1960s, where he had acquired a shallow knowledge of English literature and a predilection for alcohol and cigars. Upon his return, he had declared that his sons would henceforth be called by good English names—Bob, Pete, Mike and Tim. Somehow the nicknames didn't catch on, perhaps because their actual names were Vijayan, Shankaran, Ayyappan and Unnikrishnan, respectively. But Rajan Uncle's taste for alcohol and cigarettes endured, despite two heart attacks and a weak liver. 'Alcohol is good for the heart,' he maintained. 'Antioxidants. Rest-a-Vetta-something.'

So Mum was relieved when Vimala Aunty declared that she would just wall in her plot and leave it unoccupied. 'How can I live in the backwoods of Kerala after all our years in London and Dubai and Muscat and Sharjah?' she asked.

'Three and a half years in total,' Mum tried to remind her, but she rolled on: No, she would stay on in Hyderabad. Of course, she would be travelling to America and Paris, and Delhi and Calcutta, sharing her time equally with her four sons, so that none would feel excluded. They needed her help, she said, to bring up the grandchildren and look after their homes—their wives being too busy or too lazy, or generally not up to scratch.

Thus reassured, Mum and Dad went about building their retirement home. Architecture books were bought from the hawkers at Flora Fountain, books filled with building plans of American ranches, and English cottages with ivy creeping up the walls, and ultra-modern timber constructions with decks on the first floor, glass-fronted family rooms and swimming pools in the backyard. Dad spent his evenings dreaming up the toolshed he would build within the garage and the plants he would grow in the garden and, for a brief moment, even Mum got caught up in the excitement and said that she wanted a storeroom attached to the kitchen and a built-in closet in the bedroom.

∽

Three years, several delays and umpteen trips to and from Kerala later, the house was completed, but the grand plans of the early days had been scaled down dramatically, given the looming scarcity of the retirement years, and Mum and Dad's advancing age. Did they really need the toolshed in the garage, Mum asked— how long would Dad be healthy enough to use a power saw, for instance? Did she really require the dressing room and walk-in closet attached to the main bedroom?

During the construction, we had all pitched in with our ideas—I suggested a game room with a snooker table and a little bar in the corner, Sudha wanted one of those grand gates, and Govind and Maggie... Well, Govind and Maggie suggested a host of things. Or Maggie did. Long gone was the Maggie of our first acquaintance, the people-pleasing, worming-her-way-into-our-affections one, and in its place was, I suspect, the real Maggie, opinionated, assured and vocal. They had just built a house in the suburbs back in the States, which Maggie had decorated with Kashmiri carpets and Native Indian rugs and Mexican clay pottery and Kerala lamps, which somehow all came together seamlessly into one elegant whole. Everybody admired her house, and Maggie was bursting with helpful advice.

'Oh, you must have a sloping tiled roof like the original house, Aunty, and one of those central courtyards, with a tulsi plant at the centre?'

'I hope you're having a verandah around the house, and decorative wooden pillars and red-oxide floors?'

'Yes, yes,' Mum said, as though Maggie's word was her command, and Maggie perhaps assumed that Mum and Dad were, at that very moment, converting her suggestions into reality. 'Don't kid yourself,' I said. 'There's going to be municipal-blue tiles on the kitchen walls and a cement roof.'

'Oh no, not a cement roof, surely, Aunty? Think of the carbon footprint you're leaving behind?' Maggie exclaimed.

'If she doesn't shut her mouth, I'm going to leave a carbon footprint on *her* behind,' said Mum, dourly.

Ultimately, the municipal-blue tiles were abandoned in favour of an unremarkable brown, but the roof was flat as a dosa, the floors were covered in insipid grey mosaic tiles (the dirt won't show as much, said Mum, with good common sense) and the wrap-around verandah had been condensed to just the front of the house. When Govind murmured that Mum had ignored all Maggie's advice, Mum proffered excuses of budget and practicality—'Red oxide is very hard to maintain, Govind' or 'Wooden pillar? Do you know how much it would have cost?'—but he was convinced, quite rightly, that she had not even considered Maggie's suggestions. Sudha dismissed his complaints with an irritable 'Oh, you and your fancy American ideas!', and Govind tried to plead that not one idea had been American, but he may as well have been talking to the cloying baby-pink walls.

We all gathered for the *griha pravesham*[23]; Sudha and family from Chennai, Govind from the States, and I from Mumbai, where I now stayed in an office chummery with a couple of other colleagues. ('Chummery? What's that? A house with menstrual pains?' Sudha asked, in a rare, weak stab at humour.)

By now, our flat in Dove's Nest had been sold—to Dineshbhai, the owner of the stationery store on the ground floor, the one with the Flo-Jo thumbnail. With his cheap shiny shirt and tight trousers, tiny comb somehow wedged into the back pocket, Dineshbhai didn't look like he could afford a second-hand scooter, let alone a house in Colaba. But of course, he must have been

---

[23]House-warming ceremony

loaded. The flashy gold chain with the diamond Ganesha pendant resting on his hairy chest must have been worth a small fortune in itself.

The *griha pravesham* was a quiet family affair conducted the Malayali way—with a Ganapati homam[24] at an ungodly hour in the morning. The priest, pot-bellied and balding, chanted mantras over a sacred fire, which emitted plenteous amounts of fragrant smoke that stung our eyes and invaded our lungs, causing us to gag and choke. The fire was stoked from time to time with ghee, sending out still more smoke, and within minutes, every room in the house was clouded in a holy haze. 'Ack!' cried Prakash, holding his throat and rubbing his eyes. Preetha giggled and ran out into the garden. I wished I could follow her, but common courtesies forbade me and I retreated to the furthest corner near the window, where Govind, Ramu and Shivan Mama joined me a few minutes later. Mum, Dad and Sudha sat resolutely by the fire—Mum and Sudha covering their noses with their pallus, and Dad with spectacles clouded but apparently immune otherwise to the smoke.

Maggie was absent, as their son was unwell. For they were parents now, Govind and Maggie, of a cherubic round-faced boy whom they had named Riyaan.

'Rohan?' Dad had asked at first.

'Riyaan, Dad,' I said.

'What kind of name is that?' asked Dad.

'What's wrong with Rohan?' interjected Mum. 'Or Ramakrishnan? A nice Malayali name.'

'Nothing Mum, except that's not what they want to call him.'

Riyaan was almost a year old now, and Maggie had wanted

---

[24] A puja for Ganapati, where oblations are made into a fire

to come along, strapping the baby to her chest in a carrier, but he had come down with a stomach bug just before they travelled. So Govind was alone, but Vimala Aunty and Rajan Uncle, along with two of the four sons (Mike/Ayyappan and Tim/Unnikrishnan) and a clutch of grandchildren of different ages, had made the time and effort to come, despite Mum's lukewarm invitation.

Inevitably, the moment Mum and Dad had started building their house, Vimala Aunty had decided that she, too, wanted to move to Kerala. So she had built a huge, ugly house on her plot next door, which rose three storeys and blocked out all the light on the western side of my parents' house. It had been completed a year before ours had been finished and Vimala Aunty had announced this triumph with a grand house-warming with a catered sadya and half the village in attendance.

'Oh, she's going to blight our retirement years, mark my words,' said Shivan Mama, as Vimala Aunty peered into all the rooms in Mum and Dad's modest new home, her cheeks flushed, lips quivering with unreasonable pent-up envy. Mum boxed him on the arm. 'Shavam, can't you say something nice at this auspicious time?'

7

Gunfire at the Border

B y the time I visited my parents the next summer, they appeared to be settling nicely into their new lives. 'I can't believe it's been over a year!' Mum exclaimed. 'I still find myself staring at kitchen cabinets, wondering where I have stashed the *puttu kuzhal*[25], and rummaging through drawers to find a notebook.' Despite her resolve to have everything unpacked and organized within a month of shifting to Kerala, there were still unopened cartons of odds and ends in the spare room upstairs, in the alcove on the terrace under the water tank, in the space under the stairs and squashed between the car and every wall of the garage.

'It is all this space,' she complained to Dad. In Bombay, there was no room for excess, much less for mess. Dad had fitted his useless hoard of old paint, rusting tools and decades-old income tax returns in the small wooden loft in the corridor, or in old suitcases stored above the cupboards, from where they waged a constant battle with Mum's propensity to clean, declutter and dispose. Here, their possessions seemed to have grown exponentially with the space available, and already the cupboards were full and every spare corner occupied.

Dad, Mum informed me, was suffering none of the pangs

---

[25] A cylindrical vessel used to make puttu, a Kerala breakfast dish

of retirement, keeping himself busy by running errands and gardening and trying to help Mum around the house. 'There is no retirement for her, is there?' he said. 'And she has been cooking and washing and cleaning for as long as I have been working.' But Mum was never easy to help. If he dusted, she followed him around with a cloth to clean the spots he had missed. If he put the washed clothes on the line, she rearranged them in some manner of her own liking but of no discernible logic. And the one time that she had allowed him to cook, after weeks of Dad insisting that he could indeed cook and used to do so frequently during his bachelor days, she had breathed down his neck impatiently as he had beaten eggs for a breakfast omelette for a visiting Prakash. You have to beat them with a fork exactly one hundred times, Dad said, to get the optimal omelette, puffed up like a pigeon's chest and fluffy as a newborn chick.

'Hundred times-aw? He will get it for lunch then!' Mum had said and Prakash laughed hysterically to see his grandparents bickering; head thrown back, mouth open, gurgles of mirth catching at the back of his throat.

'Good omelette, no?' Dad asked Prakash as he wolfed down the omelette and jammed a slice of bread into his mouth. Prakash pivoted his head vigorously from side to side in agreement.

'Better than Ammamma's[26], no?'

Prakash looked from one to the other and giggled some more but wisely decided to keep his counsel.

Mum, who had been made to wait impatiently while Dad monopolized the kitchen for the beaten-to-death omelette, who had been left to clean up the debris of his culinary pursuits— fragments of eggshell and egg white all over the counter and

---

[26]Grandmother (mother's mother)

three separate bowls Dad had used to complete the task—had banished him from the kitchen thereafter, so Dad now restricted himself to setting the table and rinsing his plate in the sink. Even then, he often caught Mum rearranging the plates and glasses on the table to be just so, and wiping around the sink after he'd finished rinsing. So he gave up, and concentrated on what Mum deemed him to be best at: cleaning the drain when it was blocked, changing a bulb that had fused, screwing in the handle of the tea pan when it came loose.

This gave him plenty of time, he said, to do the things he had wanted to all his life but had never found the time: read *Freedom at Midnight* and *My Experiments with Truth* and *War and Peace* and *The Complete Works of Shakespeare*, all books he had started many times over but abandoned after dozing over them several nights in a row; watch the latest Malayalam films on Asianet; listen to all the cassettes of M.S. Subbalakshmi that they had bought over the years; brush up on the astrology he had started learning as a young man.

'So, do you miss work?' I asked.

'What's there to miss?' Dad asked. 'Finally, after over three decades, I don't have to get up in the morning and wear a pressed pant and shirt, I don't have to stand squashed up against a sweaty traveller on a bus or a train. And, thank god, I no longer have to report to a mere child!'

It was nice to see Dad so relaxed. He practically lived in his thin khadi banians and mundu now, exchanging them for indifferently ironed pants and an often stained shirt when he had to make a trip to the market. When he saw the moderately expensive branded shirt I had bought him from Bombay, he was exasperated. 'What for?' he tut-tutted. 'Haven't I worn enough of these to office?' And he placed it at the back of his cupboard, from where it would emerge for a special occasion, he promised, looking pointedly at me, the only unmarried person left in the family.

Mum had been trying to cajole me into 'seeing girls' for some time now, but I had managed to fend her off with a variety of excuses. 'I don't have the money to support anybody but myself' worked for a while, but now that I had been confirmed as a junior associate at my consulting firm, that was no longer true. My salary had been bumped up, I had exchanged my Filofax for a PalmPilot and had acquired a mobile phone as thick as a brick (although I used it sparingly because of the exorbitant rates), and that excuse was no longer viable. I'm busy, I'm travelling, I'm not ready, I said...

'Not ready?' asked Mum. 'What does that mean?'

I wasn't quite sure.

'Do you have somebody in mind?' she asked suspiciously.

I groaned.

∽

Can anyone remember when they first started noticing girls? One day, they're those shrill, silly, annoying things who can't throw a ball, will giggle at seemingly nothing and will screech if they see a frog or a cockroach, and the next they're doing all kinds of things to you. You can't look at them because you know your eyes will stray to their swelling chests, and you can't even be near them without your face turning red, your ears burning. Even the hairy-legged girls from the neighbouring school, the girl with the braces in the flat across the hallway. Undoubtedly, there are no coherent thoughts at this stage, no images of love and rosy futures. Just rampant hormones and lust–painful, all-consuming, all-befuddling lust. You deal with it as best as you can, by having conversations of raging innuendo with your friends, feigning a sexual knowledge and experience you are not likely to have for the next decade, at least. You extend your reading to the works of Harold Robbins and Sidney Sheldon, hoping that the racy bits will serve to educate and illuminate. And you start hiding posters of Pamela Anderson and Pamella Bordes—remember Pamella Bordes?—under your mattress, or among your green VIP briefs that your mother has bought for you.

After a decade in an all-boys' school, you are set free into the co-ed world of junior college. You cope as well as you can, despite the dusting of livid pimples on your cheek and the sporadic cuts from your yet-unskilled use of the razor. You live in the jeans that you buy from Fashion Street, and let your shirt hang loose over your belt to obscure the label that says 'Wangler' instead of 'Wrangler' or 'Lewis' instead of 'Levi's'. You roam around in testosterone-fuelled packs of friends, pretending to be unaware of the local oestrogen, and occasionally work up the courage to break away to talk to a girl, knowing fully well that you are being watched by the herd and that you will be tormented mercilessly on your return. At the college social, you pretend that dancing is passé and stand in the shadows nursing your orange Rasna while boys named Chris and Steven jive effortlessly in the middle of the hall and, by virtue of a slow number, get more female contact than you have ever had in your life.

Even if you surmount all odds and actually get a girl to go out with you, where do you go and what do you do? If, like me and most of the other boys of my era, your pocket money barely stretches through the month, you could probably buy her a stickjaw from the hawker of sweets and cigarettes outside the college, who you call familiarly by name to display your growing confidence as well as to flaunt your intimate knowledge of grown-up things like cigarettes. At best, you can spring for a Gold Spot and samosa in the canteen. You are no match for the rich kids, who can take a girl to the neighbourhood café for a hot fudge nut sundae and drop her home in their daddies' cars.

Despite all these hurdles, you manage to make a few female friends, you hang around in mixed platonic groups, you almost learn to flirt under the guise of intellectual debate—there is nothing quite as titillating as bickering about the pros and cons of Jack Kevorkian's assisted suicides, after all, or the long-term impact of glasnost on communism around the world—and then, you probably push off to engineering college.

Attending engineering college in the Nineties was the nearest you could get to being a Trappist monk. It should be recommended residence for brahmacharis trying to practise abstinence. The boy-girl ratio couldn't be more skewed in a Haryana village. If you're lucky, there will be about five girls for every fifty boys. Of these, one will be completely batty, two will never take their noses out of their books, one will be as flirtatious as she is unattractive and one, well, that one will keep all hope from dying.

In such a setting, your love life consists solely of sending anonymous roses to the girls on Rose Day (even to the lone girl in Mech, the one with the moustache) and reading the off-colour doodles carved on to the wooden desks. Four years of this, and you're pretty much where you started out, just rather more desperate.

For me, engineering was followed by that stint in the desert, where my love life was further simplified—there just weren't any suitable women around. Nevertheless, even at my most oestrogen-deprived, I always believed that I would meet someone, someday. She would be pretty and funny and smart, and she would get all my jokes and think me kind of special. We would get married and live happily ever after.

The threat of an arranged marriage always loomed, because that was how things were always done in our family, Govind notwithstanding. Sudha had done it, and by all rights, Govind should have. Govind straying from our middle-class script had made it only more difficult, with Mum and Dad often expressing to me how much easier things would have been if Govind had chosen from our community. They never went as far as forbidding me to 'find someone', but any female friend, especially if she was from a different religion, was looked upon with cold suspicion.

And yet, I never thought I would marry somebody my parents chose for me. It was unthinkable. Meet somebody a couple of times and then shack up for life? How does one do that? What about compatibility, what about friendship, what about chemistry? How do you sleep with someone you barely know? Who was I, Charlie Sheen? The fact that Sudha had done it didn't make anything better, because that was how Sudha was—despite her complaining and bouts of rebelliousness, she was ultimately practical and conforming, as she had shown in marrying eligible doctor Ramu and producing the two brats, Prakash and Preetha.

Come to think of it, does *anybody* really dream of growing up and having your parents choose somebody for you? Does anybody fantasize about the first meeting surrounded by relatives, the first night fumbling around a person you barely know, exposing your hairless chest and skinny legs to a stranger?

I looked with pity upon our parents, who had seen each other just once before tying the knot. Even the fact that they were reasonably happy, in their own bickering, nagging kind of way, didn't make the thought of an arranged marriage any more palatable—they lived in a different time, didn't they, when you rarely spoke to a girl you were not related to and got married before you became fixed in your ways?

We, on the other hand, knew real, live girls—they even phoned us sometimes, even though it was mostly to ask for notes or to remind you to complete your part of that joint assignment. And I had been to business school, which, after the long dry spell in engineering and Rajasthan, had been like stepping into the Playboy mansion. Really, I had no excuse for not 'finding someone'. But for all my fantasies about meeting somebody and falling in love, I was hopeless at what it actually took to get into a relationship. To make eye contact. To approach the girl and find something clever or witty to say. To get her attention. To pursue her, woo her, court her, win her over. It just seemed like an awful lot of work to me—awfully mortifying work, in fact.

I could never master that easy-banter thing that people do— what sounded terribly urbane when my friends said it always landed up sounding completely inane or slightly offensive when I did. I'll even confess to this: I'm told that a girl in college was trying to flirt with me when she asked me to massage her aching head. I hopped across to the pharmacist and bought her a Saridon instead. 'You poor sap,' my wife giggled and pinched my cheek fondly when I told her the story many years later.

Needless to say, by the time I was out of business school, with half my friends already coupled up or tying the knot, I was more single than a one-rupee note.

At last, I was rescued from complete virtue by one of the women in my consulting firm, a clever, brittle type with a sharp, trendy haircut, a voice husky with cigarette-smoking and a manner that was smug with the aura that her management degree and fancy consulting position had bestowed upon her. She took complete command over our ultra-brief dalliance—and

I mean complete command, over *everything*. When it was over I was relieved, and also a little indignant that she had been the one to dump me.

I was in my late twenties, not far from the dreaded thirty, which used to seem like middle age to me not so long ago—this was the time that an ageing actor promoted the rejuvenating benefits of a pill called Thirty Plus, keep in mind. It had occurred to me that I was hopelessly unattached, with absolutely no prospects on the horizon, while all my friends were getting hitched—I often couldn't even find an acquaintance to share a bottle of Old Monk with, let alone round up an entire gang of mates for an impromptu trip to Goa or Matheran like we used to when we were all single. So I'd find myself hanging around with the office bore, or one of the young whippersnappers who had just joined the company; I'd listen to the stories of the office bore's supposed glory days when he was on a career path to CEO, until he was thwarted by evil colleagues and fate in general; I'd try to keep up with the whippersnapper's hard drinking and chain-smoking, wondering how a generation gap had yawned open within the space of a few years. I filled my weekends with work that could easily wait till Monday, or by watching *Die Hard* and *Terminator* into the night for the hundredth time with one of my ever-changing flatmates in the office chummery. I took up a course in photography and pretended that developing a film roll was as satisfying as a warm body next to mine at night.

To make matters worse, one day I bumped into the unidimensional mugpot-topper from my engineering class and found that even he was married! He was all good cheer and smugness despite the hairline which was already beginning to recede, and she, incredibly, *unfairly*, pretty. To make things worse, it was a love marriage! Not just a stroke of luck delivered by the arranged-marriage gods—they had actually met and dated and whatnot. I couldn't imagine what she saw in him, but to think that the mugpot was getting more action than me was perhaps what made me question my notions, my lifelong stand. Perhaps any warm body was better than none?

So when Mum told me about some 'suitable' girl and asked me to meet her, I said, for the first time, 'Hmmm… Okay.'

'How long will you continue like this?' asked Mum, from force of habit. 'Being single may seem attractive now, but let me tell you…'

'I said "okay", Mum!'

'Oh!'

I was already beginning to regret it.

∽

When I got back to Mumbai, there were photos of women already waiting for me in the mail. Women in saris and more jewellery than a Bollywood heroine in a family drama. A girl who had unfortunately stood next to a rather large vase, making her look like something out of *Honey, I Shrunk the Kids*. A formidable-looking lady standing proudly in front of a shelf full of trophies and certificates. They were accompanied by 'résumés' of a sort: long lists of educational and professional qualifications, family trees running back a few generations, promises of fair complexions and homely natures. I was depressed.

'So why is it that "the boy" doesn't have to send some kind of résumé too?' I asked Mum. I found the whole practice of calling prospective brides and grooms 'girls' and 'boys' ridiculous but desisted from telling Mum so. She would have been perplexed.

'Of course you do—we sent it already.'

'You sent it! Why wasn't I consulted?'

'Oh! Big man you've become, aah? "Consulted", it seems. Why do I have to consult you? I don't know about you or what?'

I rolled my eyes but since she was over a thousand kilometres away at the other end of a telephone line, it didn't quite have the effect it was supposed to have. 'So what did you write?'

'You know, the usual. Engineering-management. Campus recruitment to an MNC firm. Fair, handsome, earning well, no expectation of dowry...'

I whimpered like an injured stray. 'And you sent a photo too?'

'Of course.'

'Which one?' I half expected her to have sent the photo she always thought quite adorable, of me at the age of five, in a dress, lipstick and a floppy hat—what can I say, a ten-year-old Sudha had been in charge of styling that day. It was worse. She had sent a passport photo I had taken for a bank account, in the days before consulting had moulded me into something more human. My hair was unkempt, I was wearing one of those early-Nineties' floppy-collared shirts and an expression that said 'feed me, please, I'm starving'.

'Why? What's wrong? Would you have agreed to get a studio portrait done? That one is very nice. You look distinguished,' said Mum.

I have to say I judged the women who agreed to meet me after seeing that photo. But nevertheless, they did, which led me to believe that there was reason to doubt their sanity.

I met a couple of them. One in Kerala, in the presence of both sets of parents. The 'girl' brought tea out on a tray and sat with her head bent for the rest of the visit, looking mostly tearful. I rummaged through my mind to find something to say, but it's surprisingly difficult to talk to someone who won't look at you. I was half afraid that her father would spring between us if I so much as addressed her.

'Forget it,' I told Mum later.

'Why?' she asked, her voice rising like a bird on a thermal. 'She's just shy!'

Another, Mum took upon herself to invite back to my chummery in Mumbai. I had to resort to some skulduggery to get my flatmates out of the house before the 'girl' arrived with her mother, a petite woman with an oiled plait and bright inquisitive eyes. The girl was some highly qualified thing who talked with great authority and laughed like an AK-47 going off. They were duly impressed by the well-appointed flat, oohed and aahed about the three-burner hob, the frost-free fridge and the fully automatic washing machine, which were all avant-garde for that time. The mother then announced that she would leave us alone to 'get to know each other' and barged into my bedroom without so much as a by-your-leave. I tried my best to keep the conversation going, and it really should not have been difficult because the 'girl' talked incessantly and filled the few silences with staccato bursts of laughter that sounded like fireworks being set off on Diwali. But my mind was on my prospective mother-in-law assessing the jumble of clothes on my bed crowned by newly washed underwear, the poster from Michael Jackson's *In the Closet*, of Naomi Campbell in half-squat grinding pose on the back of the door, the cigarette butts in the ashtray, the empty beer bottles in the corner. As soon as I could, I made excuses and sidled towards the bedroom.

'Why don't you join us, Aunty?' I said, poking my head around the door.

The lady jumped up from the side of the bed where she had apparently been combing through my bedside drawer. 'The drawer...it just fell down... I was putting the things back,' she said, without even bothering to blush.

'No, no, no, no!!!' I told Mum.

'But they're so keen! And the girl is so qualified! Where will you get anyone better?'

'Thank you, Mum, for the vote of confidence,' I said, my tone acid. 'But I don't think I can spend the rest of my life with that laugh.'

'What's wrong with the laugh?'

'It sounds like gunfire being exchanged at the Indo-Pak border.'

'Oh-ho! As if your laugh is so nice! That is what you base the rest of your life on, a laugh? You're almost thirty, don't you want to get married before we die?' said Mum, playing her trump card. The spectre of parental death was supposed to guilt one into doing almost anything.

But I had a fitting rejoinder. 'Anyway, let me just say, I think my Walkman and a couple of thousands are missing from my bedroom drawer. Is that what you want?' I parried. I was lying, but it shocked her into silence.

And thus it would have continued, the squabbling and the bargaining over the phone, the monthly instalment of studio photographs and résumés, the occasional excruciating meeting with someone completely unsuitable. But then our lives took another turn, another unexpected diversion from our well-laid-out middle-class path, a detour that made Mum and Dad and everyone else forget about my marital status for a while.

8

Paper Catching Fire

The Nineties had not quite played out. The world had gasped when a princess had died in a Parisian tunnel; TV ratings had soared with the antics of a US president and his cigar; a sheep was cloned; a fictional boy magician was about to take the world by storm.

I was taking my annual vacation in Kerala—a few stolen days from the frenetic work schedule. I pretended it was duty, but in truth it was good to get away from the endless travel and late nights at work, and from the chummery—the roulette of roommates, the communal kitchen with dishes piled in the sink and the peculiar, unfamiliar aromas of another's cooking, the pungent odour from the jumble of shoes by the door. It was good to be coddled by Mum—for, somehow, in the intervening years, due to my prolonged absence perhaps, or Govind's departure from middle-class protocol, I had been accorded the special status that Govind had once enjoyed. All my favourite dishes were being made at mealtimes, I was allowed to sleep in without Mum nudging me awake to say the maid needed to clean, and Dad relinquished his first right to the newspaper in my favour, despite protests that he really didn't have to.

Sudha and her children were in Kerala too—we tried to time our annual trips home together, so we didn't have to make endless cross-country journeys to see each other. Prakash and

Preetha were eleven now, and so starkly different that they didn't seem like peers at all, leave alone twins. Prakash was all endless appetite and boundless energy, running from room to room for no discernible reason, leaving telltale smudges on Mum's pristine walls in spite of being threatened with dire consequences if he bounced cricket balls against them, pestering me to bowl to him or play Jenga or ludo or chequers. Preetha had become shy and quiet, standing silently at the edge of adult conversations, attentive, retentive. She followed Mum around, peering into pots on the stove or helping her set the table or water the garden, or immersed herself in Nancy Drews and endless solitary games of cat's cradle with a bit of purple embroidery thread.

I remember it was teatime. A Top 20 Bollywood songs show was playing on the television; Madhuri Dixit, well past girlishness but not quite middle-aged, was flashing a smile and shaking a hip. Mum had made onion pakoras—'Bajji[27], Ammamma, bajji,' insisted Prakash, who was Southie through and through—and had brought out piles of ladoos and jalebis bought from the neighbourhood sweet-maker. Dad and Mum were bickering about how much sugar Dad was consuming, and Prakash, apparently keen to put an end to the argument, was swiftly stuffing what was left of the ladoos and jalebis into his mouth. I was savouring the tea that I had been missing all these months—strong, not too sweet and guaranteed to chase away the last slivers of midday slumber. Sudha had skipped tea and was in her room—her tummy had been playing up for the past few days and Mum's home remedies didn't seem to be working. The general consensus was that a few skipped meals would do Sudha no harm—indeed, three days of eating light, and there was no discernible shrinking of her

---

[27]South Indian term for pakora, a fried snack

ample middle. Once upon a time, Sudha had been slender, but she had never quite lost the weight she had put on when she got pregnant. Her generous belly had people nudging her coyly and asking when the baby was due, and rolling their eyes in disbelief when she insisted that she was not expecting.

Every time he met her, Govind looked at her with unspoken disapproval. Maggie had lost her baby weight almost immediately after birth—she ate like a bird and ran every other day, apart from swimming and practising Pilates and yoga. She even had Govind contorting himself into knots and extolling the virtues of padmasana.

'What can I do?' said Sudha. 'I'm on my feet all the time, but the weight just doesn't shift.'

'Yes, don't blame her,' I said. 'She's storing fat for the winter.'

Madhuri Dixit made way for a big-haired, bushy-eyebrowed Karisma Kapoor, bouncing alarmingly on a charpoy with an ageing Govinda who didn't look capable of such feats. Preetha appeared at Mum's side and tugged at her hand. I had not seen her leave the table. 'I think something is wrong with Mama,' she mumbled.

'What?' asked Mum, bemused, befuddled.

I rolled a too-hot pakora around on my tongue, allowing the steam to escape before I took another bite.

'Something is wrong with Mama,' Preetha repeated, a bit tearful. 'She's lying on the floor.'

By the time I had swallowed my pakora and digested this bit of information, Dad had scraped back his chair and rushed upstairs, and Mum had sloshed her tea all over the table in panic. I rushed after Dad, Mum behind me, while Prakash stayed behind to clear up the rest of the pakoras.

I made my way upstairs, and found Sudha crumpled face

down near her bed, blood pooling around her head. Dad was trying to lift her but was buckling at the knees under the dead weight. I hurried over and, together, we got her upright, and then back on to the bed. She started coming to, her eyes unfocused, mumbling something unintelligible. Blood oozed from a gash on her head. Mum rushed to call Dr Balan.

Dr Balan, fondly called Backside Balan by those who knew him, had a well-lit piles and fistula clinic that was blatantly located on the main road and not in some discreetly shaded street. 'People actually go there?' I had asked Mum many a time. 'I mean, what do they tell the people they run into?'

'Why, what's to tell? As though you don't have a backside!'

But he was Mum's third cousin, so he was consulted for everything from colds to stomach upsets. All he asked in return for house visits was a large glass of Bournvita and a packet of cream biscuits.

After some poking and prodding, Backside Balan declared it was nothing serious, just light-headedness caused by lack of food. 'I told her she should eat!' Mum exclaimed.

'But that gash needs to be tended to. She'll need stitches. I'd hurry, she's lost a fair amount of blood.'

So off we rushed, me in the crumpled shorts I had taken my afternoon nap in, Dad in the mundu with a hole in it, Mum left behind to look after the children. Sudha was uncharacteristically quiet, and later she would say she remembered nothing after the fall.

The closest medical facility was a fairly large hospital, two kilometres away. Despite the milling crowds, a doctor who looked no older than me promptly wheeled Sudha into the emergency room to stitch up the gash—Backside Balan had called ahead, it appeared. In a few minutes we were told it was all done, but that

Sudha would have to be checked by the senior doctor before she could be discharged. In the meanwhile, they would administer a drip, take some routine tests.

The senior doctor, Dr Kurien, strode in a couple of hours later, trailed by the junior doctor, looking appropriately servile, and a fat old woman in a nurse's uniform, who was panting with the effort of keeping up. He read the notes made by the junior doctor, and gave Sudha a reassuring smile.

'Gave everyone a scare, didn't you?'

Sudha smiled weakly.

'So, what did you eat last?'

Sudha searched for an answer. Dad chipped in, 'An idli for breakfast, a little bit of curd-rice for lunch. She's been having an uneasy stomach for days.'

'I have an uneasy stomach all the time nowadays,' said Sudha. 'I barely eat, and still I can't seem to lose this fat around my stomach.'

'Uneasy? Hmmmm. Gas?'

'Not really.'

'Loose motion, constipation?'

'No.'

'Hmmm. Have you lost weight?'

'No-oo!' we chimed in. Sudha gave us a look. 'Actually, I've been gaining weight regardless of what I eat.'

At this point, the doctor asked us to step outside so that he could examine Sudha. I was relieved to be spared further soliloquies on gas and motions and god knows what else.

I called Mum to say we would be returning home soon and went down to the canteen to get a couple of coffees. When I returned, Dr Kurien was talking to Dad. 'I'd like to run a few more tests, some more scans,' he was saying.

'Oh,' said Dad, uncertainly. 'What for?'

'Well, just to be cautious…rule a few things out.'

'Such as?'

'Sir, let's just see the test results, shall we?'

'No, no…but you have to tell me what tests you're doing, don't you?'

'Sir, her stomach is a little distended. It's probably nothing… but we have to check.'

'For what?'

'Dad…' I said. 'Just let them do the tests.' I turned to Dr Kurien. 'How long will you take?'

'We'd like to keep her overnight. We should have the results tomorrow.'

'Okay,' I said, before Dad could protest. 'Dad, I'll stay with Sudha, you go back home.'

Of course, Dad was having none of it. He tried to coax me into going home, but eventually we both stayed, after making another call to Mum. We were up most of the night as attendants wheeled Sudha in and out for blood tests and ultrasounds. In the morning, Mum appeared with the children, worry lines dug deep into her face. Prakash broke free and ran up to me as if he was seeing me after months. 'Vivek Mama, Ammamma didn't let me bring my cricket ball,' he complained. I patted him on the head. Preetha went and sat quietly at the foot of Sudha's bed. Sudha was herself now, sitting up and complaining about the fuss that was being made. 'Ate breakfast?' she asked Preetha, stroking her hand, and Preetha nodded without a word.

Dad and I went back home to freshen up, while Mum stayed with Preetha. Back at the hospital, we found the test results were still awaited. Mum was on a rant about modern doctors and their penchant for making money by running unnecessary and expensive tests. Preetha was lying by Sudha's side, while Prakash was opening and closing the blinds repeatedly, his fascination for this new pastime overcoming his fear of Sudha's ire.

'Take him home, will you?' beseeched Sudha, so reluctantly Mum left with the children while Dad and I stayed back.

Not long after Sudha had been served an unappetizing lunch, the junior doctor summoned us. 'Dr Kurien is here,' he said reverentially. 'Come to his office.'

Dr Kurien's office was on another floor, small but fairly swanky, with a potted palm in a brass planter in the corner, a couple of plaques on the wall and a sheaf of papers and piles of books on the table. Dr Kurien smiled perfunctorily as we came in and motioned for us to sit.

'Did you get a chance to go home?' he asked Dad.

'Yes, yes,' said Dad.

'Had lunch?'

'Er, no, we will go home and have.'

'Very good, very good.' I noticed a framed family photograph next to one of the plaques. His wife had an unfortunate hairstyle that made her look like a cape buffalo with jhumkis.

'Anyway,' he said, his voice suddenly business-like. He pulled out a prescription pad and started writing. 'The test results are back.'

'Yes, yes?' said Dad, polite, almost pleading. A day in the hospital, with its bleeping machines and its doctors in white coats and nurses in knee-length socks, and its swarms of patients in various stages of distress, had worn us down to that state of nervous helplessness you see in patients everywhere.

'We see some irregularities in the blood tests and ultrasounds, so we would like to bring in our specialist.' Dr Kurien continued to scribble.

I felt a flutter in my chest. I looked at Dad and he was looking open-mouthed at Dr Kurien, an uncertain half-smile on his face, willing Dr Kurien not to impart any bad news.

'Specialist?'

'Yes, yes. An oncologist.'

The flutter had become a juddering in my chest. The half-smile had disappeared from Dad's face.

'We cannot be sure—the symptoms could suggest ovarian cysts. But we suspect it might be ovarian cancer.'

Just like that. He didn't even look up from his prescription pad. If he had, he would have seen what I did—Dad recoiling ever so slightly, as though he had been given a gentle blow on the belly, and then crumpling inwards, like a piece of paper catching fire. I laid a hand on his, and was surprised at how thin it felt. Dad had always been lean, but it was a thinness borne of strength. The bone under me now felt fragile, unsubstantial, like a dry twig about to snap.

There was a long silence. 'I don't understand,' said Dad.

Dr Kurien repeated, a little louder, looking at me instead of Dad, 'Ovarian cysts, possibly cancer.'

After another long pause, Dad whispered, 'Are you sure? About the cancer?'

'About 90 per cent,' said Dr Kurien, still not meeting Dad's eyes. 'But the oncologist will probably have to do a biopsy. It's best you talk to him.' And with this, he rolled back his blue upholstered revolving chair and brought the meeting to an end.

Outside, Dad and I stood looking at each other for a while. Then slowly, he walked to one of the plastic bucket chairs in the waiting area and sat heavily down.

'Dad, it will be okay,' I said, clutching his hand, although I felt as though my insides had flowed out of my body.

He looked up at me. 'Yes, yes,' he said, reassuring me now. 'Everything will be okay.'

'It may not even be cancer.'

'But he said he was 90 per cent sure.'

And we both fell silent again.

'Don't tell Mum. Not just yet,' I said. And this made him look even more anxious.

We couldn't bring ourselves to tell Sudha, so the junior doctor told her, more kindly than the senior doctor had told us. She sat in the bed looking resigned and strong, and I couldn't take it any more. I went to her side and put my arms awkwardly around her. She patted me on the back.

'Don't worry, everything will be okay,' she said.

'Of course it will—it's you! Even if it's cancer, it doesn't have a chance.' And despite herself, Sudha smiled weakly.

We all agreed we wouldn't tell Mum just yet, nor Govind and Maggie, nor the kids, not until the diagnosis had been confirmed. Sudha was discharged swiftly and an appointment made to meet the oncologist in two days, when he would be back from a conference in the Maldives. In the car, Sudha dozed fitfully at the back while Dad and I rehearsed what we would tell Mum.

At home, Prakash and Preetha were hanging from the gate. They swung it closed behind the car and ran up to open the car door for Sudha. Preetha followed closely by Sudha's side as she went into the house, while Prakash tugged at my hand.

'What?' I said, a touch irritably.

'I found a bird's nest on the roof, come see!'

Mum came out and shooed him away. 'So?' she asked in a low voice. 'What did the doctor say?'

Dad could barely meet her eye. Before Mum could sense that something was wrong, I chimed in. 'Oh, nothing, but Sudha needs to go for some follow-up tests in a couple of days.' Even to me, my voice sounded unusually cheerful.

Mum looked dismayed. 'Why? Why are they doing so many tests?'

'Oh, it's just routine, I suppose.'

'What kind of tests?'

'Oh, I'm not sure.'

'What? Didn't you ask? What kind of consultant are you?'

'What? What does that even mean, Mum?'

'They must be checking for something.' She looked at Dad for enlightenment but he was leaning back in the easy chair, looking into the distance.

'I'm going to call that doctor and find out!' said Mum. 'How could you not check what tests they're running?'

'No, no—it's some gastroenteritis tests, I think,' I extemporized.

Mum exhaled sharply and put her hand to her chest. 'Thank god! The things that were running through my mind! I was even thinking it might be...cancer.' On that last terrifying word, Mum lowered her voice to a whisper. She continued, happy, oblivious. 'Gastroenteritis? That explains all her digestion problems. Good, good, it was worrying me. They'll give her some medicines, I expect.'

Dad gave me an anguished look. Mum caught it immediately and looked from one to the other of us. 'What is it?' she asked, her voice fearful.

I looked at Dad, his expression more helpless than I'd ever seen it. All my resolve liquefied. 'I'm sorry, Mum, I told Dad not to tell you till we were sure, but I can't do it. They are saying that it could be...it could be cancer. Sudha has to meet the oncologist in two days.'

Relief washed over Dad's face, relief at being reprieved from that role of sole custodian of that terrible secret, relief that Mum was in on it, that she, too, would share the burden. Relief mixed with that helpless distress, at having changed Mum's life in the space of a sentence, just like Dr Kurien had changed ours. Mum blinked and held the back of a chair. 'I see. Are they sure?'

'They'll have to do a biopsy.'

'Does Sudha know?'

I nodded. She looked out into the garden, her mouth pulled downwards, her eyes moist. Jasmine flowers were budding on the bush outside.

'Okay, I have to go talk to her. You stay here with your father.' She gave him a short squeeze on the shoulder as she left, a squeeze that said it would be okay, that she understood, that we were all in it together.

∽

Ramu arrived the next day. Since I'd last seen him, a dusting of grey had settled on his hair, and his features had gone a little soft. Prakash was dizzy with delight, hanging on to his father's hand wherever he went, but Preetha's happiness was tempered with worry. 'Why has Daddy come?' she asked me. 'Doesn't he have to work?'

The few days that were left of that terrible vacation were spent babysitting the children and fielding such questions from them, while Sudha and Ramu and my parents shuttled to and from the doctor's office. The oncologist confirmed the diagnosis, ovarian cancer, while adding a disclaimer that it could be confirmed only after a biopsy.

This, Ramu decided, or rather, Mum and Sudha decided and Ramu gave his inconsequential post-facto consent, would be done in Chennai, where Ramu had contacts in the medical community and could assure the best care. I was dispatched to bring forward their tickets and book a couple more for my parents, who would accompany them.

'No!' cried Prakash, lying on the diwan and flailing his arms and legs about like an oversized toddler. 'Why do we have to go back? I want to stay here till the end of my holidays!'

'But Ammamma and Ammachan[28] are coming with you,' I said, by way of consolation.

'Yay!' cried Prakash, unravelling himself from the diwan in a flash, and off he sped at full tilt. Preetha looked unconvinced but stayed quiet, and played yet another game of cat's cradle.

Sudha, who had been calm till then, fell apart at the oncologist's confirmation, but spurned tears for an all-encompassing anger. 'Why do these things always happen to me?' she asked Mum. 'What have I done? I'm moral, god-fearing, I've hurt no one...' and Mum fed her homilies about the fruits of the actions of past lives, and how she should never lose faith.

'I told you I wasn't overeating! Nobody believed me!' Here she gave me a withering look and I beat a hasty retreat.

'How did Ramu not suspect this? What is the use of having a doctor for a husband?' cried Sudha, as though prescience and X-ray vision were handed out along with medical degrees.

'How could he know?' said Mum, consolingly. 'Don't blame him.'

But when Sudha and Ramu weren't around, Dad blamed him too. It seemed to make him feel better. 'He could at least have got her to do some diagnostic tests! She's been complaining about bloating and indigestion and pain for months now. I feel bad that we didn't have her checked earlier—but does he care?

---

[28]Grandfather (mother's father)

Look at him—so laid-back! So indifferent.'

Dad was being grossly unfair, of course. It was just Ramu's way. It's a manner you see frequently in the profession—a nonchalance, a cavalier disregard for prudence. Perhaps you have to embrace a feeling of invincibility to stare death and disease in the eye every day. Like many of his peers, Ramu was completely indifferent about his own health, while advising his patients to lose weight, walk more, smoke less. He himself had at least five extra kilos around his middle, smoked ten, perhaps fifteen, cigarettes a day, and slept little. As for Sudha's prognosis, he had met it with an equanimity none of us could muster. 'There's a chance it may not even be cancer,' he said. 'And if it is, there's a good likelihood that we've caught it in the early stages—it's probably curable.' But all we could hear was the ambiguity of his words, the terrifying uncertainty of the 'likelihood' and the 'probably', and think: What if it isn't? I know this hung over all our heads, although we dealt with it in different ways—Mum by throwing herself into chores, packing up for an indefinite stay in Chennai, settling bills, closing up rooms, making arrangements for the house to be taken care of in their absence; Dad with trips to the astrologer and the temple and with hushed diatribes against Ramu; me by offering up prayers to gods I had only the slightest acquaintance with; Govind by sending my parents arcane scientific literature about malignancies and experimental treatments from across the seas.

I saw them off to the railway station a week later, worried and guilty that I couldn't be physically present to help Sudha and my parents, and yet relieved that I no longer had to be in the thick of things, that it wouldn't be me who would have to be the bearer of bad news or the maker of hard decisions. Mum briefly cupped my chin as she said goodbye, whispering, 'Sorry, monay, I had no time at all to look after you this time', and climbed into the train and disappeared before I could protest. For a while, Dad and I stood in that father-son silence that defies words, and when I squeezed his arm, I saw his eyes glisten. It disturbed me—I had never seen him tear up, not even when his mother had died. I let him go, his shoulders bent in premature defeat. Sudha was matter-of-fact, distracted by Prakash who was insisting on trying to heave a very large suitcase on to the train by himself. We exchanged a quick hug, unable to conjure up the right words to say to each other; I had already exhausted the everything-will-be-okays and don't-worrys and be-strongs and God-blesses. I shook hands with Ramu, patted Preetha on the head and stood by the newspaper stand until the train rolled out.

I locked up the house and returned to Mumbai, to my job and my chummery and my messy roommates, and to the blessed solace of work that had piled up and deadlines I had to meet and travel schedules I had to plan. Most of what I learnt of Sudha's health from that point on was second-hand, over conversations with Mum and Dad, and occasionally with Ramu.

The biopsy confirmed the ovarian cancer: Stage 1C, which was not as good as Stage 1A but vastly better than Stage 4. It had spread to outside the ovaries, but not to the other organs, which was good news. The uterus and ovaries were swiftly excised, and then there were the horrors of chemotherapy. Sudha lost her hair, practically every meal she ingested, her excess weight, her strength, her iron will, her ability to taste, the suppleness of her skin and, many months later, every trace of the malignant cells that had threatened her life. Mum and Dad stayed on in Chennai until then, shoring Sudha up over her treatment, looking after her house, her husband and children.

Despite being spared the immediacy of the disease, its shadow hung over me. When I spent a day immersed in work and looked up with a start of guilt to realize I had failed to think about Sudha's plight all day. As I caught myself humming a happy tune from *Kuch Kuch Hota Hai* or laughing at the dancing-baby animation that somebody had forwarded to me, and realized that Sudha would be in hospital, retching from the chemotherapy. As I tried to make Sudha laugh over the phone with the latest Clinton-Lewinsky joke, pretending not to notice the frighteningly tired voice at the other end. When I heard Dad on the line, his voice full of misgiving, and realized that no matter how bad I felt about Sudha's condition, I could not conjure up the depth of anguish that my parents were feeling, couldn't dig up the wells of strength they were finding within themselves to see her through this.

I told no one, not wanting to deal with the pitying looks, the well-meaning questions, the superficial offers of help. Instead, I tore down the poster of the grinding Naomi Campbell from my wall, avoided invitations to evenings out, accepted a promotion and then chucked up my job.

9

Out of the Box

I'm not sure why I did it. I was bored with my job, of course, tired of the endless travel, the late nights, the repetitive work, that feeling of being the hamster on somebody's giant wheel. But it was hardly a unique situation—everybody in my position, after a certain number of years of doing the same thing, day after day, would feel the same way. It was more than that. By all accounts, Sudha was in remission and recovering with a speed and tenacity that seemed characteristic to those of us who knew her, but in the light of what had happened, I was gripped by a restlessness that soured my days and churned my nights. It was so pointless, it seemed, to lumber on in a job that gave me no joy, to put one foot in front of the other—all just to make a living, to secure a life, to salt away some earnings. And all to what purpose, when the morrow could bring death and disease?

It was terribly clichéd, this existential angst of mine, dwelled upon on insomniac nights as I tossed and turned, images flitting through my head, refusing to let me sleep: of Sudha, sallow-faced and bald-headed in hospital, and Dad crumpling at the doctor's words all those months ago, and Mum, indefatigable, hurrying from room to room, propping everyone else up, a picture of strength. I brooded over the brevity of life, the futility of a plodding existence, as I walked, deep in thought, by the sea, the wind ballooning the shirt on my back, or around the atmospheric lanes of the Fort, brushing past the shifty-eyed hawkers trying to sell me peacock feathers and sex toys, past office-goers and college students and stockbrokers rushing by, preoccupied, unseeing.

I yearned for change. Not just change, but some chimera of control. Just when life was laughing in my face at the notion, trying to teach me that I would never have any control, over circumstances, over people, over life. But it would take me many more years to learn that.

For now, it was enough to turn my back on the job that had just brought me a promotion, more benefits and a higher salary. It was enough to escape from a city that milled around me, unmindful of my personal turmoil, of our family circumstances, of how our well-made lives had been upturned and tossed about by fate, a city that ignored my anguish and yet reminded me, in the clickety-clack of a suburban train or a Mario Miranda reproduction on a dingy café wall, in the sour-sweet-tangy taste of bhelpuri or the trundling of a dusty red double-decker bus, of happier times.

Such was my mental make-up that when one of my barely-out-of college colleagues offered me a job in a firm he was starting with some friends, I listened with growing interest. In my defence, it seemed like a promising business. It was the final flourishes of the Nineties, the era of Sabeer Bhatia and Bill Gates, and the buzzwords of the day were dotcoms, and B2B and B2C businesses, and importantly, ESOPs. Amazon and eBay had opened the eyes of the world to e-commerce, and Indian companies were following suit. 'Brick-and-mortar companies', another catchphrase, were now as passé as public-sector companies once were, and dotcoms were where the money, and the stock options, were.

The dotcom in question was going to be an e-commerce site that would sell all kinds of household goods, from fresh fruits and vegetables to detergents and toiletries to imported perfumes and cheeses. Customers could order their groceries online, on that wonderful new thing called the Internet, and the company would deliver to their doorstep. Since the company wouldn't have to spend on expensive retail space, it would be able to offer deep discounts to lure customers away from their neighbourhood store. The initial capital expenditure was being funded by the partners, but they were already talking to venture capitalists and were expecting to shake hands on a deal that would bring a huge infusion of funds to the maiden venture.

I would be in charge—in charge!—of charting out and implementing the strategy of the firm. I would be doing everything from plotting marketing and advertising strategy and overseeing web design to deciding the logistics of the supply chain. It was extremely seductive. Until now, despite my recent promotion, I had been a mere cog in the wheel—a large multinational wheel, no doubt, but a cog nevertheless—doing the grunt work on presentations and consulting reports, crunching numbers, manipulating charts, spending hours on PowerPoint. But now, there would be none of that, no more sitting on the fringes of business meetings, an extra body whose presence justified the many man-hours we were billing the hapless client. From now on, I would be master of my own fate.

If I hesitated, it was only because of the colleague in question, a chap called Purab with a flawless shiny complexion and overly gelled hair who said things like 'believe you me' and 'low-hanging fruit' even in casual conversation. Inevitably, he was considered to be something of a rising star in our consulting firm, and he was as much in demand for his impressive presentation skills and his ease with graphics as he was for his ability to spin yarns. About the dotcom they were about to start, he said it would be a paradigm shift in the way consumers bought groceries, that they would be really pushing the envelope and thinking outside the box.

In due course, he convinced me to meet one of the other partners, a tubby Tamilian called Ramalingam with a bushy moustache and a reassuring air of stodginess, who also worked in our consulting firm. Our paths had not crossed, but he was spoken about in water-cooler conversations with equal parts of reverence and scorn; reverence for his number-crunching skills and his jaw-dropping ability to recall arcane points of corporate law, and scorn, for his propensity, among other things, to eat the same lunch of rasam-rice every day, cooked by his mother and packed in a stainless-steel tiffin carrier. Over lunch—a greasy mutton curry and bright yellow pulao from the office canteen for Purab and me, occasionally supplemented by some surprisingly tasty pappadams and other fried bits that Purab kept filching from Ramalingam's tiffin carrier despite his glares—we discussed the nuts and bolts of the business. Ramalingam started talking numbers—potential sales, untapped markets, profit margins— and suddenly, the empty words with which Purab had been clothing the venture began to take a form, a form with flesh and bones, and hot, hungry blood coursing through its veins.

The business was going to be set up in Bangalore, not a centre of commerce like Mumbai was, but the most technology-savvy city in the country, and therefore one which would be most likely to embrace the e-commerce proposition. The salary was attractive, with an expense account and perquisites and ESOPs—benefits that only senior management ever got. And for accommodation, I would be given an entire flat to myself. No roommates! No wet bathrooms and oily kitchen countertops! It would have taken me several more years of toil before I could hope to aspire to any of these in my multinational consulting firm.

'And you'll get a fundoo designation, man!' said Purab. 'Chief planter!'

'What?' I said.

'You know, like a VP-Strategy, man, but waaay cooler!'

'Can't I just be VP-Strategy?'

'That's so passé, dude. Everybody's into these out-of-the-box designations these days. Believe you me.'

I tried to explain all this to Dad, skipping the chief planter bit, but he remained sceptical. 'Yes, all that's very good, but it's senior management in a very small company. A dotcom,' he said, adopting the modern lingo, but saying it with distaste. 'I don't mean to discourage you, but…'

'I know, Dad, I see what you're saying, but that's where all the business is nowadays—in start-ups, in dotcoms…'

'I don't understand these dotcoms. How do you earn money? How many people have Internet? How big is the market?' he asked.

'Small,' I conceded. 'But that's where the potential is, Dad. It's expected to grow in leaps and bounds in the coming years.'

'And till then, what? How do you sustain yourself?'

So I told him about the venture capital funding.

'But they haven't got it yet, have they?'

'No, but it's as good as signed and sealed.'

There was a long silence, the kind that Dad used where other fathers would have substituted a lengthy rant. 'And what value are those ESOPs they're offering you?'

'Not much today. But potentially, millions,' I said, and endured another long silence.

'Anyway, think about it, will you, before you do anything rash?'

I didn't tell him that I had already handed in my papers.

Within a month, I moved to Bangalore.

∽

In the Nineties, Bangalore was still small enough to retain its sobriquets of Pensioner's Paradise and Garden City, but it had also become the home of a number of wildly successful software companies, earning it grand titles such as the IT capital and the Silicon Valley of India—perhaps by those who had never actually visited Silicon Valley or an IT capital, for Bangalore was still relatively small and provincial then. The city seemed to be defined within a ten-kilometre radius that barely grazed Koramangala in the south, Sanjay Nagar in the north, Lingarajapuram in the east and Malleswaram in the west—everything else was distant suburb. The airport, its decor and ambience frozen in the 1980s, was twenty minutes from the central business district. There was barely a smattering of skyscrapers, even in the commercial areas, and the few residential apartment buildings were small and low-slung, as though apologizing to the neighbouring bungalows for their forwardness in reaching skywards. There were no suburban trains, no taxis, just autorickshaws that careened through the narrow clogged roads, and wheezing buses that had their routes displayed only in Kannada. Stores reluctantly opened their shutters at noon, and streets got deserted by 9 p.m. The fanciest movie theatres in the city were half the size of those in Mumbai and most of them were not even air-conditioned.

In my condescending, big-city way, I found it charming. I liked the wide roads, flanked by trees whose names you wanted to learn—expansive rain trees that stretched across streets, flaming gulmohars, tall African tulips and jacarandas that showered the streets with a carpet of lavender blooms. I liked the quiet residential streets lined by modest bungalows, with gardens of rose beds and crocus bushes, and pink and white bougainvillea tumbling prettily over their low walls. I liked the rambling public gardens with centuries-old trees and pelicans circling the lakes, and the atmospheric restaurants: Victoria Hotel, where the waiters seemed to be as old as the enormous trees in the garden and getting served was an afternoon-long affair; India Coffee House, a dingy little hole, with passable scrambled eggs that they advertised as poached eggs and a robust South Indian filter coffee that could revive a corpse. And I loved the smoky, unpretentious pubs where the pitchers were cheap, the music was loud classic rock and the clientele an alloy of impoverished post-grads trying to stretch a pitcher out for the whole evening and pot-bellied middle-aged men still wedded to their youth.

The locals, I would find in the months to come, were a good-natured bunch, who were slow to incite and quick to adjust: to the pot-holed roads, the crazy traffic, the perpetually late help. Nobody seemed to own a watch, or break out of a sedate pace, and everyone looked at you askance if you tried to impose schedules or deadlines. Their idea of road rage was to make a vaguely querulous rotating gesture of the hand that could at best mean, 'What are you doing?' And everybody smiled at you genially when they talked to you, from the passer-by who was confidently giving you wrong directions ('go straaaiiiight, turn left at the dead end' was routine, even when there was no such dead end) to the autorickshaw driver who was asking you, quite affably, for ₹50 over the meter.

And the famed weather lived up to its reputation: Chilly mornings that made early walkers and building watchmen scurry to pull on their monkey caps. A winter that actually required a different wardrobe from the summer, something I never would have imagined necessary in perennially sweltering Mumbai. A summer that was short and merciful and often punctuated by refreshing evening showers. And a gentle monsoon, with brief placid drizzles that you could easily wait out under the awning of a shop.

The new millennium was less than a year away, and there were all kinds of anxieties around Y2K, from doomsday predictions to fears of major computer glitches. The previous generation of hardware engineers had not accounted for the new millennium when they had abbreviated the years in digital calendars to two digits, thus making the year 2000 indistinguishable from the year 1900. So everybody was scrabbling to get their systems corrected and upgraded, and yet fears abounded of worldwide computer crashes at the dawn of the twenty-first century, leading to everything from plane crashes to the obliteration of digital identities, bank accounts and so on.

Our office was on 100 Feet Road in Indiranagar, which my local colleagues told me, with an apologetic smile, was quite a hike from the central business district around MG Road. To my delight I found it to be a ten-minute auto ride. At the time, 100 Feet Road was exclusively residential, with the exception of a couple of schools that tried not to make their presence felt. There was one restaurant at the very end, where it met the old Airport Road, and a couple of small grocery stores. Ours was one of the first offices in the area, smuggled into an unassuming bungalow which had an entrance hall that served as the reception area, a living room that had been partitioned into cubicles and multiple interlinking rooms that served as cabins—mine afforded a view of the jackfruit tree in the back garden. It was flanked by the cabins of Purab and Ramalingam, who, inevitably, we had now started calling Paschim. It was just us and two more partners, and a local geek who was responsible for setting up the e-commerce website.

The first few months were frenetic. I was talking to suppliers and warehousing people and advertising types on the one hand, and accompanying Purab and Paschim on presentations to potential investors on the other. We were working seventy-hour weeks but we were happy and excited and looking forward to Monday mornings. I felt some of the heaviness that had been pressing on me for months now lifting, and an almost-forgotten lightness of being returning. While it would be going too far to say I was jumping out of bed every morning—I was never a morning person—the spring had returned to my step, the laughter had returned to my chest.

It helped that Sudha's check-ups were all showing her to be in remission. Mum told me that Sudha was dealing with the angst brought about by her cancer by reading from the scriptures and chanting from her bhajan books. She had asked Mum to join her when she undertook a pilgrimage to Badrinath, Kedarnath, Haridwar and Rishikesh as soon as she was able, and was even contemplating going vegetarian. This seemed completely in character—Sudha was always the religious one among the three of us. Even as a child, it was she who was the happiest to accompany our mother to the temple to break coconuts for Hanuman and Ganapati every Tuesday and Saturday. It was she who could recite the *Vishnu Sahasranamam* and *Hanuman Chalisa* and *Gayatri Mantram* by heart. While all of us found god in the weeks before the exams, Sudha went the extra mile, filling notebooks with mantras to invoke the heavens, written in a neat, girlish hand. As soon as she married, she started fasting on Mondays for Ramu's well-being, and Preetha and Prakash were sent to bhajan sessions at the local temple every weekend, despite their strident protests. Even in college, when any right-minded teenager would worry about the cool quotient of their attire, Sudha would wear rings and necklaces with enormous stones that were eye-catchingly hideous to ward off evil and bring good fortune.

Mum and Dad viewed all of this with mixed feelings. On the one hand, they were thankful that Sudha was channelling her bottled anger, her existential angst into religion. It meant that there were fewer conversations about the unfairness of life, the futility of existence, fewer expostulations of why-did-it-happen-to-me? On the other hand, they were increasingly being subjected to Sudha's pious lectures about the meaning of life and the purpose of suffering, and had once been forced to endure a television production of a baby Krishna who lisped preciously through lips glossy with pink lipstick.

Nevertheless, they let all this pass without comment, although Mum scoffed at Sudha's overtures of turning vegetarian. As if Krishna and Arjuna didn't eat non-veg, she said, as though she has been informed by some divine source that they were dyed-in-the-wool carnivores. 'They were warriors,' she would go on to qualify.

Now, it might have been Mum who had initiated Sudha into religious fasts and visits to the temple, but Mum's spirituality was tempered with her firm common sense. Mum's visits to the temple were regular but brief, and she was far too particular about her attire to ever consider marring it with rudraksha malas and ugly rings. Her religious fasts were not fasts at all, just an abstention from non-vegetarian food and, for some reason, rice. She compensated by drinking copious amounts of sattvic wheat gruel and Champion oats sweetened to dessert-like consistency, and staved off her hunger pangs with soothing slabs of chocolate and badam halva. 'Why is chocolate okay but not rice?' I asked Mum, but never got a satisfactory answer. Dad would accompany Mum uncomplainingly to temples and had even started spending half an hour meditating before the gods in the puja room at twilight; he had also read more of the scriptures than Sudha ever would, but he would have never thought to lecture anyone about religion, not even his own children.

∽

My conversations with Sudha, and Mum and Dad too, no longer revolved around health worries and blood counts and worst-case what-if scenarios. Inevitably, it came back to their next most immediate concern—my single status.

Mum and Dad had been far too distracted until then to actively pursue any alliances, although proposals that had come in had been dutifully forwarded to me, even when Sudha was in the midst of her chemotherapy.

'Really, Mum?' I had once asked. 'You want me to get hitched now? Where are we going to have the wedding—in the oncology ward?' If Dad had directed his ire and helplessness at Ramu, my anger at the world, much as I tried to conceal and suppress it, seemed to bubble up to the surface and explode frequently in conversations with Mum.

'You have to live your life, Vivek,' she had said quietly. 'Your world can't come to a standstill because of all this.' I don't know how she did it, keep a steely calm while dealing with Sudha's body-wracking nausea and tears over her falling hair, Dad's fears about the possibility of a return of the malignancy, Govind's well-meaning manila envelopes of medical notes, and my bitter, unhelpful outbursts followed by periods of penitence, when I tried to act my age, keeping my childish rants to myself and acquiescing meekly to pleas of going through matrimonial résumés and meeting strange women.

In retrospect, I was lucky that I didn't meet the girl with

the AK-47 laugh during one of these phases, for, out of sheer guilt, I would have possibly found myself being rushed to the pandal, nosy mother-in-law and all. I did, however, have a couple of stilted telephone conversations with prospective 'girls'. After one particularly fraught discussion with a girl who asked me, between long pregnant pauses, what my favourite colour was, who I considered my best friend and how quickly I wanted kids, I told my mother that there were to be no more telephone calls.

I was, therefore, less than enthusiastic when Mum set up yet another meeting, but Sudha's routine check-up was looming and I couldn't bring myself to add to my parent's woes. 'She's over twenty-five, and her mother died when she was young,' Mum said apologetically, as though these were black marks against the girl's name. 'Raised by her father. Not very fair, I'm told, but she's well qualified, an architect, I think, and the family is very good.'

Yippee, I thought, my embodiment of a perfect woman, the one with the good family. But I kept my mouth shut.

It turned out that she lived in Bangalore—was a true-blue Bangalorean, in fact. My parents spoke to her father, and it was decided that we would meet up at Koshy's for coffee on a particular Sunday. 'The father is away visiting his son who lives in Spain,' Mum said, 'so it wouldn't be right, you going to her house.'

'Why?' I asked. 'Does he think I'm going to drag her to the bedroom and ravish her?'

Mum ignored me and rattled on. 'Ideally, you should wait until he returns, but he seemed okay with the both of you meeting.'

Koshy's was the Café Leopold of Bangalore—the place to see and be seen. Theatre people rubbed shoulders with teachers and geeks; it was a good place to people-watch. I reported on time, my punctuality honed by years of pacing myself back in Mumbai to catch the morning 7:13 or the evening 9:32. I got a table in a corner and squeezed myself on to the Rexine sofa so that I could watch the door. Ten minutes in, I hunted down a waiter and asked for water. Half an hour later, I lit up a cigarette and started picking absently at the sofa stuffing, which was peeping out from a tear in the Rexine. Another ten minutes later, when the waiter refilled my glass of water and proffered a menu for the second time, I contemplated whether I should order a coffee for good manners or just leave with as much dignity as I could muster.

'Vivek?'

I looked up to see a very tall girl before me. 'Oh my god, I'm so sorry, I got stuck in traffic!'

I struggled up, pushing the table forward with a clatter as I unravelled myself from the sofa. 'Hey, no problem,' I said, smooth as premium whisky.

'I'm Malini, by the way,' she said with a laugh, and stuck out a hand. It was warm and a little sweaty, and a little rough. The fingers were long and thin, I noticed, artistic, although the nails were chewed down past the fingertips.

We ordered filter coffee and chicken patties, and embarked on the usual stilted back and forth: What do you do? How long have you been in Bangalore? Do you like it here? Where did you study? Etcetera. But by the time we were pushing the crumbs of the patties around our plates and contemplating the rings in our coffee cups, it didn't seem stilted any more. I liked her easy laugh and her no-nonsense air, her kohl-rimmed eyes and big toothy smile, the way she teased me about abandoning engineering for management and selling out to the lure of Mammon, the manner in which she threw back her head and laughed when I likened architecture to the kindergarten of civil engineering. I liked the fact that she ignored the circumstances of our meeting; talked as easily as if we were friends meeting after a while. I couldn't ever imagine her asking me what my favourite colour was. Even the fact that she said 'haitch' for 'aitch' seemed endearing somehow. By the time we shook hands and said our very-nice-to-meet-yous, I was wondering if I should take her number or give her mine or ask her if I should meet her again. In the end, I said nothing, terrified that I would be breaking some arranged-marriage code of conduct and bringing both families into disrepute if I did so.

'So?' asked Mum, abandoning STD-call prudence, and calling me that very night. 'What did you think?'

'She seems okay,' I said casually.

'Okay? What is okay?'

'Okay is okay, Mum. She didn't seem too weird.'

'So what do I tell her father? Can we go ahead?'

'We could meet again, I suppose,' I said grudgingly.

Mum made a little strangled noise of excitement that made me smile.

The next morning, I was woken up by the sound of the telephone ringing. 'Hello?' I said, sleepy, annoyed, my heart racing with anxiety.

It was Mum. 'We spoke to the father! They also want to go ahead! He will start planning the wedding as soon as he's back! We're going to the astrologer right now to fix an auspicious date!'

'Wait, wait, what, what, WHAT? Hold on, Mum! What are you doing fixing dates?'

'Why? You said to go ahead.'

'I said we could meet again.'

'So what does that mean? It means go ahead, no? Why do you want to meet her otherwise?' she questioned, her voice taking on that suspicious tone now, which made me feel like a thirteen-year-old all over again, caught with a stash of *Debonair* magazines.

'No, but Mum,' I protested. 'How can I just marry her after

meeting her once? Don't I need to get to know her a little better? What if she turns out to be a weirdo, after all?'

'What "get to know better"? You think if you meet her three times you will know her any better? You have to live with a person for years before you know them. Next you will tell me you want to date her for two years before marriage!'

'Well, ideally…'

'Really, Vivek! Why are you objecting so much? Tell me now, truthfully, do you have someone in mind?'

'What?' I spluttered like an old scooter being kick-started.

'No, if you do, don't waste everybody's time. What am I going to tell her father? That you want to date her for two years and then if you decide you don't like her, they should go to hell?'

'No, you don't have to tell them anything like that, but you…'

Mum interrupted me, but in a calmer tone. 'This is how things work in arranged marriages, Vivek. The family is good, the horoscopes match, people we know have spoken highly of the girl and the family, what more can we do?'

'At least let me meet her a couple of more times,' I said.

Mum was silent for a while. 'Okay,' she said finally.

So my parents called up her father once again and it was decided that I should take her out for a movie. I pored over movie listings as though they were client spreadsheets. I ruled out *Runaway Bride*—no girl was worth that kind of torture—and much as I wanted to watch *Austin Powers: The Spy Who Shagged Me*, I settled for *The Matrix*. Later, she would tell me that she almost rejected me on that count alone.

But at the time, I was blissfully unaware, and enjoyed the afternoon in the darkened theatre, her hand brushing against mine on the armrest, our fingers briefly touching as we plunged into the popcorn we were sharing. By now I had learnt that she was fond of seafood, so, afterwards, I took her to a five-star hotel—I was looking to impress, and could write it off on my expense account—and watched as she dipped sannas[29] in Mangalore fish curry and dug expertly into crabs with those long fingers. I remember telling her that I should take her to Mahesh back in Mumbai for their butter-pepper-garlic squid, and before either of us could dwell on the implications of such a statement, I started feeling queasy. An image of a suspect prawn I had taken a bite out of a short while before trembled before my eyes; not wanting to seem coarse by spitting it out hastily as would have been prudent, I had let a coy delicacy get the better of me and had swallowed it whole, resisting the inclination to gag. The rest of its companions I had hidden on other parts of my plate under curry leaves and a decorative rose made of carrot, and had continued talking as though nothing was amiss. Now, halfway through the gajar ka halwa, the prawn appeared to be waging a lone mutiny somewhere in my nether regions and was threatening to forge a way out, one way or another. I only half listened as she prattled on, and gestured for the bill as soon as I could.

'Do you think I could get your number?' Malini asked. 'I'm tiring a bit of having to fix our meetings through our mummy-daddies, aren't you?'

'Yes, yes,' I said, now sweating profusely from the effort of not being sick. 'Of course.'

I scrawled my number on the back of a paper napkin and handed it over. I fought back an upsurge of bile.

'Listen, do you think I could drop you off at an auto stand?' I said weakly. 'I just remembered I have to be somewhere urgently.'

'Oh, okay,' she said, and even in my food-poisoned state I

---

[29]Mangalorean rice cakes

could make out that her tone was flatter than usual, and patently more icy, but to her credit, she didn't throw the napkin back in my face. We had talked of visiting Tipu Sultan's summer palace after lunch. It was hidden between markets and hospitals in an old quarter of Bangalore, and Malini had gushed about teak pillars and Indo-Islamic architecture and assured me that it was something I had to see.

That was not to be. After evacuating her unceremoniously at a corner, not even waiting to see if she was able to hail an auto, I sped back home and, for the next seventy-two hours, was very, very sick. I ignored the doorbell and the telephone and got out of bed only for multiple visits to the toilet. Somewhere around Hour Fifty-One I realized I had forgotten to ask Malini for her number in return and wondered what she must have thought. I threw up nervously.

'Where have you been?' shrieked my mother, when I felt strong enough to answer the phone. 'I've been trying you for two days!'

She piped down when I told her. 'Oh. Are you better now? What medicine did you take? Swallow methi seeds whole and eat half a bun after that, it will stop immediately. And don't eat bananas—that's for constipation, not diarrhoea or vomiting. You're drinking a lot of water, I hope?' After ascertaining that I was better, she continued. 'So I visited the astrologer, and he's given me a couple of possible dates.'

'What?' I asked, still a bit disoriented.

'The marriage dates! One in December, the other in March the next year. They are also okay with it.'

'What?'

'What "what, what"? Are you really okay?'

'You fixed the marriage date? And told Malini's family? Why?

I never told you to.'

'Aiyyo, if I wait for you to tell me everything, Malini will marry someone else and have three children by then! Two days I've been trying to reach you! And why are you acting so innocent and all? You only told Malini you are going to take her to Bombay to eat at Mahesh! If you didn't want to marry her, you wouldn't have said that, no?'

This stumped me. How did she know that? Had she employed someone to plant bugs on my person? Or perhaps hide under the tablecloth? At this point, it didn't seem impossible.

'And she asked for your number! What more do you want? That means go forward, no?'

I didn't know what to say to that. I tried to protest about the unseemly haste with which things were going forward, the way my mother had taken things into her own hands, how, although Malini seemed like a nice girl, I still wasn't sure if I wanted to actually marry her, in that forever-after, no-turning-back kind of way. And she did say 'haitch' for 'aitch'. I was met with a barrage of don't-be-silly-you-can-never-be-sure, no-not-even-after-ten-years-together, what-will-I-tell-her-father and don't-worry-everything-will-be-okay-the-astrologer-said-so.

So that was the romantic way in which I got hitched, through a mixture of parental arm-twisting, cajoling and emotional blackmail. I tried to reassert my authority by insisting it couldn't be a December wedding—no, not on the eve of Y2K, when I would be indispensable if problems cropped up at work, although I was a bit foggy as to what those problems would be and how exactly I could help.

Despite all the hectic behind-the-scenes manoeuvring, Malini had not yet called me. I managed to get her number through Mum and called to explain and apologize profusely. 'You did look a little green,' she chortled unsympathetically. 'I was wondering if it was the food or the company.'

'Well, you'll be happy to know that we are now officially betrothed by virtue of me offering to take you to Mumbai to eat at Mahesh and you being so forward as to ask me for my number!' I paused. 'I wonder how they found out?'

There was a long silence on the other end of the line, and then she said quietly, 'I am going to kill my father!'

This time, it was my turn to chortle.

10

Black Friday

Inevitably, the wedding was fixed for December. Mum countered my protests with a volley of 'you can't make girls wait so long' and 'they wanted it early, what could I say?' and 'the astrologer says the December date is most auspicious'. I suspected that both families were conspiring to hasten matters along, thus allowing us no time to think things through, develop cold feet or somehow mess things up. I visited Malini's house, a small bungalow in a quiet lane in Jayanagar where she had grown up. There was a kolam[30] on the threshold, the ceilings were high, the fans creaked and the rooms led into each other. Her father, Mr Pillai, had just retired as a mid-level scientist from a government agency called, to my delight, the National Bureau of Agriculturally Important Insects. With his large round eyes, sharp nose and halo of unkempt white hair, he looked like some agriculturally important locust himself, and I listened to him intently as he talked about the cassava mealybug and long-haired wasps. I might have been intimidated by his erudition if only he hadn't been dressed in a pink Hawaiian shirt, which, I was to discover, was just one of the many he possessed, in various colours. Malini and her father made a reciprocal visit to meet my parents in

---

[30]An auspicious decorative pattern drawn traditionally with rice flour in front of houses, similar to a rangoli

Kerala, where I gathered all went well, despite, Mum reported, Dad subjecting Malini to a monologue about the rising price of petrol—'42 paise per litre when I was a child,' he said, while cleaning his ears absent-mindedly with the twirled-up edge of a thin towel.

'He's a doll,' said Malini, when I apologized on his behalf. 'And in any case, my father was regaling your mother with the life cycle of a coconut hispine beetle.'

My telephone conversations with my parents now featured long discussions on the colour of paper for the invitation card, which relatives would be invited and whether or not Maggie would take the trouble to come.

Meanwhile, our dotcom got its first tranche of seed funding—a half-million-dollar deal which got us featured in a couple of national papers. Mum cut the features out and used them to make Vimala Aunty green. We celebrated with a pitcher at Peco's, accompanied with masala peanuts and Jim Morrison and shop talk, followed by carrot-coloured kebabs at a roadside stall at Shivajinagar and midnight cups of Suleimani chai.

And then we promptly threw ourselves into putting the money to good use. The website was upgraded, a warehouse with refrigeration systems and conveyor belts and the works was leased, goods were stocked, advertising space was bought in national dailies and on television, and people were hired. Our little bungalow-office was now crammed with twenty employees.

'We're ready to roll,' said Purab.

What with our budding start-up and Malini's construction projects, which took her zigzagging across the city to various work sites, we barely had time to meet. But somehow we did, sometimes for a movie and a meal, sometimes for window-shopping at Commercial Street followed by two-foot-long paper

dosas at Woody's or hot gulab jamuns at Bhagatram's or roadside
cups of bland boiled corn that I was too polite to say were no
match for the monsoon bhuttas in Bombay, sometimes for a
stroll in Cubbon Park, sometimes back to my company flat so
Malini could borrow books or CDs and generally get acquainted
with the lay of the land, after which we would drive down to the
shabby Indiranagar RTO complex and sit in the car eating oily
kathi rolls from Nizaam's.

In these months, I learnt the following things about her:
that she was congenitally unpunctual and always blamed the
traffic, that she was blind without her contact lenses, that she
loved anything with chocolate in it and could eat mountainous
quantities of it without putting on a gram, that she knew where
to find the sturdiest timber and the cheapest tile, that she liked
dangly silver earrings and large stick-on bindis and Kolhapuri
chappals, that she could draw and paint like an artist with those
long nail-bitten fingers, that she read weighty books about
incestuous love and the pangs of the diaspora, that she listened
to Leonard Cohen and Eric Clapton and secretly enjoyed Boyzone,
that she was once in love with a classmate who jilted her to
go abroad (I loathed this ghost of boyfriend past instantly and
in absentia), that Govind-inspired endearments like 'honey' or
'sweetie' ventured hesitantly on my part made her guffaw like a
car backfiring.

On one of our drive-throughs at Nizaam's, I wondered aloud
if she thought it would be a good idea if we invested in a home.
Although property prices were high, interest rates were lower than
they had ever been, and I would, at last, be able to afford the
EMIs—we had given ourselves a modest pay hike once the seed
funding had come in. Malini was so excited about the idea that I
started wading through the classifieds immediately. Many of our

hours together were now spent driving around town looking at apartments, and finally, we settled on a modest two-bedroom with marble floors and a niche in the dining-room wall that served as a puja space and kitchen tiles decorated with baskets of fruit which delighted Malini inordinately—all this was standard issue for Bangalore, but practically palatial by Mumbai standards. I made a down payment, and we were slated to close the deal soon after we got married.

Mum was excited about this turn of events. To her, my willingness to nest indicated that all was well, that I was devoid of cold feet, that I had embraced the idea of my traditional arranged marriage. It also gave her something to brag about to the likes of Vimala Aunty—Vivek is buying his own home, yes, full marble flooring and Jaguar fittings in the bathroom! 'Jaquar, Mum, not Jaguar,' I corrected her, and she was so delighted that she forgot to retort that it was she who had taught me the alphabet and not to act too smart. Mum was not vain in the traditional sense, but she took much pride in her children's achievements and would make sure that she would broadcast our little successes to anybody who would listen. And although Mum had seemed invincible in the face of Sudha's illness, still cheerful, still hopeful even in the darkest days, even when the rest of us were seized with fear and doubt and sinister thoughts, those of us who knew her well saw the erosion of her spirit in her inability to produce a boast about our small triumphs—not about Govind being eligible to apply for US citizenship, not about my latest business trip to Stockholm. But now that Sudha had been cancer-free for over a year, Mum's pride had started returning, cautiously, in small measure, and instead of being exasperated with her embarrassing displays of maternal pride, as I had frequently been as a teenager, I found myself relieved that she finally felt strong enough to flaunt.

Dad, on the other hand, was more circumspect. In their times, taking a loan from a bank was inconceivable—admittedly interest rates were over 25 per cent at the time, even if you could get a bank to agree to lend to you. 'Are you sure you can afford the EMIs, Vivek? For the next fifteen years?' I would be paying EMIs roughly equal to Dad's salary when he retired. He made me show him the math, and he didn't argue with my logic of using my HRA to fund part of the EMI, but I could see that he was perturbed nonetheless.

∽

It was time to get hitched. Mum and Dad came down a couple of weeks early and settled down in my guest room; Sudha and Ramu drove down from Chennai with the kids and took over the rest of the house. Sudha looked healthy and pugnacious once again, and was, alas, back to her pre-cancer weight, only the hair that was growing back in short, tight curls around her head a reminder of her chemotherapy. A large rudraksha mala hung around her neck, a badge from her recent pilgrimage to Gangotri/Yamunotri.

Sudha and Malini eyed each other warily; Sudha with the instinctive disapproval that a dowdy woman feels on seeing a fashionable one, Malini with the defensiveness of one who knows she's being judged. But Preetha and Prakash took to Malini instantly—Preetha sat by her side and stared admiringly at her silver nose-stud and the way she talked with expansive flourishes of her left hand, while Prakash showed his approval by sharing with her his endless stash of Lay's chips and Haldiram's mixture. Ramu, his hair now more salt than pepper, and profuse, growing out of his ears and along the lobes, sprouting from his nose and merging into his bushy moustache, sat around looking uncomfortable and answered Malini's polite questions in awkward monosyllables.

Mum and Dad found a new diversion as soon as Govind and Maggie arrived, in the shape of their grandson, Riyaan. He was now a quiet five-year-old who asked his parents for permission to leave the dining table when he was done, carried his own little Mickey Mouse backpack with hand sanitizer and tissues and mineral water and an energy bar, and dutifully observed his bedtime of 7 p.m. He was never reprimanded, although small misdemeanours were met with timeouts and long, murmured conversations with either Govind or Maggie, who explained how his behaviour was wrong, and how they had been disappointed with his actions but still loved him. Riyaan loved everyone, it seemed, and expressed it often, throwing the endearment casually over his shoulder like a discarded orange pip when he was taking someone's leave, even at Ramu, who looked at him askance, when so addressed.

The contrast with Prakash and Preetha was stark. Prakash talked at the top of his voice and thought nothing of wiping his running nose on his collar, and Preetha had taken to flouncing off if she didn't get her way, even daring to mete out the silent treatment to Sudha for days when she wasn't allowed to go for an out-of-town school trip.

Mum and Dad worried that Riyaan was painfully thin, which Mum put down to Maggie's strict control of his diet. 'No, no butter on the toast? And that's way too much jelly… And candy only once a week, and never in the night, the sugar rush makes him too hyperactive?' she instructed Mum and Dad as soon as they arrived.

'What is this sugar rush?' Dad asked me, and I shrugged, equally puzzled. In a few days, Dad had convinced Riyaan that gulab jamuns and ice cream didn't count as candy, not if you didn't tell Mummy and Daddy, and stealthy afternoon visits to Bhagatram's in Commercial Street and Corner House on Residency Road, Preetha and Prakash in tow, became the norm. Govind and Maggie worried a little about Riyaan's diminished appetite in the evenings but put it down to jet lag and culture shock. By the time the wedding came around, Riyaan, too, was eating with his mouth open and tearing around after Prakash, and forgetting to say his I-love-yous before he departed.

The wedding took place in a Jayanagar choultry, which I had come to learn was, in fact, the Bangalorean's term for a wedding hall and not a vast, mechanized chicken farm, as I had envisioned. The whole family turned up: Vimala Aunty and Rajan Uncle came with their four sons and their families, and ran up vast bills, Mum complained, for whisky (Rajan Uncle) and milkshakes (the grandchildren) in the unassuming hotel in which we had booked rooms for them. Shivan Mama appeared bearing a gift pack of his favourite old records and an illustrated copy of the *Kama Sutra*, laughing heartily at the expression on my face when I opened it in the presence of Malini's entire family. Malini's brother flew in from Madrid, a strapping handsome-looking fellow who made me feel quite inadequate.

I don't remember much of the actual wedding. I do remember sitting shirtless on the stage, nipped by a brisk December wind that had found its way into the hall and directed itself squarely at my chest, making me look like a slightly furry participant in a wet T-shirt contest. I know there was a small commotion as Prakash chased a by-now-rambunctious Riyaan down the aisle and to the stage, where Riyaan had a spectacular fall that elicited gasps from the gathered crowd. Then there was that terrible clamour of wedding chenda[31] and nadaswaram, which made me bite my tongue and brought tears to my eyes, and when I looked up, Malini was sitting by my side, looking completely unrecognizable in a heavy sari and flowers in her hair and make-up iced on to her face. The thaali[32] got stuck in the mass of flowers in her hair and my parents struggled with it for a while before it broke free. After the ceremony, the guests surged towards us and presents were pressed into our hands, a million introductions were made and promptly forgotten, a hundred photos were posed for. Prakash found the packet of dried fruits that was supposed to be gifted to Malini's family, and after making a small hole in the cellophane, managed to wolf down all of the apricots and most of the walnuts, and was slapped tightly by Sudha, regardless of the fact that he was almost a teen. At the evening reception, Rajan Uncle, who had squeezed into the seat to my left and was entertaining me with mangled quotes from *Wuthering Heights*, 'Be with me always—take any farm—drive me mad! Only do not leave me in this abscess, where I cannot find you!', stopped mid-sentence and asked me, 'Uh, how are you related to the couple?' Vimala Aunty jumped up and said, 'Aiyyo Rajan, what are you saying? This is our Vivek, the groom,' and Rajan Uncle giggled absently and said, 'Yes, yes, of course, of course.'

And then it was all over, and it was just the two of us, all smiled-out, exhausted and ready to collapse. 'So, Mrs Menon,' I said. 'Committed for life. Scared?'

'Petrified,' she smiled.

'Come here Pooky,' I said and she threw her head back and

---

[31] A percussion instrument
[32] A necklace worn by a married woman in Kerala, like the North Indian mangalsutra

let out a bellow of mirth. 'Angel?' I tried. She snorted. 'No? Bunny? My little parakeet?' I ventured. 'My dear old warthog?' She slapped me on the side of the arm and fell on to the bed, clearly overcome by my wit.

And then it was on to other findings: that at night, Malini exchanged contact lenses for a pair of round spectacles that made her look like a rather endearing fish owl, that she had a beauty spot where her ear met her neck and a tiny amoeba-shaped birthmark at the base of her spine, that although her hands were rough, her touch was soft...and that first-night fumblings were not as awkward as I had supposed.

∽

The new millennium dawned, and despite the ominous predictions, passed without incident. I spent the night at the office with Purab and Paschim, and we split a bottle of whisky and toasted to the modest sales that we were now clocking and the imminent arrival of our second tranche of funding, which would make us big and rich.

In the first month of the new millennium, we swiftly closed the deal on our apartment and whenever we had a free moment, Malini and I tramped the bylanes of Infantry Road looking for a cheap bed, a sofa and a TV cabinet to furnish it with. Malini gave me dubious looks as I looked longingly at commodious La-Z-Boy replicas in faux leather, and managed to coax me into buying one of those flimsy, elegant-looking wooden sofas that were as comfortable as a railway-station bench, while costing an arm and a leg. We splurged on a wrought iron bed, all the rage then, and skimped instead on a workman-like plywood TV cabinet, that was all straight lines and devoid of embellishment. Purab laughed seeing me rushing out of office on yet another Saturday shopping expedition, this time to buy dhurries, which were apparently indispensable. 'Look at you, dude, all domesticated already.'

The millennium was not even two months old by the time we moved into the new house, which Malini started filling up with completely useless things—vases of dried twigs, the aesthetic value of which I couldn't quite grasp, and bowls of potpourri and floating candles, and creepers that peeped out of old rum casks and wine bottles. Occasionally, her friends, all uniformly loud and giggly, dropped in to gush at her handiwork, usually when I was just back from office and wanting to sag in front of the television.

We had grown to almost fifty employees by now. Our advertising campaigns had started attracting customers, but not in the numbers we had been expecting. In retrospect, it is clear that customers were still suspicious of buying anything without seeing or touching it. And honestly, in those days of dial-ups, Internet speeds were so slow that it was faster to just to step out to the neighbourhood store and buy what you wanted. So the massive warehouse we had poured some of the seed funding into was lying underutilized for several months. We started promising same-day deliveries and offering deep discounts to move the goods, but as the orders came in, the delivery channels were unable to live up to the promises made by the marketing team. Goods were reaching customers days after they had ordered, leading to returned purchases, bad press and further reduction in sales.

And then came 14 April 2000. Black Friday. Markets around the world collapsed, and leading the retreat were dotcoms like ours. Overnight, we became untouchables.

'It's just a temporary blip, dude!' Purab said, as Paschim slumped glumly over the pink pages of *The Economic Times*. 'The markets will rebound, you watch!'

They didn't. A couple of months later, our investor informed us that the second tranche of our funding would be postponed until we lived up to the sales targets and the other conditions of our contract that had been laid down based on the early promise of our business. Our creditors started calling. Purab promised that they would get paid soon, in one week, by the next month, in a few months. Paschim travelled the country looking for alternative funding. In September, we cut back our salaries. In November, we no longer had enough money in the bank to pay wages to our employees. They left en masse, abusing us on the way out.

The first year of the new millennium ended in a very different way from how it had started. An irate creditor marched into our office and left with two computers and Paschim's laptop. Malini was pregnant with our first child, but all I could think of was our mounting losses and unpaid creditors and that huge housing loan we had taken. We fought incessantly—about the long hours I was keeping, about how she had left oily smears and crumbs on my keyboard from the chips she seemed to wolf down by the bagful nowadays, about how I had chucked a dirty shirt just outside the laundry basket instead of lifting the lid and putting it inside, at how she bit her nails off instead of clipping them like civilized people did, at how I had, in a completely innocent attempt to whisper sweet nothings to her, called her 'my sweet giant panda' in her sixth month of pregnancy.

By the spring of 2001, as the avenues of Bangalore were getting painted pink and yellow with the blooms of the tabebuia trees, the writing was on the wall. The firm would have to wind up, and I would be out of a job. Unemployed and overleveraged. And with a baby on the way.

For months I looked for alternative employment, shuttling between gynaecologist appointments and meetings with headhunters. But the market was as depressed as I was, and despite my fancy consulting job, it was clear that my brief stint at a failed start-up was a blot on my résumé. 'Don't worry,' said Mum. 'Your dashas[33] are changing, that's all. It's a temporary hiccup. The next dasha is excellent. By next year you will have an even better job, mark my words. Things can change in an instant.' I was so worried that I hoped against all my indifferent beliefs, against any remaining trace of scientific temper, that she might be right.

Dad was not quite as calm, asking how I was meeting the EMIs for our home, worrying if I would be evicted, and offering to send me some money by breaking one of his retirement investments. 'What is there, it's for you children only,' he said, but I couldn't contemplate the thought. Here I was, even now, buying olive oil and imported cheese without even throwing a glance at the price tag, still hanging on to my house, despite the monthly dents the mortgage was making on Malini's salary and my quickly diminishing savings—how could I contemplate taking a handout from my parents, who visited three different shops to get the best value for their monthly groceries, and rationed their consumption of mangoes in an exorbitant year, who thought nothing of standing in lines and filling in multiple forms for an extra per cent of bank interest or an exemption on tax?

But I would be fibbing if I said that Dad's offer didn't seem more and more attractive as the months of unemployment ticked on. But as I reached the depths of despair, Mum's predictions came true. By the end of the year, not only did I have a daughter whom we named Chand ('How about Chandrika?' suggested Mum. 'You can always shorten it to Chand at home.') but I had

---

[33] Astrological phases

indeed managed to land a better job at a UK-based consulting firm, which seemed to think that my start-up endeavour displayed leadership and enterprise and not complete stupidity. I entered as a senior associate, a level above what I had been at when I left the earlier firm. The company was in many ways a replica of the consulting firm I had left—large, multinational, prestigious, and the job was as stressful, mundane and repetitive as my previous one. But it offered the security of a large firm, a fat reliable salary, an EPF account and superannuation benefits that would help me in retirement—things that were suddenly important again.

More than a decade later, I bumped into Purab at the latest microbrewery in town. With its wooden tables and benches and naked metal pipes running overhead, and fat barrels displayed proudly like animal trophies in a hunting lodge, it was indistinguishable from the rest of its ilk. For a brief while, it had been populated by underage girls in short shorts and juvenile boys with earrings, until the novelty—and their parents' cash—had worn off. Now it was full of well-travelled techies who knew their Hefeweizen from their Schwarzenlager—and their wives girded into the latest from aLL, who swayed self-consciously as a Beyonce number played over the chatter.

He had just co-founded another e-tailing company, Purab told me. 'It's past the start-up stage now, boss, and it's growing organically,' he said, and I pictured aisles growing out of soil fertilized with nothing other than Purab's pure manure. 'We've just been valued at half a billion dollars!' I stopped picturing, started listening. 'See, we were just ahead of our times!' he said.

I nodded, oddly comforted.

'You want to join us, dude?' he asked.

I won't lie, I was tempted. 'What's Paschim doing?'

'Oh, he's back into consulting. A big shot now, a partner at some mammoth firm, bro—but bloody boring, believe you me.'

That doused whatever vestigial streak of adventurousness I might have nursed in my bosom. 'Maybe when I pay off my mortgage, bro!' I said with a light laugh, ignoring Malini's look of derision at my middle-aged use of the word.

Part Three

....

Towards Childish Treble

11

Big Fat Monster

I was well entrenched in my boring new/old job, once again clocking seventy-hour weeks and travelling twenty days a month. I now spouted a second language: I said things like 'cost metrics' and 'deliverables' and 'leverage' and even 'boiling the ocean' with no sense of irony. Chand grew up mostly in my absence from the mewling, wrinkled, vulnerable little bundle whom I used to pick up gingerly as though she were a piece of glass, to a tottering toddler who made me unreasonably delighted by calling me 'Mapa' for a while, and then into this energetic, slightly stubborn young individual who went to school and wanted a particular hairclip on a particular day, and could make me melt just by climbing into my lap and putting her head on my chest. With Chand's entrance into our lives, Malini had transformed from the laid-back wife who slept in on Sundays and seldom sweated a dusty bookshelf, to a slightly neurotic young mother who never went anywhere without a wet wipe and nearly fainted when I fed Chand an Iyengar Bakery chip. Now that Chand was almost five, Malini had settled into a formidable, multitasking dervish who packed lunches before setting off for work and thought nothing of getting into pitched battle with the school attendant who was flirting with one of the student's maids instead of keeping an eye on the children crossing the road to the school bus.

Mum was five years into senior citizenship, a fact she never failed to mention at opportune moments—to the young traffic cop who had stopped them when Dad had inadvertently skipped a red light and was levying them with what she considered an exorbitant fine, a fine particularly exorbitant for long-retired senior citizens, to the unfortunate student who came knocking at their door to ask for donations for charity. 'Donations for charity? We're senior citizens ourselves—we need donations for charity, what with the rising prices!' Dad was about to turn seventy, and although his walk had slowed and he stooped ever so slightly, he still ambled to the market to buy the day's groceries, to the electricity office and the water board to pay the bills, to the temple with Mum in the evenings. He spent his days googling the benefits of gobar gas and monitoring online lotteries, deriving much pleasure in the few hundreds he won once in a daily draw, and dreaming what he would buy himself with the bumper prize of a few crores when he won it. 'A round-the-world trip, an original M.F. Husain and a decent gardener!'

Govind and Maggie were in Germany now, where Govind was teaching Developments in Nanomedicine to international students in Munich. Mum and Dad visited them there, and sent us photographs of Mum in her cardigan, and socks with sandals, at a biergarten[34]; of Dad in his balaclava and button-down sweater (which he proudly told people was seventeen years old, of premium quality and bought for only ₹170) on the hanging bridge in front of the fairytale castle at Neuschwanstein; and of both of them with Riyaan, looking awkward around drunk revellers at Oktoberfest. From our brief conversations I could tell that Mum was spending her time making childhood favourites for Govind

---

[34]A German beer garden

in the kitchen while Dad occupied himself saving Govind some money by pinching the stickers off the organic fruit that Maggie insisted on buying and pasting them on to the ordinary fruit that he bought surreptitiously at grocery stores with severe-sounding names like Kaufland. 'One-third the cost,' he informed me, in a conspiratorial whisper.

Maggie had put her inclination for excessive exercising to good use and was working as a personal trainer at a local gymnasium. She was also training for her first marathon. She had meal plans, supplemented by smoothies spiked with algae and wheatgerm which she swore were delicious, and a training schedule that was more rigorous than Govind's teaching schedule—even weekends were spent doing 2,500-metre swims and 100-kilometre bike rides. She looked like tracing paper, Mum pronounced, thin and sallow and almost transparent, and had crow's feet around her eyes. 'White skin ages fast,' she said, with some satisfaction, and Sudha agreed with a sage, 'It's not good to be too thin after an age.'

Riyaan had morphed from the sweet little toddler to a talkative boy, who had taken to calling Mum and Dad Latha and Achuthan, respectively, until they set him right. He lounged, Mum complained, with his feet up on the sofa without even removing his shoes, and wandered around the house with a can of Coke perpetually in his hand. 'What happened to sugar rush now?' asked Dad.

Sudha, not content with bhajans and fasts and pilgrimages, had found herself a guru—a man whom we all referred to as Gurudev instead of trying to recall his name, which ran into multiple syllables. The photo of Gurudev which hung in Sudha's puja room revealed him to be bearded and long-haired like a mendicant, and a little wild-eyed, like the urchins sniffing glue under the railway bridges back in Bombay.

Gurudev had started out with a small ashram on the outskirts of Chennai, where he taught the scriptures to a modest following of troubled locals, along with his own brand of spiritual exercise that combined chanting, yoga, tai chi, meditation, deep-breathing and belly laughter. His following grew moderately until a few years later, when he was discovered by a wealthy tycoon with family problems. In return for spiritual succour, the tycoon had poured in lakhs of rupees into the ashram, lakhs that would have otherwise been spent on cars and women and a generally decadent lifestyle. Within a few years, the ashram shifted to a sprawling campus with multiple buildings and grounds as vast as a botanical garden. Famous actors, models, businessmen, doctors and politicians joined the flock, attracted in equal measure by the fashionable coral and green batik robes of Gurudev and his disciples, the catchy names of the spiritual courses, such as Soul Regeneration and Stretching for Success, and Gurudev's assertions that 'Renunciation Does Not Mean Renunciation of the Material but Renunciation of Evil'. More centres were opened around the country, charitable schools and hospitals were set up and Gurudev now spent many months of the year touring the world to meet his growing number of followers. When he was in Chennai, you had to take tokens to get his darshan, and were often made to wait an entire day before you could see him.

'You won't believe, such a humble person,' Sudha told me. 'Truly a realized soul.'

Sudha had signed up for weekly satsangs at the local ashram, volunteered to teach twice a week at one of their schools on the outskirts of Chennai and to serve food to the homeless at their temple every weekend. To Mum's consternation, she had also given up eating non-vegetarian food. She kept separate vessels to cook non-vegetarian food for Ramu and the kids, but only after her attempts to talk them off meat had failed. But they weren't kids any more—they were both in college; Preetha had got admission into medical college, while BCom student Prakash now spent his days staring uncomprehendingly at balance sheets and Keynesian theory.

So there we were, immersed in our ordinary lives, ready to take on another completely ordinary day. Chand was feigning stomachache to get out of going to school and Malini was practically bundling her into her uniform. I had just fought with Malini myself, convinced that the maid had somehow managed to shrink all my pants while doing the laundry. 'They're all tight!' I yelled, and instead of being properly contrite, she retorted quite disrespectfully, 'Have you thought of going easy on the frappes at Coffee Day?'

I was searching for the brown shoes which would go with my lucky brown belt for an important presentation I had to make that morning, when the telephone rang. I cursed at the intrusion and considered ignoring it, but it went on insistently until Malini hollered, 'Get it, will you!'

It was Sudha. There was something in her tone at the end of the line, her 'Hello?' shrill, her voice breaking, which made me remember that it was that time of year again—when she was due for her routine check-up. Eight years had passed, and every time the scans had come up clean, not a trace of malignancy. But each check-up had us collectively holding our breath and trying to banish what-if scenarios from our minds until the results came in. Now, hearing Sudha at the end of the line, I knew. The cancer was back.

'Hello, Vivek?' I could hear now that she was crying.

'Yes, I'm here Suds,' I said, my heart sinking. I sat down

heavily on the side of the bed, forgetting the shoe for the moment.

'Vivek...' she was bawling now.

I didn't know what to say.

'It's Dad. He...he died.'

∽

From a very early age, we live with the spectre of our parents passing, with a consciousness of their frailty, an awareness of our own dependence on them. And yet nothing prepares you for a parent's death. You know with certainty that it is going to happen one day; you pray for its postponement; when you're young and dependent, you wonder how you will get by without them; you know, with certainty, that once it happens, your life will never be the same. You know there is nobody who will know you as well, love you as unselfishly, criticize you as bluntly, drive you mad quite as uniquely, wish you well as constantly—and you realize that there will be a hollow in your heart, and your life, when they are gone.

My earliest fears swirled around my mother. I vividly remember spending an entire schoolday, my stomach tied in knots, my mind twisted with worry, as lessons went on around me. All because a classmate had, during recess, casually mentioned to me that there was a monster prowling the street outside our school, the street my mother took every day as she came to pick us up from school.

'Liar!' I shouted.

'You're a liar!' he shouted back, face smeared with the jam from his short-break sandwich. 'Big, fat monster—as tall as that tree there, as big as that building! His teeth are as big as...as that blackboard...and...and...he's already eaten twenty people. And stomped on fifty—no, hundred!'

When the end-of-day bell rang, I rushed outside and scanned the waiting faces anxiously—David Ling's grandfather who practically lived in school, bringing him exotic-scented soups and prawn-dotted rice for lunch, a couple of aayahs, sweaty-faced and indifferent, and a sea of mothers, tall, short, fat, thin, fanning themselves with sari pallus, powdered and rosy in pastel midis, unsuitably attired for the Bombay heat in woollen pants and synthetic blouses. And among them Mum, neatly turned out as ever, her cotton sari stiff with starch, not a hair daring to stray out of her fake-hair-enhanced bun. I had rushed up to her and hugged her around the knees tightly, and she had paused from the gossip she was having with Aloo Poonawala's mother—a riveting conversation about the PT teacher being caught with the school secretary under the assembly stage, I would later learn—and gave me a bemused look, confused with this show of affection from the son who usually trudged up to her reluctantly, dragging his water bottle behind him, averting his face if she bent down to kiss him.

We grow older, but the monsters still lurk, salivating and multiheaded, in the shadowy corners of our minds; death, disease and infirmity are the terrifying ogres of our adulthood.

Thoughts of my father's mortality began to torment me when he was diagnosed with high cholesterol in his forties. It was stolid middle age in those days, but high cholesterol, diabetes and hypertension were not the lifestyle diseases that they are today, afflicting the young with as much impunity as they do the old. They were undeniable markers of an approaching old age, and harbingers of that frightening and almost always fatal heart attack. He was still too young, too important, too indispensable to die! It was about that time that I started praying for his health.

We spoke often about death in our family. Mum had lost her

own parents when she was young. In addition, three astrologers, one palmist and a parrot fortune teller had told her that she wouldn't live beyond the age of forty-seven, so she was determined to prepare us for a future without her. We were often counselled to be strong, to look after Dad when she was gone, to stop bickering with each other and keep a united front. She would remind us that she had had a happy life and that we shouldn't mourn her when she was dead. In her forty-seventh year—and for a couple of years after (we had to account for human error, after all), the probability of her immediate demise poisoned our little pleasures. It made Sudha quite tearful and I was a little nicer to her for a while, but eventually we scoffed at the astrologers' predictions and forgot them completely thereafter.

But Mum remained convinced that she would never live to a ripe old age, and death still remained very much part of her conversations, although it attained a different hue. She used it to blackmail us—'You'll know when I'm gone!' she would exclaim, and she used this line so frequently that one day, I retorted, 'Yes, perhaps then I'll have some peace!' To her credit, after an initial shocked silence, she burst into laughter and never held this unforgivable trespass against me.

Dad, on the other hand, never really spoke of his own death, although he was calmly accepting of its inevitability. And he always made provisions for its possible imminence—for instance, when a few years before, he had been given a chance to choose a life membership to the Automobile Association, he had scoffed at the sales lady's description of the lumpsum payment for life membership as more cost-effective than the annual membership fee. 'I'll have to live at least 12.2 years for that to be true. At my age? No, no, it would make more sense to take the annual,' he had said, waving off the sales lady's entreaties that he had at least a couple of decades left. He had lived just six years after that, and for that economy, I imagine he would have been pleased.

∽

As we booked tickets to Kerala and made funeral arrangements, we cobbled together the story of how it had happened. Mum and Dad had had a brief tussle in the morning over whether he should have eggs for breakfast, as he had woken up with an upset tummy. Mum had relented when Dad had agreed to boiled eggs instead of his usual omelette, but when he had started holding his belly and groaning an hour later, she had laid into him with a ton of I-told-you-sos and you-never-listens.

By 11 o'clock, after self-administered doses of antacids, Dad had declared himself better, then insisted that he would go down to the electricity office to pay the bill.

'It can wait. I will pay the bill later in the week, or I'll send the gardener,' Mum had said, but Dad was having none of it.

'Stop fussing,' he snapped. 'I'm perfectly fine now. I'll be back in half an hour.'

'But it's so hot! It's Monday, there will be a long queue as well.'

'Nonsense! There will be no queue.'

'Why do you want to exert when you're still not fully well? What is the need to go?'

'There is a need,' he argued.

'At least take an umbrella for the sun!' she had called out, just as he was reaching out for it, so he had obstinately withdrawn his hand and walked away, letting the gate bang shut as he left.

At the grocery store by the corner, he had stopped to ask for one of those tetrapacks of coconut water, unmindful for once of the shocking cost for what was, in the end, only coconut water. He was sweating so much that the grocery store manager had drawn up a rusty metal chair and made him sit down for a while. 'Why didn't you carry an umbrella, saar[35]?' the manager had asked, and Dad had smiled sheepishly and left, disappearing around the corner towards the electricity office, with a stray dog trailing behind him, sniffing at his mundu.

At the electricity office, the queue snaked around the corner of the building and Dad had paused for a while as though debating whether to turn back. Perhaps the thought of facing Mum's I-told-you-sos made up his mind. He joined the queue behind Mr Varghese, one of their neighbours, who looked at his pale, sweating face and insisted Dad take the place in front of him. Uncharacteristically, Dad accepted, and joined the queue behind a short fellow in a checked mundu folded up almost to his behind, who stood swaying slightly, the strong aroma of alcohol wafting Dad's way.

A lady at the front of the line rummaged in her bag for change. One strap had fallen off her shoulder and the zip on the side pocket was open, displaying a sanitary napkin and an embroidered handkerchief. 'Why do women carry such large bags?' Mr Varghese had asked Dad. 'And nothing is in its place, ever. She knows she has to pay the bill, why doesn't she keep the money ready?' Finally, she had produced a ₹500 note and argued with the man at the counter when he claimed he didn't have change. By then, Dad was wiping his sweating face with a handkerchief and massaging his left shoulder with his right hand. Eventually, the lady paid her bill, and Dad nudged the drunk in front of him, who was snoozing with his head on the wall, to move forward.

'Silly woman,' said Mr Varghese, and as Dad turned to talk to

---

[35]A corruption of 'sir'

him, something flitted over his face. A distant look, Mr Varghese said, as though Dad was mining his subconscious for a deeply buried memory. Then Dad's eyes rolled back in his head and he crumpled to the ground. Mr Varghese cried out. In minutes, the line disintegrated and rearranged itself around Dad in a circle. Somebody called for water. Others tried to open his shirt to give him the air that he could no longer inhale.

Mum was standing at the living-room window, looking out from behind the curtain. It had been over an hour since he'd left and she was worried. He must have stopped at the barber's, she told herself, on purpose to annoy me, knowing that I'm waiting for him to serve lunch. Or perhaps he's run into that senile old bore, Rajan. And he had forgotten to take the mobile phone with him, the one Govind had bought him the last year. Occasionally, she darted away from the curtain to rearrange something nervously, and a little angrily—the embroidered cloth over the television, the books on the shelf.

There was a clang as the latch on the gate was lifted and dropped. She darted back to the window and saw it was not him. She opened the door and came out to the front porch. She saw Mr Varghese entering, followed by the manager of the grocery store. And the drunk who had tagged along. As they approached, she noted the sombre expression on their faces, and she knew, she told Shivan Mama. Her knees buckled and she sat heavily down on the planter's chair with the shaky arm, which Dad had just begun to repair. Even before they could speak, she was crying, quietly, resignedly.

Within minutes, the maid, Banu, put her head around the door to investigate who the visitors were. When she heard the news, she reacted in a way that Mum would never have been able to, bawling hysterically and beating her head with her hand.

Seeing her, the drunk also burst into tears.

'It is okay, it is okay,' Mum consoled them, almost smiling at the irony while wiping her own eyes with the end of her pallu.

∽

Vimala Aunty took charge of the funeral arrangements, Shivan Mama of informing people about Dad's demise. Dr Balan arrived, scribbled out a death certificate and administered Mum a sedative.

We got there by early evening, us from Bangalore, Sudha and her family from Chennai. The house was full of people—my father's one surviving brother, two brothers-in-law and many nephews and nieces, my parents' neighbours, and other people who had materialized from somewhere to help—or perhaps to goggle—as they always did when there was a death in the locality. Dad's body was on the floor, washed and dressed in clean clothes, and covered with the robes of death, the red pattu and white kacha that were the symbolic pieces of cloth placed atop a body. He looked peaceful, and he might have just been asleep but for the fact that he wasn't snoring, that a piece of cloth was tied around his head to prevent his mouth from falling open, that his ears and nose were covered with cotton wool so that body fluids would not leak out, that a couple of fingers of both hands and his big toes were tied together so that the arms and legs would stay in place. A ring of rice encircled the body, an oil lamp burnt at the head. Verses from the *Bhagvad Gita* played on the two-in-one. Chand looked gravely at Dad's body, apparently not recognizing it for the grandfather who stumped her with magic tricks and could touch his nose with his tongue.

Sudha and Malini were crying afresh, and I had to swallow hard to prevent myself from tearing up. Malini had started crying inconsolably on hearing the news that morning, and Chand had followed suit, standing in front of the mirror and watching herself bawl hideously with a detached curiosity, until she had learnt that she was no longer required to go to school that day. 'Yay!' she had yelled, tearing around the living room.

Mum was in the bedroom, exhausted from hours of crying. And she was refusing to eat. 'His bo…dy,' she bit back a sob, 'must leave the house first,' she told Shivan Mama, who was trying to coax her to have a morsel of rice, at least.

'He wouldn't have worried about all that,' Shivan Mama said, and rightly so, but she would not be moved.

As she saw me, her face crumpled and she started crying again. 'I fought with him before he left,' she sobbed.

I didn't know what to say. It was the most awful thing, of course, last words spoken in anger that could never be retrieved. I couldn't find the words to console her. Malini gently elbowed me out of the way, went and sat by Mum on the bed and put her arms around her.

'Mum, what are you wearing?' hissed Sudha.

I now saw that Mum was swathed in a bright Kanjeevaram sari, and had patted on large quantities of talcum powder, which stood out against the redness of her eyes. It made me smile.

'It's probably just the side effect of the sedative. Let her be,' I whispered to Sudha.

'Let her be? How can I let her go out all decked up? What will everybody think?'

'It doesn't matter. Just leave her alone,' I said, but Sudha couldn't contemplate that option.

'Mum! Are you crazy? Dressing up as though you're going for a wedding! What will people say?'

Mum looked down in puzzlement at her hand, which was brandishing a Lakme brown matte lipstick. 'Oh my god! You are right.' She let out a shaky laugh. 'I don't know what I was thinking.'

Outside, Preetha and Prakash stood, quiet and wary, a little away from Dad's body, until Ramu instructed them to prostrate before it. They did so hurriedly, a little nervously, then stood in a corner, whispering to themselves. Seeing them, Chand started prostrating repeatedly at Dad's feet, giggling delightedly at this new game, until Malini dragged her away.

The crowd parted to allow a tall middle-aged man in a crisp white mundu to enter. From his air of confidence, we deduced that he was the person from the Nair Sabha, who Vimala Aunty had summoned to take charge of the ceremonies. The man surveyed Dad's body lying in the middle of the room and then questioned some bystanders, 'Doctor issued death certificate? Cremation organized? What time?' He took out a compass and grunted with satisfaction that somebody had thought to place the head in the south, in the direction of the kingdom of Lord Yama.

He quickly identified me as the doer of rites, and barked instructions at Shivan Mama, without making eye contact with me, clearly recognizing me as the type who was ignorant of rituals and possibly unfamiliar with Malayalam. Has he bathed? Worn the new mundu? Will he be able to do the rites for his father?

Vimala Aunty started making a fuss that the funeral would be conducted without Govind, who, of course, would only be able to come after a few days. 'Aiyyo, funeral without the eldest son doing the rites? How can that be?'

A helpful woman, who I had never set eyes upon until that moment, suggested embalming the body, preserving it till Govind arrived. Seeing the intense discussion that this fuelled, the man from the Nair Sabha drew up. 'What's the matter?'

'The eldest son will arrive only after a few days. We want to embalm the body,' said Vimala Aunty.

The Nair Sabha man looked at her with thinly masked dislike. To him, a delayed funeral could only mean deferred fees, a wasted trip. 'Embalm?' he spat. 'What are we, Christians? You want to bury the body next? Have a mass? Don't you know the soul cannot leave the body until it is cremated? Maybe you would like to watch over the body in the night? Perhaps you are not worried that the soul might enter your body?'

Preetha and Prakash started giggling. Chand also broke out into uncomprehending but loud chortles. Malini gave her a pinch to make her subside but it only succeeded in making her howl with indignation. Malini hustled her upstairs.

'I didn't mean it like that...' Vimala Aunty whimpered. 'You are the expert, you must decide.'

'I should think so! Bunch of nonsense!' muttered the Nair Sabha person, and Rajan Uncle snorted with inappropriate laughter.

Mum, face scrubbed clean and dressed in a simple cotton sari, appeared in the doorway, causing a hum to pass through the crowd. They watched her as she looked at Dad's garlanded body on the floor. After prostrating before it, she made her way to the straight-backed wooden chair in the corner and sat with her eyes closed. As people drew up to give their condolences, she briefly opened her eyes and allowed her hand to be clutched, her body to be embraced, before shutting them tight again.

It was time. Freshly bathed, chest bare, a mundu draped around my waist and secured by a string taken from one of Mum's petticoats, I followed the Nair Sabha man's orders. I placed rice and tulsi leaves in Dad's mouth, circled the body, prostrated at his feet. Mum was ushered to the body to prostrate at Dad's feet once more. She took one long look at his lifeless features, her lips quivering, her eyes filling up. Sudha put an arm around her, honking into a checked handkerchief. Then a stretcher made of bamboo was brought in and I, Shivan Mama, Ramu, a couple of unfamiliar neighbours and Manikandan, the gardener, lifted Dad's body on to it. Even Rajan Uncle, who had just had a triple bypass surgery a couple of months back, tottered up to make a stab at pulling some weight. We lifted the stretcher on to our shoulders and took Dad out to a waiting hearse to the cries of 'Om Namah Shivaya' and 'Hari Om'.

There was a short wait at the crematorium and a few more rituals, but all I remember is lighting the pyre. As I watched the flames leap up and consume his body, it sank in. That he was gone, forever. I would never hear his voice over the phone again, deep, measured, comforting. He would never worry about how I was going to pay my EMIs, or if I was working too much, or sleeping too little. I would never be able to roll my eyes in Malini's direction when he started to talk about the price of Berkeley cigarettes in 1972. I would never be able to get him to teach me how to paint with oils or draw with charcoal, things I had been meaning to do but had left for too late. I would never hear him tease Mum about serenading him when they first met, or gurgling with gleeful laughter when he won a few hundreds in a lottery. He would never be sitting in the easy chair on the verandah when we came home on vacation, peering through his reading glasses at the headlines, or frowning at the crossword. Regret mingled with the smoke from the pyre, stinging my eyes, making my breath catch in my chest.

12

Three Score and Ten

'Look at him—11 o'clock in the morning and already sozzled,' said Mum. 'Eighty-one years old, two heart attacks, a triple bypass surgery, drinks like a fish, smokes like a fire and still going strong.' We were looking at Rajan Uncle, who was dead to the world on the faux Rajasthani swing in their verandah. Although Vimala Aunty had managed to get Rajan Uncle to abstain for about a year after his triple bypass, he had fallen off the wagon with a vengeance.

'It has to be the alcohol,' I ventured.

'What?'

'The alcohol must be preserving the organs. You know, like those hearts and lungs floating in big bottles in medical schools, pickled in spirit...'

Mum burst out into a laugh. 'Perhaps we should ask Vimala to donate his body to science—find out the secret of his longevity.'

It had been three years now, and the laughter was back in our lives. It was a different laughter, at first forced, as though to drive the tragedy out of our lives, later often weighed down by underlying sorrow. In the first year of Dad's passing I had woken up every day with a heaviness in my heart, not even knowing why in those first moments of wakefulness, a brief instant of blissful amnesia before memory returned, bringing with it the full realization of my bereavement. Every day had been shadowed by loss, every happiness curdled by sorrow.

'A good way to go,' people would tell us soon after he had died. 'At least he didn't suffer.' And although we wanted to stick a knife in their throats and slowly twist it around, we knew this to be true. It is what he would have wanted—what any sane person would want, a sudden, painless death.

But I wondered if indeed it had been sudden and painless, or if he had gasped for breath, doubled over with pain, tried to call out for Mum. 'Yes, immediate death, he wouldn't even have felt it,' Ramu told Mum smoothly when she asked him, but his answer was so pat, so mechanical, that we found ourselves questioning how he could know this to be so. Nevertheless, for my own peace of mind, I chose to believe him. I wondered where Dad was, somewhere in the cosmos or reincarnated as a little boy or girl in some house, and whether we would meet again in another life, whether he would be my father again or related to me in some way.

I know Mum felt that he had been robbed of some years. '*The Bible* describes a lifespan as three score and ten, but that was before modern medicine and flushing toilets,' she had said more than once. In those initial days of loss, when the newspapers came in the morning, she had taken to turning to the obituaries first, sometimes reading them out to me or Sudha over the phone: 'Kunjan Pillai, 86, sad demise', 'Ammukutty Nedungadi, 81, dearly beloved', 'Abraham Tharakan, 95, slept in the Lord'. Ninety-five!' The statistics revealed what she suspected—that sixty-nine was too soon for him to have passed. We had been cheated of a decade at least.

We had all moved on with our lives, of course. Govind had finished his assignment in Munich and was back at MIT. Maggie had opened her own gymnasium in the States, was training for her first triathlon and had started a healthy-living website where she extolled the virtues of green tea and organic clothing.

'What's organic clothing?' Mum asked.

'Cotton?' I ventured and Mum made a wheezing sound of derision which brought to mind the noise our apple-green Ambassador used to make when you were trying to choke-start it on a rare wintry morning in Bombay.

She now sported a buzz cut—Maggie, not Mum—which, along with her petite frame and muscled limbs, made her look like a teenage boy. 'Aerodynamic,' she said, running her hand over her stubbled head. 'For the swim part of the triathlon? Chic, yeah?'

When I visited them in the States, she playfully pinched the spare tyre I carried around my trunk. 'Ouch!' I yelped.

She eyed me sardonically as I reached for a second pancake. 'Try this,' she said, pushing a juice the colour of grass at me. 'Kale, cucumber, spirulina, hemp, flax, banana, spinach? Miracle drink!'

'Yum!' I said, squeezing the bottle of maple syrup more vigorously, and Riyaan snorted through the chocolate milkshake that was *his* breakfast.

Govind, on the other hand, gamely scarfed down Maggie's shakes and trail mixes and couscous salads, and made Mum quite cross by picking at her glorious curries and refusing to eat rice when he came home to visit. 'Too many carbs, Mum!' he would say apologetically.

Sudha, when she was not after the children to study, was immersed in the workings of the ashram, attending satsangs and conducting bhajan sessions for the neighbourhood children. 'Poor children,' I said feelingly, and Mum's small tentative smile suggested she agreed. Preetha was immersed in her MBBS course, and Prakash, after scraping through his BCom course, had incensed Sudha by opting to post-graduate not in accountancy or management, as would have been customary, but in the Culinary Arts.

'He wants to become a chef, it seems! Two-year course costing thousands of rupees! And for what? Some diploma or something which is probably not worth the paper it's printed on,' Sudha fumed. 'It is Mum's fault, praising him so much when he made that batch of brownies last summer!'

Sudha tried to convince Prakash to take something that might be less esteemed than Chartered Accountancy but more socially acceptable than Culinary Arts: 'MCom? MCA? Travel and Tourism? Hotel Management?' she suggested, the last proffered in a mournful whisper.

'He's going to become a chef?' asked Mum, doubtfully. 'Won't he just eat up everything before it reaches the customer's table?'

But Prakash was unusually adamant, and Culinary Arts it was. Now, he prattled happily to anyone who would listen about the importance of knife skills and kitchen hygiene and the difference between béchamel and hollandaise. Sudha, in the meanwhile, gave circuitous answers when people asked what Prakash was doing, and every time they went out to a restaurant to eat, she spent most of the meal looking dejectedly into the kitchens, picturing Prakash as the one in the toque tossing the roomali rotis, the one the maitre d' was imperiously clicking his fingers at.

I was now in charge of a team of young trainees who I had to watch over like a secret service agent guarding the President, so that they wouldn't copy entire industry reports and sector analyses from Wikipedia. When I looked in the mirror, I saw thinning hair speckled with grey, dark circles under the eyes and that spare tyre around the middle. But I was the proud owner of an iphone 3G, a fully fitted Skoda Octavia which promised a top speed of 170 kilometres per hour but was usually inching along at 30 in peak-hour traffic, and a villa being built in a gated community in the suburbs that was gnawing away half my salary in large bites of mortgage payments.

But the villa was deemed necessary for our growing family. The previous year, Chand had acquired a little sister, Tara, who she regarded with equal measures of love and envy—well, mostly envy. And Malini had convinced her father to come and stay with us, a task that had been proving difficult. He was in rude good health, boarding public buses with a jauntiness I could seldom summon, and taking himself off on conducted tours to the Taj Mahal and the sun temple at Konark, feeling not even a little uncomfortable in the company of family groups munching on Haldiram's mixture and honeymooning brides in jeggings and white lacquer wedding bangles up to their elbows. But he had become increasingly hard of hearing and Malini had been worrying about his safety in the bungalow in Jayanagar that he still lived in, although it was now surrounded by apartment buildings on three sides and a commercial complex on the fourth. Since he couldn't hear the doorbell or people banging on the gate, he often left the front door open, and when Malini showed him newspaper reports of the latest robbery and murder, he would wave her off with an airy, 'Oh, nothing will happen, don't worry.'

And then, something had happened. As he had sat catching up on the latest headlines in entomology, a couple of thieves had walked in right behind his back, carried off the television and the DVD, and walked out undetected. The thought of how much worse it could have been made Malini quite hysterical and I had been roped in to convince him to move in with us. Eventually he had relented, and just as our villa was being constructed, his bungalow was being put up for sale.

Mum, too, had moved on as best as she could. For the most

part, she was philosophical, remarking that life had an ebb and flow about it—good times followed in the wake of bad, the advancing tides of adversity mingled and swirled with the eddies of retreating good fortune. But, of course, for her especially, life had changed completely. 'I still find myself setting the table for two,' she confessed, 'or turning to talk to him when I'm watching television.'

His absence filled the house, despite the large photo that hung on the living-room wall, Dad looking uncharacteristically grave and well dressed in a dark suit and tie. The house had grown forlorn without him, as though it, too, was grieving his demise. It mourned him in the planter's chair with the rickety arm which still lay unrepaired three years after his death, in the clogged filters of the bathroom taps that he would regularly clean, in the dead battery and dusty bonnet of the car that was now seldom used, in the overgrown parts of the garden and the fungus that had infected the banana plant.

In the first few days of his passing, we worried how Mum would cope without him. I remember stirring awake at night, listening to the sounds of stray dogs barking and a watchman sounding his hourly whistle, the rev of an engine as a late-night reveller returned home and the whirrs of the lift as the milkmen came to make their morning deliveries, and wondering if she was awake too, listening to the nocturnal noises of her own house, the sighs and creaks of the cupboards and doors as they stretched their limbs in the night, the sudden mysterious hums and grumbles of the fridge and the caws of the first crow at dawn. I wondered if she started at alien noises, held her breath at moving shadows. And I wished that somebody was with her, to calm the racing of her heart at the sudden noises, to soothe away the unease left behind by a bad dream.

As we had scattered back to our lives in the immediate aftermath of the funeral, leaving her alone with her loss—we would regroup for the sixteenth-day ceremonies—Sudha had asked Mum's maid, Banu, to stay on at night, despite Mum's protests that she would be fine by herself. 'Just for a month,' we cajoled. 'Try it and see.'

Banu was hesitant herself, to spend the night in the home of a departed soul, superstitious as she was about everything. The moment she stepped into the bedroom, she looked in horror at the urn carrying Dad's ashes, which Mum had placed above the Godrej cupboard.

'Aiyyo, that is not supposed to be inside the house, Amma. You should bury it in the garden.'

'Oh, be quiet,' Mum had said and refused to move it.

Banu had fallen silent, but she had eyed the urn warily as she made up her bedding on the floor furthest away from the cupboard, and somewhere in the middle of the night Mum was awakened by Banu's piercing screams.

'What? What? What is it? What is it?'

Banu pointed to the cupboard. 'Saar! Saar is sitting on the cupboard!'

Mum switched on the light and looked to where she pointed. 'What? Where? There's nothing there.'

Banu looked again, squinting against the light. 'But I saw him, Amma. He was trying to get out of that urn all night, and just now he was sitting on that cupboard.'

'Keep quiet!' said Mum, furious. 'Enough of that!' The next day, she had the urn buried in the garden, but by the time we returned for the sixteenth-day ceremonies, Banu had been politely told that her nocturnal company was no longer required.

'But I'm not alone,' she would protest, if we tried to coax

her into hiring full-time help. 'Banu is here till noon, and Shivan comes for lunch almost every day, your father's brother drops by occasionally, Manikandan comes to garden in the afternoons, and Vimala drops by with her tasteless biryanis every now and then—frankly, I wish I had more time to myself.'

Later I wondered if Mum ever longed for the uneventfulness of those intervening years. Maybe she thought she would play out the rest of her life like that—doing ordinary things, marking time till the grim reaper called. To me it seemed like a bleak way to live out the rest of her life, but in time, I would come to yearn for the ordinariness, the lack of drama, of those years.

13

All He Has

It was in 2008—as housing prices plummeted and mortgage defaults surged in the United States, as economists were predicting that history was repeating itself, that the Great Depression of the 1930s was going to be revisited—that Govind began to suggest to Mum that he would like to return to India. He was worried about Mum, he said, he wanted to use some of his skills to help his own country. He would come first, and Maggie and Riyaan would join him later, after tying up some loose ends.

A long time ago, before Maggie, before the green card and citizenship, Mum had nurtured a hope that Govind would return to India, so that seas and continents would not separate them in her old age. It was a dream that she had long given up on, so in the ordinary course, Mum would have been ecstatic at the thought of Govind's return. But given the turbulence of the American economy, she was worried. In India, my private banker—yes, I now had enough in the bank to be deemed worthy of a fresh-out-of-management-school private banker who would hard-sell me mutual funds and pension funds I didn't want but would mess up the simplest of service requests—my private banker insisted that India was different, immune even, that the plummeting stock markets were merely a correction, a correction that should be taken advantage of by ploughing even more money into equity. Nevertheless, I could sense the tension in the air at my workplace, in the freeze on fresh recruitments, in the murmurings in the granite-paved corridors of downsizing and cost-cutting and the imminent dangers of being taken over by a rival firm.

'Do you think Govind's lost his job?' Mum asked me worriedly.

'It seems unlikely, Mum. He's a tenured professor, not an investment banker.'

'But still…something doesn't feel right.'

'Don't be silly, Mum, lots of NRIs are returning to India these days—so many opportunities at home now, you know. Or maybe he saw *Swades*, decided he wanted to be Shah Rukh Khan.'

But in the end, it turned out that Mum's unerring instinct had been accurate. Something was not right at all.

Before the year was out we learnt that Govind was not returning with Maggie and Riyaan, that it wasn't patriotic fervour or filial love that was guiding him home. It turned out that he had had a breakdown, and a spectacular one at that. In the middle of a lecture on The Use of Nanomaterials in Tissue Engineering, he had stopped mid-sentence, returned to his seat at the front of the class and cried for several long minutes while his students had looked at him nervously and wondered what to do. It ended with a complete meltdown in the department head's office and Govind offering to tender his resignation.

Completely out of the blue, it seemed to us at first, but it transpired that Maggie had asked for a trial separation. It was not working for her any more, she said.

'What does that even mean?' asked Mum.

Although it took us by surprise, it appeared that there had been rumblings for a while. Maggie's fitness centre had now acquired quite a following and she had been spending long hours there. At first, Govind had not minded, until he had met the newest recruit, a ripped young man called Matt, with eight packs, bulging biceps and something called lats, and hair like someone out of a 1980s' Head and Shoulders ad, all blond cascading waves. Govind himself was completely bald now, a far cry from the hairy twenty-something with floppy hair and IIT moustache who had gone to the States so many years ago. He had taken to shaving his head to remove the stray wisps, revealing dents and crenulations that made him look like an oversized wasabi bean. Prakash said approvingly that he looked 'dope'. 'What?' I said.

'Fly,' said Malini, who seemed to be more tuned into the zeitgeist than I was.

'Huh?'

'Hep. Cool. Trendy. It's an *American Idol* thing.'

Mum was horrified. 'He looks like a gangster!' she said, clearly thinking of Amrish Puri as Mogambo, and although there was a fleeting resemblance if you squinted and pretended that Govind was four inches taller and thirty kilos heavier, Govind would never look formidable enough to be mistaken for a gangster, not even if he flaunted skeleton tattoos on his arms and a diamanté cross dangled from his ear.

Matt and Maggie had become something of a work item— when they weren't training members at the fitness centre, they were off taking part in 10Ks and swim meets and cycling classics across the country. Govind never actually voiced his disapproval but he glowered at Matt when he came by to pick up Maggie, and Maggie had, on more than one occasion, caught Govind checking her cell phone and trying to hack into her emails.

Then Maggie had announced that an investor had shown interest in her fitness centre and wanted to finance a chain of franchises around the country. The first one would be opened in Los Angeles. 'Isn't that grand news, darling?' she cooed to Govind, sitting on his lap and stroking his bald head (or so I pictured).

'Mmm-hmm. Will you have to travel there?'

'I'll have to move there for a bit? But not for long, babe, six months maybe, a year at the most? But think of the opportunity? You can hold the fort here till then, can't you, angel?'

Govind probably jumped up, decanting her unceremoniously on the floor. 'Is...is Matt going with you?'

Maggie picked herself off the floor and rolled her eyes. 'Yeah, but you're not going to make a thing of that, are you, baby?'

An uneasy silence had prevailed between the two as Maggie had started making arrangements to move to LA. But a few days later, a thousand-page tome, *The Basics of Electrochemical Nanotechnology*, had flown through the window of Matt's house, frightening his dog and nearly beheading his wife. 'You have a wife? Shame on you!' cried Govind as he was being ushered, head first with a firm hand, into the back of a police car. On Maggie's intervention, Matt didn't press charges but a restraining order was served on Govind.

'What's a restraining order?' asked Mum, and inhaled air sharply through lips puckered o-shaped with shock at my explanation.

Things had gone quickly downhill thereafter, and Maggie had moved out, taking Riyaan with her. For a few weeks, Govind appeared to be holding it together in the classroom, although the other teachers noticed that he now preferred to sit by himself in a corner of the staff room, lost in thought, starting if anyone addressed him and occasionally swatting at imaginary flies. And then had come the cloudburst of tears in front of a classful of students.

'Take a sabbatical,' the department head advised. 'Your job will be waiting for you when you're ready.'

And so, Govind had taken the sabbatical and decided to come back home to spend it.

Maggie tried to explain herself to Mum in a conciliatory letter, accompanied by an appeasing box of gluten-free chocolate made with sunflower butter. Govind had become unstable and paranoid, she said, it had become untenable to stay under the same roof. Aunty, she wrote, I hope you will be able to give him the help that he requires at this point.

'Of course she's having an affair,' said Mum, spitting out a square of the chocolate. 'Pah—how can chocolate taste so bad? Anyway, what was I saying? Yes, she's definitely having an affair— these foreigners are all like that…they don't have the same sense of values we do.'

I shook my head at Malini, who was listening in on the extension and trying hard to stifle a giggle. Despite almost two decades' acquaintance with an American daughter-in-law, Mum's image of the Western world was based on a stereotype loosely stitched together from years of watching *Bold and the Beautiful* and *Santa Barbara* back in the Nineties.

'He's leaving Riyaan behind?' I asked.

'Yes! Riyaan's already moved across the country with Maggie. Govind says he'll fly him out here during his vacations. Till then, he'll talk to him on the sky.'

'On the what?'

'You know, that thing you connect on the computer and you can see and talk to the other person?'

'On Skype, Mum.'

'Sky or Skype, what does it matter? He's leaving his son on another continent and coming here, isn't he? I wish your father was here. He would have known what to do.'

'No, he wouldn't,' I said. 'He would have worried about

how much money Govind is going to lose in alimony and child support.'

'Oh my God, she's going to milk him for all he's worth, isn't she?'

'I don't know, Mum.'

∽

It was a familiar Govind who emerged from the spanking-new international airport in Bangalore. His cheeks were a little hollower and there were dark shadows around his eyes, but I put it down to the many hours of flying—Mum would no doubt blame Maggie's neglect. But as we sat down at a café outside the airport, I noticed that he was even more quiet than usual, that his customary soft voice had dropped almost to a whisper, and that he seemed not to hear our bright chatter, our cautious questions. When a child shouted, he started like a frightened doe, and I observed that he had acquired a nervous tic; a cross between a wink, a grimace and a shrug. He had refused to stay on in Bangalore, so after feeding him breakfast, we bundled him into an inter-state taxi that deposited him at Mum's front door that evening.

'So how was your flight? Was it on time? Did you get sleep? Are you jet-lagged?' Mum questioned him with the firm cheeriness of one trying to skirt a sensitive topic, and Govind replied in slow, distracted monosyllables as though it was an effort even to speak.

He looked glumly at the table laden with dinner—all his old favourites, of course, Malabar chicken fry and Alleppey fish curry and palada—which Mum never gave up making, even when Govind had been insisting for years that he preferred salad and bread, that rice made him bloated and spices gave him heartburn.

'I'm not hungry,' he said.

'What? But you've travelled such a long way.'

'I ate on my way.'

'No, no, you must eat something,' Mum said, but Govind looked so tearful at the suggestion that she didn't insist.

'At least some payasam then?'

'No, nothing.'

'Some fruit?'

'No,' he said, and retreated to the upstairs bedroom, which Mum had made up for him, complete with bottled water, hand sanitizer in the drawer and toilet paper in the bathroom.

He didn't emerge the next morning, not even as the smells of his old favourite, idli-vada, wafted through the house.

'It's probably jet lag,' thought Mum, but when noon came and went without any sign of Govind, she started to worry. When soft knocks on the door went unanswered, she threw it open, to find the curtains drawn against the afternoon sun and Govind lying face down on the bed.

Mum cleared her throat. 'Would you like lunch, monay?'

'I don't want any food,' he mumbled.

Mum was not sure what to say. In our family, it was rare that people didn't want food. 'But you have to eat something. You haven't had a morsel since last night.'

'I'm not hungry.'

'Please,' Mum found herself pleading, as though Govind was a recalcitrant toddler and she a novice mother. 'Have something. For me.'

'Do you think he's anorexic?' asked Vimala Aunty, eagerly. She had come over 'to check on Govind', and had tut-tutted theatrically at his skeletal frame and the way he had grimaced at her from his darkened room.

After much cajoling from Mum, Govind dragged himself to the table at dinner time—'without even brushing his teeth, I suspect,' Mum said—and sat staring at the empty plate until Mum leaned over and filled it with mounds of red rice and steaming chicken curry and little stacks of vegetables. Seeing Govind still staring absently at the plate, Mum commanded, 'Eat!', and Govind flinched and began eating, but with little enjoyment.

Weeks passed, then months, and still Govind lurked in his bedroom, curtains drawn against the outside world. Wisps of hair grew back on the sides of his head, revealing that he was almost completely grey. Occasionally he talked to Riyaan 'on the sky' but showed little interest in anything else. Even when terrorists attacked Mumbai on 26-11 and Mum stood transfixed in front of the television watching endless live telecast of people shot dead at CST station, smoke belching from the windows of the Taj, soldiers taking cover behind double-decker buses and rappelling down from helicopters to the rooftops of Colaba buildings that we once walked by without a backward glance at—he remained in his room, apparently oblivious to the images, to the defilement of our shared past. He dutifully came out to the living room when Shivan Mama or Vimala Aunty came over, but would sit lost in thought, disinterested in chitchat, unresponsive to their questions, and would often get up abruptly in the middle of a conversation and disappear into his room. When Mum tried to talk to him about Maggie, he sat mute and unresponsive, his face registering no emotion but for the nervous tic.

'We never liked her, you know,' Mum said over breakfast one day, sliding one more dosa on to Govind's plate. 'I tried to, but never did. Too artificial, all smiles, no character.'

Govind chomped on the dosa dreamily, not seeming to hear. When he was done, he got up without even offering to put his plate in the sink and disappeared into his room.

'Do you think I should take him to a psychiatrist?' Mum finally asked me. This was Mum's equivalent of admitting that it was the end of the world as she knew it. In her mind, psychiatrists were a cross between the charlatan who sat on a plastic sheet under the banyan tree outside the temple, advertising his healing touch on a sign tacked to the tree—'100 pur sent cure for all alemints'—and the young medical student who had once poked her fifteen times while trying to draw blood for a test. Her knowledge of psychiatry, it must be said, was based on the treatment, in the distant past, of an unhinged uncle who was administered ice-water baths and 440 volts (fortunately, never at the same time).

'He's just having a good mope,' I told her. 'Wait and watch for a while.'

Somehow, in the years following Dad's death, I had become Mum's confidant, her sounding board. It was me she called these days to complain about the help, or to gossip about Vimala Aunty's fourth son, Unnikrishnan/Tim, who had lost yet another job, or to wonder aloud after a fight with Sudha whether she should slip her some ashwagandha[36] for her stress. I was not sure how it had happened—apart from Dad, it had been Govind and Sudha who had been her preferred confidants for long; as a callow youth, I had been far too disinterested in household matters, far too preoccupied with Azharuddin's latest score or Claudia Schiffer in her Guess jeans, to listen to her with the attention she expected. But distance had crept into Mum's relationship with Govind a long time ago, even before she knew it perhaps, back in the days when she was hunting for suitable 'girls' while he was secretly courting Maggie in a foreign land. And Sudha no longer enjoyed a good gossip,

---

[36]Winter cherry plant, used in Ayurveda for its medicinal properties

having elevated herself to a higher plane. She was likely to get sanctimonious if Mum confided that she suspected Unnikrishnan/ Tim had been fired from his job for pilfering office supplies—after all, Rajan Uncle seemed to have boundless quantities of A4 paper, staplers, Post-its, Scotch tape and even three printers. I was not entirely at ease taking on this mantle of confidant, certainly not when Mum was reminiscing about her childhood collection of butterflies when I was trying to dash off an urgent mail, or when she was narrating unrelentingly the entire story of *Delhi 6*, complete with snippets of dialogue, when I was trying to catch a rerun of *24*. 'Talk,' said Malini, when I complained, no doubt thinking of her own mother who was no longer around to converse. 'You don't know how lucky you are.' And so I talked.

Sudha, Mum told me, felt that Govind would benefit by spending some time with Gurudev. Sudha had now started taking an advanced course at the ashram, which would ultimately make her proficient to teach Gurudev's patented form of spiritual exercise to new followers. She was also learning reiki on the side ('Using energy to heal,' she told me, 'It's been proven to be miraculously effective'), and faithfully signed up for the half-yearly trips that the ashram organized to different places of pilgrimage in the country. She had already visited the Char Dham, Amarnath, Mathura-Vrindavan, Dwaraka, Kancheepuram, Thanjavur and Palani.

Mum worried about her frequent absences from her home. 'Poor Ramu, he makes his own tea when he comes home from work!' she said, as though Kalki[37] had just thundered up on his horse to destroy the world. 'And often he has to heat up and eat his own dinner—and the children's—all by himself, if she's late

---

[37]In Hindu mythology, the final avatar of Lord Vishnu, who destroys mankind and ends the darkest age, Kaliyuga

in getting back from the ashram!'

'You don't say!' I exclaimed, feigning astonishment.

'Poda!' she said and rabbited on about a neighbour's daughter who had got divorced because she had taken up work in another city, leaving her husband alone and lonely, so lonely that he had been forced to have an affair with a colleague. At the other end of the telephone line, I eye-rolled heavily.

co

'Maybe I should get a medical opinion about the psychiatrist thing,' said Mum. 'Perhaps I'll ask Dr Balan to come over, you know, observe Govind discreetly in the guise of a visit.'

'Who, Backside Balan? You're thinking of the wrong end, Mum!'

'Oh, be quiet!'

So Backside Balan came over to observe Govind and after snorting up a big cup of Bournvita and a packet of Bourbon biscuits, he pronounced that it was just heartache, and all Govind needed was lots of good food and plenty of occupation. So Mum threw herself into making lavish feasts and getting Govind to help around the house, and roped in Shivan Mama to take him around the village to see the sights. Govind complied meekly, accompanying Shivan Mama to the spice market and library, which were the highlights of the little village, setting the table, dusting the curios, sloping off to buy vegetables, but his efforts were lackadaisical and distracted. At the library, he wandered off to a corner, where he stood staring intently at a shelf of Harlequin romances for half an hour. When he set the table, he forgot to place the glasses, or slopped water on the table. When he returned from the shop, it was with the wrong vegetables or having forgotten to buy the chicken. After he dusted, Mum had to wipe down surfaces he had neglected. Once, he ambled off, preoccupied, into an unfamiliar neighbourhood and took three hours to find his way home.

And yet, Mum persisted. She complimented him on the indifferently dusted counter. She tried to get him to talk about work. She piled back issues of *Popular Science* in his room, because in his teens he had pestered Dad to buy him the magazines from the vendors at Flora Fountain and she didn't know what Govind read nowadays. She took him with her on her evening walks to the temple, pointed to the beggars outside and said, 'When I look at them, I feel we're not so badly off, don't you think?', but such homilies seemed to influence Govind in no way whatsoever. She sent his horoscope via Shivan Mama to the astrologer, covertly conducted the pujas the astrologer directed her to, and cajoled Govind into wearing the sacred orange thread that the astrologer had sent across. She commanded Sudha and me to call and speak to him, although when I did, I found that I couldn't keep the conversation going for more than a couple of minutes. At the best of times, Govind had not been garrulous, but now it was like talking to a tree, a dead one at that. My questions were met with weary monosyllables; my bright chatter about the goings-on in my own life and my weak jokes to lighten the conversation were greeted with long and deafening silences.

'That's the last time I try to talk to him,' I said, after a particularly tedious phone call.

'Please,' said Mum. 'We're all he has.' So, of course, I called him again, enduring the unending minutes of silence for her.

Sudha persisted as well, sending him motivational articles and prayers over email, until three months later, they started bouncing back. 'Did you block her?' asked Mum suspiciously, and Govind did not confirm or deny the accusation.

'Don't you think he's wallowing?' Sudha asked me. 'I mean, it's not like…' What she wanted to say, I knew, was: It's not like he has cancer.

And frankly, I agreed with her. Yes, his marriage was failing, his son was a continent away, but it had been months now. Sudha and I were taking time out of our lives to call him, to reach out to him—and he didn't seem to care. Nor did he seem to care that his almost seventy-year-old mother was cooking and cleaning and hobbling around and doing her best to cheer him up, to make things right.

Mum, on the other hand, was always trying to find a silver lining, trying to read something positive in Govind's every little action. 'He opened the curtains today,' she would say, or 'He got the groceries right yesterday, every single one on the list,' or 'He smiled at Vimala today, with no prompting from me,' and this would always be followed by a 'I think he's getting better'. When he went back to curling up in his dim room, looking through visitors and slumping in apathy at the dinner table, she would get a little deflated but would keep her chin up. 'You have to show patience, it takes time,' she would say. 'I read it in a *Reader's Digest* article.'

ᔕ

Govind's sabbatical came to an end, and yet he showed no signs of wanting to go back to the States. Maggie was still in LA with Matt. By some luck, or by the goodwill that he had accrued in the days when he had been diligent and deliberative and one of the best teachers around, the university had agreed to grant him an extension, but there were hints that there would be no more. Govind seemed unconcerned, and even implied that he might not go back, that he would look for another job, perhaps in India.

'But what about Riyaan?' Mum asked.

'Riyaan?' asked Govind, looking quite befuddled. 'Oh, Riyaan. Yes, there is that.'

Mum was still displaying admirable amounts of patience, for dealing with Govind continued to be as tricky as handling a very small child—he had to be reminded to bathe, to eat, to change his clothes; he had to be told when and how to talk to visitors.

But sometimes, I could see her forbearance flickering like an oil lamp in a lively breeze. And in weaker moments, she would allow herself to complain just a little bit. 'Doesn't even make his own bed! I have to sneak into his bedroom when he's away running errands, and he doesn't even notice when he comes back that the sheets are changed, the pillows are fluffed, the bed is made. Just plops down on it like a sack of onions.'

It was bound to happen, a sudden gust of irritation extinguishing that flame of grudging tolerance. Perhaps it would have flickered some more, its wick oiled by maternal concern. But then, one day, Govind came home with a duck.

A live one, quacking and all, and leaving white splashes on the porch. 'It flew into my windshield and hurt its leg! They were going to kill it,' he told Mum, a little tearfully. 'Right there in the middle of the road. How could I allow that? So I bought it off them. A hundred dollars only.'

'What?' asked Mum, feeling faint.

'You should have heard the way it was quacking,' said Govind, eyes moist.

'What will ducks do other than quack?' asked Mum.

At this point, the duck emitted a loud squawk and flew on to the dining table and began to peck inquisitively at Mum's beans thoran[38].

---

[38] A Kerala vegetable preparation with coconut

And this was when the forbearance that Mum had shown over the months crumbled like a badly packed biscuit. It didn't help that her maid had chosen that very day to bunk work, citing a mother-in-law who had died for the fifth time.

'Out, out,' Mum cried, flying at the duck with a fork. The duck, taking quick evasive action, escaped being impaled by a short feather. She chased it out of the house and into the garden, crying 'Out, out,' all the way.

'Okay, that's quite enough!' she glowered at Govind, when she returned. 'Yes, you have problems, I understand that. Your wife left you, which is of no surprise to any of us—you shouldn't have married her in the first place. But the deed is done, you are a middle-aged man with a son and a job and a life. Enough of this moping! Enough of this lying around! Enough of this nonsense!'

Govind gaped at her open-mouthed. And then in the silence that filled the room in the aftermath of Mum's outburst, his lips quivered and he broke into tears. 'Loud, messy, gasping tears,' Mum reported.

She looked at him horrified. Then she dropped the fork and rushed to him. 'Aiyyo monay, I didn't mean any of that. It's that damn bird that's making me say these things.'

There were more tears from Govind and apologies from Mum that day, and a snivelling Govind and a subdued mother sat down to a meal that had gone cold. The sounds of chewing and occasional sniffs from Govind filled the silence, until Govind said, in a remorseful tone, 'I have been moping, haven't I?'

'No, no!' said Mum.

'No, I have. I know I have.'

'Maybe just a little bit.'

'I'm sorry, Mum. I know I've been a pain in the…butt. I'll stop that, I promise.'

'Oh, how can you be a pain in the butt, monay? But yes, maybe it's time to stop moping.'

∽

There had been no more mornings spent lying in bed, contemplating the ceiling. No more evenings cooped up in the darkened room. No outbursts, no slumping on the table, no self-pitying asides. Govind had started bathing regularly, making his bed, rinsing his plate and shaving off the wisps of hair from his head, displaying the shiny gangster pate once again.

Then one morning, he emerged from his room wearing small silky shorts, expensive-looking running shoes, a headband, wristbands and a sleeveless vest that displayed long tufts of hair under his arms whenever he gestured. Banu, the maid, looked shyly away. 'This must be some Western fad,' Mum said to me later. 'Didn't your father teach you boys to shave your armpits every now and then?' But she watched quietly as this new avatar waved his hands and touched his toes and twisted his body.

'Going for a run,' he said. 'I think the fresh air will do me some good.'

'Going for a run, it seems,' grumbled Mum. 'Hasn't running caused him enough trouble?' But she didn't dare to say anything to Govind, so scared was she that she would spook this upbeat apparition away.

When he returned, glistening with sweat, he was brandishing a loaf of bread and a bunch of bananas under one of the hairy, and now sweating, armpits.

'What is that for?' asked Mum.

'That's my dinner Mum, if you don't mind. I can't keep eating like this. These three-course meals, four times a day—I can't take it any more. Look, look how fat I've become,' he said, pinching at a tiny tyre around his waist. 'If Maggie sees me now...' and he trailed off, seeing Mum's expression. 'And all these spices are getting to me...'

'Spices getting to him! What was he brought up on—bland half-raw meat and boiled potatoes?' raged Mum to me. 'Half his problem is this—eating all this Western nonsense instead of proper meals. He may deny it, but this is what he craves deep down, the food he was brought up on. Why is he trying to be someone he isn't?'

Nevertheless, she kept her counsel, because Govind seemed to be shaking off the worst of his pathos, replacing it instead with a manic busyness. When he wasn't exercising, he immersed himself in impenetrable tomes on science that he had unearthed at the library, and occasionally emerged to help around the house, repairing a leaking tap or a faulty emergency lamp. In the evening, after Skyping with Riyaan, he would spend some time playing with the duck.

Yes, the duck had stayed, in spite of Mum's hostility. It gave Govind some pleasure, and despite signs of his improving spirit, Mum was still handling Govind delicately, picking her words carefully, ignoring minor trespasses and always on the lookout for a relapse. So she refrained from saying anything as the duck waddled around the house, quacking angrily at Manikandan, the gardener, chasing visitors, even flying at Shivan Mama and pecking at his head once. 'Can't you train him to do that to Vimala?' asked Shivan Mama testily. But with Govind, the duck was as amiable as a well-fed baby, snuggling up to him as he caressed its feathers, not once pooping on his lap, and accepting breadcrumbs from his hands without ever pecking a finger off. In that imaginative way he had, Govind named him Donald.

'Donald, it seems!' Mum muttered. 'Damn duck!'

14

Bedlam

By the summer of 2010, the days of solitude in the wake of Dad's passing were well and truly forgotten, for Mum's house was jam-packed. There was Govind, virtually back to his old self; the nervous tic had almost completely disappeared and he could even talk with a measure of equanimity to Maggie, who had returned home from LA. And, he said, he was looking forward to returning to America at the end of his sabbatical. Sudha put it down to the prayers and reiki that she had done for him, Mum to the loud, messy tears he had shed that day he had brought home Donald, and Govind himself to his increasingly healthy lifestyle.

For Govind had gone back to his diet of salads and smoothies and could run a 10K quite effortlessly now. Preetha, whose bedroom in Chennai was adorned with posters of a pretty-faced Ranbir Kapoor with a towel clinging perilously to his waist, and Shah Rukh Khan with arms akimbo and open shirt flying behind him, was impressed. 'Govind Mama is going to have a six-pack like John Abraham, Mama!' she told Sudha admiringly. Mum was unimpressed, even when Govind declared that he was going to train for a half-marathon. 'Why?' she asked bewildered, and listened, sceptical but silent, as he talked about runner's highs and endorphin surges.

'What's he up to?' I asked. 'Trying to impress Maggie?'

'You think so?' fretted Mum, and eavesdropped intently but

with little success the next time Govind skyped with Maggie.

Even Mum was not spared. Govind tut-tutted at the amount of ghee she was putting in her biryani, printed out articles about the dangers of sugar for the arthritis that had become so severe that one of her fingers looked like forked lightning. He had even taken to rationing out her desserts for her, which made Mum quite cantankerous. 'Who has just one cup of payasam?' she grumbled. 'Or eats just one piece of cake?'

He had taken over many of Mum's chores as well, and made much work of them, making spreadsheets for grocery-shopping and rationing out precise numbers of curry leaves and garlic pods to Banu, the maid, who he insisted on helping in the kitchen, wearing a checked apron that fell over his silky shorts and made him look as though he was naked below the apron. This caused Banu to blush a deep red and prompted Mum to suggest that perhaps he could find something else to do.

So he turned his attention to Riyaan, who was down visiting during his vacations. 'Want to visit the temple, son?'

'Already been,' answered Riyaan, barely taking his eyes off the television which was tuned into a *CID* rerun.

'A bike ride, then?'

'Nope.'

'How about we take a short trip to Munnar then?'

'No thanks, Dad.' Rumour had it that Riyaan was quite an accomplished boy, having finished the intermediate level tests in piano, and being promoted to an advanced class in science, although there was little evidence of this when he visited India— all he wanted to do was lie in front of the television, laughing hard at the elaborately bejewelled women in the melodramatic soaps and the news anchors shouting at their guests on the nightly debates. Occasionally, he would be persuaded to accompany

Govind on a jaunt around the village, and he would come back mighty pleased with himself for the photographs he had taken, of the backsides of cows being transported in open-backed vans or of signs that said 'Anus Tailoring Shop'.

Sudha, Prakash and Preetha were also there, for the Pujya Gurudev was setting up his ninety-seventh centre about forty kilometres from Mum's house. It was her suggestion, Sudha hinted proudly, to set up the ashram there. 'Excellent,' said Mum, somewhat bleakly.

Sudha was part of the founding committee for the new ashram, and now that the building had been completed, she had been selected from a clamour of eager volunteers to travel to Kerala and oversee matters till the inauguration ceremony. Workers had to be hired, managerial staff appointed and administration staff employed, because a spiritual centre was like any other institution, which required cleaners and cooks, secretaries and typists, managers and assistants. Stocks—of brochures and religious books for the shop, incense and oil for the temple within the ashram, furniture, bed linen for the dormitories, table linen for the canteen, utensils for the kitchen, all in pristine white and monogrammed with the ashram's logo—had to be selected and ordered, accounted for and stored. Plans had to be made for a grand inauguration ceremony. The locality had to be surveyed for its awareness about the Pujya Gurudev's brand of spirituality—the word had to be spread.

'What about Ramu? What about the children?' Mum asked Sudha.

'The "children" are in their twenties, Mum!' Sudha replied. 'They will be with me, initially at least. The work starts during their summer holidays.'

'And Ramu?'

'Ramu will manage. He's not a child.'

So Sudha and her 'children' had arrived at Mum's doorstep, along with six suitcases, two kit bags and the dog, the last a recent addition to Sudha's household. It was a black Lab that the children had whimsically called Clooney, but if there was anything superstar-like about it, it was hard to locate. Thanks to a diet of macaroons gone wrong or slightly scorched puddings fed to him by Prakash, who was now in the patisserie stretch of his Culinary Arts course, he seemed to be taking after Sudha in the waistline department. Since the twins were in charge of looking after him, he was indifferently maintained, with a bedraggled coat and emitting that awful smell of unwashed dog.

Mum, who disliked dogs more than she did ducks, recoiled as the poor old thing waddled up to her and gave her a tentative sniff. 'Get that thing away from me! Why is it here?'

Prakash laughed. 'What Ammamma, so scared you are of this poor thing, ma!'

'I'm sorry Mum, but there's nobody to look after him there— Ramu's hardly ever at home, and I can't trust the help,' said Sudha.

'Chee! Hutt!' Mum squealed, as Clooney licked her hand. 'Take it out! Out! Into the garden!'

Prakash, laughing hard, dragged Clooney into the garden, where he was promptly assaulted by Donald the duck. Clooney yelped and turned tail, seeking refuge under a hibiscus bush.

∽

Within a few days of Sudha's arrival, Mum's neatly kept house was turned upside down. Preetha's bed was strewn with vampire romance novels and padded lace bras. 'Eight hundred rupees for one,' confided Mum to Malini, clearly scandalized. Prakash and Riyaan were constantly in front of the television, ostensibly watching cricket or football but clearly mesmerized by Mandira Bedi's strapless blouses and Shakira's hip-shaking. A half-dozen eggs that Mum had kept aside for a curry vanished into thin air, only to reappear in a new avatar, as a crisp-on-the-outside, soft-on-the-inside meringue that displayed Prakash's patisserie skills. Sudha squeezed in a large framed photo of the Pujya Gurudev beside the gods in the puja room. Religious books lay haphazardly around the coffee table, the dining table and the sofa, the last of which was also lined with Clooney's dog hair. For, despite Mum's repeated attempts to banish him from the house, Clooney always managed to worm his way in somehow. It didn't help that Donald the duck kept flying in his face when he showed up outdoors.

'Poor thing, Ammamma, let him come in, no,' said Prakash. 'That crazy duck will peck his eyes out otherwise.'

'He's frightening poor Donald,' Govind told Sudha indignantly. 'Why don't you tie him up?'

'Why don't you tie the duck up?' parried Sudha.

So Govind did, fashioning a little collar for Donald's neck with a piece of ribbon and tying the duck to a railing of the verandah, where it paced around quacking belligerently.

Every day, ignoring Mum's protests and concerns about safety, Sudha took the early-morning local train to the site of the spiritual centre, travelling second-class, proudly sharing the berth with vegetable vendors and fisherwomen, and probably blighting their morning commute with sermons about the benefits of yoga and the importance of meditation. She was usually back home only late at night, leaving Mum to flit about disapprovingly as Prakash and Riyaan cheered on Brazil in a World Cup match, the vuvuzela blaring continuously in the background, and Preetha constantly texted God-knows-whom.

'Is Sudha monitoring all of this? Who is she talking to and

messaging all day?' she asked me. 'Should I ask her?'

'Stay out of it, Mum,' I warned.

'The whole day. Ting! Ting! Message after message! Do you know she hasn't gone out for three days? And Prakash? Have you seen his hairstyle? Spends half an hour styling it every morning, and it looks like he went for a long ride on a motorbike and forgot to smooth his hair down! And whatever happened to hair partings?'

By the time the holidays ended, Sudha had barely made a dent in the work that had been allotted to her.

'Ask them to find someone else. You have a husband and children to attend to,' Mum said.

But Sudha wouldn't be budged. Prakash and Preetha were dispatched home and Clooney and Sudha hung back for what was to become an extended stay at Mum's house, a stay that would last the better part of a year and a half. At first, the delays were due to the unavailability of suitable candidates for the staff, for Sudha's standards were high, her requirements stringent. Then, there were hold-ups in the delivery of stocks. Just as the stocks arrived, a bunch of employees left, some to join a budget hotel, others a pure-vegetarian restaurant and some more a polyclinic, all of which had sprung up in anticipation of the crowds the ashram would attract once it was functional.

On every other weekend, Sudha would travel down to Chennai, to see Ramu and the children, to leave instructions with Prakash and Preetha that invariably would be ignored, and to generally see to things that she thought would not get done in her absence. Although Mum protested that she missed Sudha, that the house was too quiet, it was a small moment of calm from all the bedlam, when she could once more spend a few moments drinking her morning tea on the verandah, poring over the newspaper and kicking away Clooney as he tried to make advances to curl up at her feet. The more Mum resisted him, the more Clooney seemed to warm up to her, scratching at her door at night, trying to follow her into the kitchen, jumping on to her bed the moment Mum was distracted. If he got too close, Mum would throw her bunch of keys at him, a formidable weapon on a massive Ganesha keychain that could inflict serious injury, for Mum had dozens of keys, which locked storerooms and cupboards against the light-fingered machinations of the maids. Clooney would run away yelping but would return to be assaulted again a few hours later.

When Sudha returned from Chennai, Mum's house would be abuzz once more, with visitors from the ashram, prospective employees coming to drop in biodatas, and painting and cleaning contractors wheedling for an extension or yet another advance. Moreover, without bothering to consult Mum, Sudha had organized a bhajan session at the house on Saturdays, rendered by a group of women so musically disinclined that the renditions of the *Lalitha Sahasranamam* and the *Hanuman Chalisa* sounded, Shivan Mama said, like stones being ground in a Sumeet mixer. On Sundays, the neighbourhood trooped in for a satsang with the resident brahmachari, a triple divorcee who had eventually decided to eschew the carnal and temporal. 'We are using your house only till the ashram is ready, Amma,' the brahmachari told Mum soothingly, swallowing a few bondas, made without onions to his dietary requirements as Sudha had instructed. 'And, by the way, can I have Seven-Up instead of coffee the next time? The heat, you know. Also, there's no need to stick to only Indian snacks. I like pizza too, for example,' he said. 'But Jain pizza, without onions, garlic, etcetera.'

'To think I keep quiet!' said Mum. 'A few years earlier, I

would have given him a piece of my mind.'

'Mellowing with age, are you, Mum?' I laughed. 'Or can't summon up the energy to cross swords with Sudha?'

'The thing is, my voice doesn't rise like it used to any more, and half the time, I can't remember the words I want to use! The side effects of age,' she sighed.

So she endured the unmelodious ladies and almost warmed up to Clooney as he howled equally unmusically to the bhajans. She provided coffee and snacks for the satsang, suffered the ladies who peeped into the bedrooms and asked inquisitive questions about the presence of Govind in the house, even smiled brightly when they gave her unsolicited spiritual advice.

When the house emptied, Sudha would switch on the TV to some religious channel and insist that Mum join her in watching a spiritual lecture or in listening to some uplifting bhajans. Occasionally, Mum nodded off in front of the television, awakening with a snort just as a commercial came on. Looking through bleary eyes at Sudha, she would gush, 'Excellent talk! Wonderful bhajan!' and wonder why Sudha was looking at her so balefully.

If Mum was lukewarm about Sudha's efforts to improve her lot, Vimala Aunty, on the other hand, was hotly interested. Now, Vimala Aunty was pugnaciously pious, eager to do pujas, make offerings and air her knowledge of spiritual matters, which was somewhat limited, to say the least. In the Seventies, Shivan Mama had found her doing her evening puja with great devotion, eyes shut and swaying to the strains of '*Dum maro dum, mith jaaye gham, bolo subah shyam, hare Krishna, hare Ram*'. When Dad tried to convince her that the Bollywood song was actually filmed to the backdrop of a group of junkies high on more than devotion, she had been disbelieving and indignant—until she had seen the movie for herself.

Now Vimala Aunty insisted on visiting the under-construction ashram with Sudha, attending every bhajan session, every satsang held at Mum's house. She cozied up to the brahmachari and spoke of her long faith and deep knowledge of the scriptures. She visited the ashram in Chennai and returned with emblems of her devotion—a large photo of the Pujya Gurudev, spiritual books, CDs of the Pujya Gurudev's talks, two rings and a locket imprinted with the ashram's emblem.

In the ordinary course, Vimala Aunty's flamboyant display of piety would have rankled Mum, but she had other things on her mind. For one, Banu, the maid, who had been with her for almost a decade, had given notice. Mum was convinced this had been brought on by Govind's display of skinny leg and armpit hair, although Banu maintained it was due to increased responsibilities in her own home.

And then, Govind had given her something to think about. 'So Maggie was saying that perhaps we were too hasty to separate,' he told Mum one day, beaming like a car on a dark highway. 'She wants to meet, talk about reconciling.'

'What?' Mum asked, indignant. 'Who does she think she is—upped and walked away two years ago, and now she wants to reconcile?' She looked up to find that Govind's beam had dimmed a little, as though in deference to oncoming traffic. 'You aren't thinking about it, are you?'

'No, no,' said Govind, after a moment's hesitation. 'Of course not.'

But the moment of hesitation had Mum worried.

15

Milk of Human Kindness

Mum was watching Kate Middleton marry Prince William in Westminster Abbey ('Not as pretty as Diana,' she pronounced) when Govind announced that Maggie was taking him back. Mum had suspected it all along, for the announcement had been preceded by months of Skype conversations behind closed doors, which often resulted in Govind emerging from the bedroom with a bashful smile on his face, and launching a tentative salvo:

'Maggie says Riyaan misses me,' or

'Maggie says that the house is empty without me,' and

'I think I overreacted about Matt, there was nothing there ever,' and eventually,

'It's best for Riyaan if we reconcile.'

That Mum could not argue with, so she bit back her caustic remarks about Maggie's treachery and pretended to be happy for them.

So as Osama bin Laden was being hunted down in a walled house in Pakistan, Govind bid a tearful farewell to Donald and a not-so-tearful farewell to Mum and Sudha. 'You'll look after him, won't you?' he asked Mum, 'I would have taken him with me if I could.'

'Yes, of course,' said Mum. 'Like he was my own.'

After Govind left, Mum tried to convince Kamakshi, the

latest in a line of new maids, to take Donald home.

Kamakshi recoiled with horror. 'Chee! No, no Amma. It will dirty my whole house.' Manikandan, the gardener, who had overheard the conversation, swiftly offered to take Doe-naald off Amma's hands, but seeing the way he was gulping down his drool as he said this, Mum didn't have the heart to hand the duck over to him. Instead, she opened the box of banana halwa she had picked up as soon as Govind had left, and while mulling over the dilemma of Donald, she chewed through six of the eight pieces that were inside.

'I hope you're following your diet?' Govind asked her from across the seas.

'Of course, of course,' she said. 'Strictly.'

Meanwhile, the spiritual centre was complete, and the Pujya Gurudev was due to sweep in for a final inspection. Of course, Sudha had invited him home, and brushing aside Mum's protests, insisted that the house be whitewashed, the garden weeded and the bathrooms acid-cleaned. Kamakshi marched up to Mum and threatened to resign as soon as Sudha announced her intentions.

'We will get somebody else to do it, you don't have to do anything,' Mum pleaded. Yes, pleaded, for this was what Mum had been reduced to, the same woman who could make the help quail with just a look in her heyday. But she was pushing seventy now, her joints so stiff and painful that it took her several minutes just to get out of bed, her quick walk grown sluggish and even her temper slower to ignite. For the eventualities of age, she frequented a young Ayurveda doctor called Dr Gopi who practised out of a ramshackle old clinic. It appeared as though Mum was Dr Gopi's only patient, for his clinic was usually deserted when she visited and he would be playing solitaire on an archaic computer, killing the screen with a guilty giggle when she appeared. Nevertheless,

Mum was a faithful client, because Dr Gopi charged only half of what other doctors did, never asked her to do medical tests, something she looked upon with the same suspicion as she did psychiatrists, and smiled indulgently if she negotiated with him about the extent to which she should follow the prescribed diet restrictions—'Once in a way, I can eat chicken, no? One sweet a day won't kill me, eh?' Ignoring these geriatric eccentricities, Dr Gopi supplied her with all kinds of foul-smelling oils and potions which she applied rigorously, without any benefit, it seemed.

All of us had been exhorting her to spurn the oils and potions and visit a proper doctor, but ever since Sudha had been diagnosed with cancer, Mum believed that visits to the doctor only ended with bad news. Mum also believed that modern medicine was responsible for many evils, chiefly the extension of lifespan which had passed Dad by, but which threatened to be bestowed upon her despite the dire predictions of the astrologers. So she would insist, 'It's just old age. Human beings aren't supposed to live for so long.'

'But seventy is the new sixty, Ammamma!' Prakash would say.

'Tell that to my bones,' she would retort.

Nevertheless, chores had become increasingly difficult, and maids had become essential, although she still insisted on doing all the cooking herself. 'I will become useless if I don't do anything,' she would say.

Eventually, Kamakshi was coaxed to stay on, but only after Mum had given her two days' leave while the house was being whitewashed, so that Kamakshi would not be inconvenienced in any way.

When the Pujya Gurudev arrived, he turned out to be rather more personable and far more charming than his wild-haired photo suggested, and with a few complimentary words about

her house and the deliciousness of her food, he charmed Mum
utterly. 'He's charismatic,' she allowed, but refused to sanction
anything more.

'She refuses to come for the inauguration,' Sudha complained
to him.

'How can that be, Amma? If it wasn't for your nurturing,
your lifelong support, could Sudha Akka[39] have achieved all this?
You must come.'

Mum murmured something about joint stiffness.

'I will arrange everything. A taxi to the centre, a golf cart
to take you to the building, people to help you up the stairs—in
a chair if you like.'

'No, no!' protested Mum.

'Yes, yes!' insisted Gurudev.

ᘒ

So it happened that the day of the inauguration found Mum,
Vimala Aunty, Rajan Uncle, Sudha and Prakash squeezing into a
rented Innova and driving down to the ashram. Sudha had shaved
off her hair on her latest visit to Tirupati, prompting Vimala
Aunty to lean over to Mum and ask in a penetrating whisper
and with exaggerated concern, 'Is the cancer back?' Prakash had
finished his Culinary Arts course and had landed a job as a
pastry chef, where, as far as I could make out, he was mostly
responsible for separating and whipping up eggs, kneading and
proving dough and cleaning up kitchen spills. As a commis 3
chef, he was on the very lowest rung of the kitchen ladder, but
the kitchen was in a seven-star hotel, and in the two years that
he had been pursuing Culinary Arts, the world had awoken to

---

[39]A term of respect in Tamil, literally 'elder sister'

the glamour of chef whites. *Masterchef* had come to India and everybody seemed to be talking croquembouches and macaron towers, and even Vimala Aunty looked at Prakash with respect when he gushed about chocolate sculpturing and artisan breads.

Ramu had stayed back with Preetha, who was swotting for yet another exam of her interminable medical course, and Shivan Mama had invented a stomach upset to avoid the ordeal. 'Lucky rascal,' muttered Mum. 'You think Sudha will believe me if I said I ate the same thing you did?' Shivan Mama shook his head.

After a two-hour car journey, the Innova drew up to high walls and enormous gates manned by walkie-talkie-toting security men and sniffer dogs. As they made their way up a long winding driveway past landscaped gardens and grand buildings, Sudha pointed out the sights: 'That's the temple, Temple of Tranquillity, here's Asana, our yoga centre, that's Bhakti, our meditation hall, this is Milk of Human Kindness, where all the cows are housed.' Mum smiled brightly, holding her pallu up to her nose against the waft of cow dung.

A large pandal that could seat over two thousand guests had been set up in the vast grounds for the inauguration ceremony. It was already packed, but Sudha was led up to the front where twenty rows had been reserved for VIPs. Mum found herself sitting behind a well-known television newsreader and a yesteryears Bharatanatyam dancer. They settled in their seats and, as they waited for the programme to begin, Mum fanned herself against the heat and looked around at the crowd: ladies in heavy silks, men in pristine white mundus, khadi-clad foreigners, a smattering of holy types in the signature coral and green batik robes of the ashram. Prakash whipped out his mobile and took an ironic selfie behind the dancer's back, his right hand in what he imagined to be an authentic mudra and eyes slanted to the side in a pose he deemed dancer-like.

Just as the din in the audience was reaching fever pitch, a young MC, looking uncomfortable in her Kanjeevaram sari, shuffled over to the mike, cleared her throat and, in a nervous high-pitched voice, muddled through a welcome speech. Then the Pujya Gurudev came on to the stage to a great big cheer of 'Jai Gurudev! Jai Gurudev!' A lamp was lit, the chief guest—the state home minister—was honoured with a marigold garland. Then Gurudev launched into a rousing speech. 'We will be opening our hundredth centre in India this year!' he thundered to quite unholy whoops and cheers. 'And our twentieth hospital, our thirty-fifth school! Leading the way will be this centre, your centre, dear friends, built with your donations, your sweat, your faith!' Sudha became quite pink with pride when he mentioned the tireless efforts of the founding committee. There followed a two-hour-long spiritual and cultural programme with Carnatic musicians singing bhajans, a Mohiniattam performance, a presentation of yoga and a display of Kalaripayattu. Rajan Uncle, who had managed to sneak in a snifter before leaving that morning, snored softly beside a transfixed Vimala Aunty, while Prakash played games on his phone. The programme ended with an interactive demonstration of Gurudev's spiritual exercise. Mum lumbered to her feet, her handbag falling to the ground as she rose, her sari crumpled. She went through the motions half-heartedly, throwing her arms around with less enthusiasm than suggested, whispering out 'Om's that were meant to be guttural and not throwing her head back and guffawing as you were supposed to for the laughter section of the exercise. Prakash, on the other hand, threw himself into the exercises with hyperbolic eagerness, clipping the Bharatanatyam dancer's jasmine-adorned head with his arm at one point.

Lunch was served in an adjoining pandal, a glorious sadya served on banana leaves with innumerable curries and vegetables and pickles and pappadams, and no less than four payasams.

'Can we go now?' asked Mum, sated and drowsy with the four payasams.

'But you have to see the main building!' said Sudha, and so the geriatric gang waddled and tottered down the enormous driveway to the spiritual centre, a grand white semicircular building. 'Doesn't it feel like it's opening its arms to embrace you?' asked Sudha, waving at the two arcs of the semicircle, and Vimala Aunty nodded sagely while Mum wondered how she had given birth to such strange children. Inside, in a large front hall paved with Italian marble, a two-armed staircase led to the floors above, a staircase of the type seen in Hindi films of a certain vintage, in mansions that had pipe-smoking villains in bathrobes and molls with blonde wigs. Vimala Aunty shadowed Sudha as she made her way upstairs, while Rajan Uncle doddered behind her, and Mum plodded torturously behind, hoping Rajan Uncle wouldn't fall on her. Prakash brought up the rear, holding Mum up with a finger in the back when she swayed precariously on a step.

Upstairs, Sudha took them to see the enormous halls where daily yoga sessions and evening aartis would be conducted, the café and restaurant which served wholesome Indian food and organic pizzas, and the rooms for visiting devotees and brahmacharis. Here, they bumped into the Gurudev.

'Amma, I am so glad you have come! Did you eat?'

'Yes, yes, thank you!' interjected Vimala Aunty. 'What a beautiful programme, so much culture.'

'But what was that nonsense at the end? Throwing your arms around, laughing like a hyena?' asked Rajan Uncle, irritably. He was missing his afternoon peg. Gurudev, the smile still plastered on his face, turned to look at him, but Vimala Aunty was already towing Rajan Uncle away.

Gurudev, seemingly unperturbed, turned back to Mum. 'So, Amma, did you like the programme?'

'Of course, of course. Very much! Beautiful,' said Mum.

'And how is your health?'

'Nothing to complain about.'

'Do you know what is the best thing for health?'

'Ayurveda?'

Gurudev threw back his head and laughed, as though he was conducting another session of his spiritual exercise. 'Yes, medicines, Ayurveda or otherwise, but do you know what is the best medicine?'

'Laughter?' asked Mum, remembering a snippet from *Reader's Digest*.

'Yes! And yoga!'

Mum simpered in the sycophantic way she had seen his followers employ with him.

'So you must come for our sessions regularly, Amma. All your ailments will go away.'

'Yes, yes, certainly,' said Mum, looking wildly around for Sudha, 'Er, I think we have to leave now.'

'Of course, of course. Let me see you to the entrance.'

'No, no!' Mum protested. 'There is no need. You have so much to do, so many guests…'

'All that can wait, Amma. It is such an honour for me that you came. Come, come,' he said.

So Sudha, Prakash, Vimala Aunty and Rajan Uncle were herded together, and as all the holy types turned to gawk enviously at the party that had been blessed with the Gurudev as personal escort, Gurudev started telling Mum about the plans he had for the local centre: the setting up of five rural schools and two charitable hospitals in the neighbourhood, hosting annual yoga meets and monthly satsang sessions, the introduction of the ashram's own brand of organic produce, from spices and honey to flour and oils.

'There is only one thing, Amma—we need funds,' he said. Mum felt a slow unease creep over her. She had already been made to fork over a few thousands for the ashram to Sudha, which she had done unenthusiastically, only for the sake of keeping the peace.

'If all members contribute, we can achieve all our goals.'

They had reached the top of the two-armed staircase. Gurudev leaned against the banister.

'Not much, Amma, maybe ₹30,000 or ₹50,000 each.'

It was at this point that Mum felt her legs buckle. She fell sideways, like a heroine fainting in a Bollywood movie, and despite Gurudev, Sudha and Vimala Aunty all reaching out to steady her—Rajan Uncle was asking a brahmachari he had just met if he had read *Lady Chatterley's Lover* and Prakash was still immersed in his phone—she keeled over and started rolling down the stairs. Halfway down, she rolled into the banister, which broke her fall, and her injuries were limited to a badly sprained ankle, a very sore back and a terribly bruised ego.

Later we joked that it was the shock of Gurudev's blatant fundraising that had caused Mum to collapse.

Part Four
....
Sans Everything

16

Knife in the Wound

The house now emptied of her daughter and grandchildren and Clooney, Mum must have been looking forward to some respite. But barely a month after her first fall, Mum stumbled again, this time as she was bringing out a tray of tea to Shivan Mama who was waiting for her on the verandah. Mum managed to break her fall by hanging on to the railing, although the net effect of buckling knees and falling crockery and hot tea splashing all over was quite dramatic. 'That stupid Kamakshi, she never wrings the mop, always leaves the floor wet,' Mum griped.

'There was not a drop of water on the floor,' said Shivan Mama.

'Yes, there was, how do you think I fell?'

'Be honest, you're still reeling from the Pujya Gurudev's fundraising efforts, aren't you?'

'Oh, poda!' Mum laughed.

Barely had the memory of that fall receded when Mum fell again. She was standing in front of the puja room, just about to light the lamp. She didn't tell any of us about it for long, but later we found that she had crashed head first into the pictures of gods on the marble-topped counter. 'One minute I was standing, the next minute I was down, I don't know what happened,' she admitted eventually. She hit her head on the edge of the counter and lay there, stunned and bleeding, for who knows how long. Eventually she pulled herself upright, holding on to the wall to steady her shaking legs, and made her way to the bathroom to wash away the blood.

Then, a few weeks later, she fell yet again. I had arrived in Kerala with Malini and the kids, and Mum was crossing the road outside her house to where a vegetable vendor was selling her favourite white bitter gourd at a cut-rate price. Mum got excited about groceries, especially if they were on discount, the way I got excited about the latest gadgets. While others came back from holidays with new clothes and souvenirs, Mum's acquisitions would often be less exotic: ripened long beans that were not easily available in the city and brinjals that were cheaper in the village, lugged along good-naturedly by Dad, who would always mock her but would never demur from carrying them home. So when Mum spotted the vegetable vendor from an upstairs window, she rushed down the stairs and out of the gate as fast as she could, to accost him before he decided to meander away. Just as she reached the middle of the road, she toppled over like a bowling pin, causing an oncoming motorcyclist to weave and wobble and crash into the vegetable vendor's cart. The bitter gourds rolled everywhere, causing more motorists to weave and wobble and honk, outraged. The motorcyclist who had crashed his bike advanced menacingly on Mum to berate her and possibly to try to extract some compensatory hundreds from her. Mum tried to retort but, stunned and breathless and indignant, couldn't summon forth her voice.

Just then, an unexpected knight in shining armour appeared in the shape of Manikandan, the gardener, who had spotted all the happenings from the gate where he was leaning, enjoying a beedi after a difficult half-hour of weeding. He rushed across the road and helped Mum up and shoved away the advancing motorist roughly. 'Get lost, you rabid dog,' Manikandan snarled, much like a rabid dog himself. 'Can't you see that Amma is hurt? So what if your bike is scratched? Did Amma scratch it on purpose? She fell down just to scratch your bike? Advance one more step and I will break your blasted bike into two!'

The motorist backed away, trying to save face by spitting out the filthiest abuses as he retreated, but patently not so much rabid dog as cowardly cur. Manikandan helped Mum back to the house, by which time all of us had been alerted to the commotion on the street outside.

'What happened, Mum?' I asked, as she settled down to catch her breath.

'Oh, I don't know, I was rushing, I suppose, not looking where I was going...'

'What, Amma, second time this month,' said Pappikutty, draping herself over a chair. Pappikutty was the latest in a line-up of maids, for Kamakshi had left, for a higher salary and less menial work, she mentioned on her way out. Pappikutty was an affectionate old lady, who was as sloppy as she was garrulous, and she thought nothing of abandoning her work to join in on family discussions, despite Mum having hinted several times that her participation in every household conversation was not mandatory.

'What?' I asked. 'What do you mean, second time?'

'Nothing, nothing,' Mum said. 'Pappi, don't you have work to do?'

'Second time she fell this month, saar! Two weeks back, in front of the puja room and nobody around to even help her! Didn't you know?'

'No, I didn't,' I said and turned to fix Mum with an accusing glare.

'Oh, you children would have just fussed!'

'But this is your third fall in a few months, Mum!'

'Ha, ha, that Gurudev really got me, ah?'

'Stop joking, Mum. This may be a small thing, but you must get it checked by a doctor. They will probably just give you some medicines for it.'

'Okay, okay. I will go to Dr Gopi tomorrow.'

'What, that solitaire-playing quack?'

'He's very good, monay.'

'I mean, at least if he played Angry Birds, you could credit him with being up to date.'

'What is Angry Birds?'

'I rest my case. He will probably ask me the same thing. I'll bet he still thinks that arsenic is a legitimate cure for venereal disease.'

'Oh, be quiet.'

'No, but seriously, Mum, let me ask Ramu at least.'

'No need, no need. That Sudha will fuss so much. As it is, I often wonder who is the mother and who is the child? Will you stop worrying? It's nothing—all old people have falls once in a while. This is why I didn't tell you in the first place!'

After I returned to Bangalore, Shivan Mama informed me that he had accompanied Mum to Dr Gopi, who had given her his usual prescription of foul-smelling potions and a long list of dietary restrictions. 'As far as I can make out, she's religiously taking the potions, but ignoring the diet restrictions completely. When I call her out on it, she tells me, "Oh, 'don't eat' doesn't mean 'don't eat *completely*'! Little-little I can eat."'

'Yes, that sounds like her,' I said, shaking my head.

Eventually, Shivan Mama decided that he would contact Backside Balan covertly for a second opinion. He arrived one morning and after downing his large glass of Bournvita and finishing a packet of cream biscuits, which he ate like a child, opening the halves and licking off the cream filling inside before polishing off the biscuits, he broached the topic with Mum.

'So Shivan tells me you've been having some falls?'

'Cheh, that blabbermouth, it's nothing, really.'

'Hmm. Yes, probably. Low BP perhaps, or an ear problem. Easily remedied.'

'Yes, yes. Dr Gopi prescribed some kashayams[40] and all.'

'And have they helped?'

'I haven't fallen since then.'

'Hmm. But maybe you should get some tests done?'

'Aiyyo, no need. These doctors just prescribe tests to make money.' She looked up to find Dr Balan looking sternly at her. 'Not you, of course, Backsi...Dr Balan.'

And then, two weeks later, Mum fell again. This time her knees buckled as she was standing over a pot of boiling sambar, which she grabbed at instinctively to break her fall. Mum and the pot came crashing down, leaving Mum with hot curry all over her and Pappikutty rushing screaming from the kitchen to call Shivan Mama.

'Okay, you can ask Ramu,' Mum told Shivan Mama, in a subdued kind of tone, when everybody had recovered somewhat from the pandemonium.

Ramu directed Mum to a doctor he knew at a hospital in her neighbourhood, who conducted a retinue of tests: blood tests, blood pressure tests, eye tests, tests to rule out osteoporosis, tests of the inner ear, CT scans, ECGs, X-rays, MRI scans. The good news, Sudha informed me, was that they had located no signs of anything serious. The bad was that they still didn't know why she was falling.

---

[40]Water-based Ayurvedic concoctions

'I told you it's nothing,' Mum grumbled. 'A thousand tests for nothing. You children don't realize I'm almost seventy! These things happen with age.'

'Do you think her speech is a little slurred?' asked Malini. I listened for it but couldn't tell any difference, but I alerted Sudha nevertheless. Mum was taken for another round of tests which yielded no results.

'Could she have had a stroke?' asked Malini, but Ramu said no, there were no indications.

Then, about a year after her first fall, Mum found she could not move her feet. She was trying to shoo away Donald, who was attempting to invade the house, but her legs refused to respond.

'What is happening to me?' she asked Shivan Mama, suddenly apprehensive.

The legs responded after a while, but Mum did not complain when Ramu asked for another round of tests to be done.

This time, Ramu called me from Chennai after seeing the results. The fact that it was Ramu who called me and not Sudha made me fear the worst. Ramu and I had a cordial but somewhat indifferent relationship—he was an amiable chap and, at times, I felt a little sorry for him that he was married to Sudha. But we inhabited different worlds. Our conversations when we met revolved around the form of the cricket team or the transformation of Djokovic after the gluten-free diet. Malini and Sudha, too, seemed equally remote from each other, meeting one another with polite questions about each others' children and maids, but little else.

After some awkward chitchat, I asked about the results of the latest test. 'We think it might be atypical Parkinson's,' he said.

'Parkinson's?' My heart lurched. Those monsters were rearing their heads again. 'But there are no tremors, no...'

'Yes. That is why it is atypical. The symptoms seem to fit—falls, possible speech impediments, now problems with movement.'

'I see. And why is it caused?'

'It could be a neurological issue, or a series of small strokes. New research suggests that it might be an autoimmune disorder.'

'I see. What is the cure?'

'There is no cure. Only palliative care, at best.'

'Oh.'

'There are treatments that may improve the symptoms, although we know very little about the disease. We think Parkinson's is due to the lack of dopamine, which is a chemical in the brain, but atypical Parkinson's patients rarely respond to treatments that increase dopamine levels.'

'Oh.'

'I hate to tell you this, Vivek, but the symptoms are likely to get worse. It is a degenerative disease.'

'Oh.'

'I'll send you a couple of links. Read it and call me if you need any more information.'

Then Sudha came on the phone, snivelling, shrill. 'It's a horrible disease, Vivek. I've read all the literature. All the muscles will start degenerating one by one. She will have problems with movement, vision, even swallowing food and water in the long run.'

Before I could digest this, Ramu came back on the phone.

'Is this true,' I asked, 'what Sudha says?'

'Yes, symptoms of atypical Parkinsonism include ataxia, dysphagia...' He was hiding behind medical jargon now. 'But the disease progresses at different rates in different people. She may just die of old age before the symptoms become too bad.'

There was a silence as I absorbed this, and then Ramu said in an undertone, 'You should probably pray for that.'

'Could it be something else?' I asked, hopefully. 'Could the diagnosis be wrong?'

'It could. But it probably isn't.'

I wondered if Ramu was this comforting with his patients as well.

'So what can we do now?'

'Start some therapies to slow down the progress of the disease. Physiotherapy, dopamine treatments perhaps, there are other things. She should probably move here so that we can oversee the treatment.'

Sudha came back on the phone.

'How is Mum taking it?' I asked.

'I haven't told her, Vivek, how can I? Tell her she has a disease which will make her a vegetable? I've told her it's something to do with cells, something which will require some treatment in the short term. I told her she should come here, but she's resisting. Will you talk to her?'

I will, I promised, but as I put the phone down, I wondered if I could—there would be questions I had to fend off, suspicions I would have to parry. This was, after all, the woman who could smell one glass of beer on my breath when I was young, no matter how many Polos I had popped into my mouth to conceal the odour. The one who used to detect an adolescent crush by the slight heightening of the colour on my face, the same person who could sense my mood from the cadence of my 'Hello' over the phone and would cross-examine me relentlessly if she thought I was despondent, even if I pretended to be just fine.

'Can't you talk to her?' I asked Malini.

'Don't be silly!' Malini scowled. 'You will have to do it.'

I called. As expected, there were questions.

'But what is wrong? There must be a name for the condition.'

'It's some nerve problem, that's all I know, Mum. It requires some treatment.'

'Nerves or cells? Sudha said cells. Are you hiding something from me? Is it serious?'

'No, don't be silly, Mum! It's nothing serious. '

'Then why should I go and park myself at Sudha's? Why can't I take treatment here?'

'It's better if Ramu sees you... He will be able to monitor things better in Chennai.'

'How long will it take?'

'A month or two...'

'My god! Two months of Sudha's tantrums and lectures and bhajans. No, no! I can't do that! And I have so much to do here.'

'What do you have to do?'

'Some people don't have secretaries and trainees under them to delegate their work to, you know,' she said icily, and I threw my hands up in defeat.

'You have to tell her the truth,' Malini said, when I put the phone down. 'Sooner or later, she's going to see through these lies you both are peddling her.'

'Oh, be quiet, will you?' I shouted, somewhat satisfied to see the wounded expression spreading over her face. 'What do you know?'

But a week later, I was making a trip to Kerala, and over a cup of tea, the news of Kasab's hanging playing behind us on the television, I told her as gently as I could, feeling much like I was headed to the gallows myself. I told Mum about the disease she had, passing lightly over what it could do to her, how there was no cure. I had spent the flight staring blankly at my Kindle, wondering how I would tell her, how I would comfort her, how

I would cope with her tears. But there were no tears. She just sat there, calmly digesting the news, as though she had known all along.

'Hopefully I will be dead before it becomes too bad,' she said.

And I couldn't say anything, because I was hoping for the same thing, for her quick and merciful demise.

'You will try the treatments, won't you? You never know what might help. And it may slow things down—keep you active for longer,' I said. Every word sounded like driving a knife in the wound, but, under the circumstances, that was me being kind.

'But I have to stay with Sudha? Listen to all those spiritual talks and...and subject myself to her reiki?'

I laughed. 'I'm afraid so. At least for a little while.'

'Okay,' she said, and the placidity with which she said it, her complete lack of fight, broke my heart more than tears could have.

A month later, just a day after her seventieth birthday, which she had spent quietly, fielding our calls and settling bills, she left for Chennai. She had already handed over Donald to a salivating Manikandan, who promised to look after him 'like it is my own moustache, Amma!' She had handed over the house keys to Shivan Mama for safekeeping, and bid goodbye to Vimala Aunty and Rajan Uncle. Vimala Aunty was unusually subdued. 'You get well soon, okay?' she told Mum, giving her a kiss on the cheek. 'Don't worry about anything here, we'll take care of it.' Pappikutty brought sacred ash from her family temple and smeared it all over Mum's forehead. 'Very powerful, our Deva. You will become alright very soon,' she said, blinking through her tears.

Shivan Mama dropped her to the station, making sure the porter settled her in and hefted her suitcase on to the luggage rack. It wasn't heavy; Mum had packed some starched cotton saris for the Chennai heat, a prayer book and a framed photo of Dad. At the time she didn't know that she wouldn't use the saris for long. And she didn't know that she would never return to her own home.

17

Lab Rat

I visited Mum often, taking the Shatabdi down from Bangalore and arriving just in time to be assaulted by the mid-morning swelter of Chennai. It had been several years since I had been to Sudha's house—Sudha and I would coordinate our trips to Kerala so that we could meet there instead. It was one of those bungalows whose vintage could be easily placed in the Eighties, and it had probably been trendy in its time: flat roof, asymmetrical, arc-shaped front elevation, a pattern made from broken tiles climbing over the facade. I'm quite sure I designed something similar in my Civil Engineering days—or copied them from the unidimensional mugpot, at least. The large kitchen had a counter made of Cuddapah stone, the hall and dining areas were on two levels separated by a couple of steps, there was a sink in the corridor outside the dining room. The floors were of grey patterned mosaic and the tiles in the bathroom were of the shiny white six-inch-square type that was customary for that era. There was an external room and bathroom at the back for the help, and a generous garden with a lawn and potted plants.

I had expected some clutter, because Sudha had never been house-proud, but it appeared that in the intervening years, Sudha had not once cleaned her house. Mum had warned me about this—'I think she has lost interest in the worldly after her illness,' Mum still found it hard to say cancer, 'and Ramu is too frightened to have an opinion.'

I had put it down to Mum's inclination to exaggerate, but in actuality, she had been tactful. The house was in complete disarray. The sofa in the living room was covered with dog hair and the dining-room sideboard was piled with books—medical tomes, spiritual books, Prakash's cookbooks splashed liberally with turmeric powder and oil. Dusty artefacts occupied every space: framed photographs and garish landscapes, plaques from medical associations, artificial flowers in hues no god could have created, a gaudy blue plastic Krishna, brass artefacts crying out for a lick of Brasso, a cupboard full of ghastly imitation crystal. The space under the stairs overflowed with old newspapers and magazines, from which Prakash occasionally pulled out a *Femina* from 1992 or a *Reader's Digest* from 2007 for Mum to peruse. In the kitchen, the Cuddapah stone counter was pockmarked and greasy, the sink was edged with a green slime that was an amalgam of years of Vim bar and dishwater, the cups were ringed with tea and coffee stains dating back to the last millennium. The fridge was of an ancient vintage and the exhaust fan groaned as it rotated and sprayed sticky grime.

Mum said it was Sudha's way of rebelling against all things temporal—why should she do something as inane as cleaning when her body could let her down again and her mind had been elevated to a higher plane? On a previous visit, Mum had suggested to Sudha that it might be a good idea to detach herself from decades-old magazines and devote herself to a mop every now and then, but this had resulted in a heated argument, an argument that somehow led to Sudha berating Mum for everything from forcing her to have ghee-laden Ayurvedic preparations after childbirth, which she held solely responsible for the stubborn extra kilos around her frame, to marrying her off to a man with

210 頃 *The Monsters Still Lurk*

a ridiculous name like Ramu, a name he shared with our old milkman from Bombay, the one who used to get us milk in the Seventies, in bottles sealed with caps of striped foil. So Mum had given up trying.

But now, none of that mattered. We were all relieved that Mum was being treated, and monitored, that she wasn't keeling over all alone in her house in Kerala.

Here, there was Ramu, his hirsuteness now having spread to his eyebrows, which had sprouted hairy antennae that quivered above his reading glasses when he spoke and made him look like a cockroach; a cerebral cockroach, one with a master's degree and a stamp collection, no doubt, but a cockroach nevertheless. Ramu, who, despite that air of contented inefficiency reminiscent of proprietors of dusty antique stores, seemed to have friends in high medical places and could have hospital queues jumped and insurance paperwork completed in a trice and exorbitant medicines subsidized by just a word in the right ear.

Prakash and Preetha were there, both flitting in and out of the house to be sure, but available to run to the medical store to get a tablet or accompany Mum to the doctor. Prakash had now moved a rung up the kitchen ladder and was entrusted with baking basic sponges and loaves, whipping up icings and making the chocolate twirls and decorative roses that sat atop chocolate ganache cakes and butterscotch pastries. Because of the sauna effect of long hours in a hot kitchen, he had lost all his puppy fat, and now looked lean and fit and handsome in his skinny jeans in bright hues, his hair teased and gelled into impeccable carelessness and a diamond stud in his ear.

'Is that the gay ear?' Mum asked me worriedly, and I was so astounded that she knew such a thing existed that I didn't reply. She went on to mutter something about it being a sure sign that

Kalikaalam[41] was upon us; men dressing as women and women acting like men.

Preetha was still toiling away at her endless medical studies; she was in her postgraduate course now. On the one hand, she attended classes on paediatric ophthalmology and specular microscopy, and on the other, she participated in candlelit vigils for Nirbhaya, and wrote earnest blogs about the need to remove the stigma around menstruation, citing the example of a temple in the Northeast built on the site where a goddess's yoni was said to have fallen from the heavens, and which celebrated the goddess's menstrual cycle with a festival every year. 'What's yoni?' asked Mum, and looked quite glum at the answer.

There were the ladies from the ashram and junior swamis, who came several times a week to sing cacophonous bhajans and do pujas and conduct spiritual lectures in the tumult of Sudha's living room. There was Gurudev, who dropped in whenever he was in town, and entertained Mum with tales of his recent travels—spreading the word to the housewives of Texas, being detained by hardliners in Malaysia, having a Shah Rukh Khan song sung to him by a German girl in Munich. There was a cook and a maid and a driver, and there was Clooney, of ancient vintage and arthritic now, who refused to leave Mum's side, apparently having no recollection of past inflictions of kicks and well-aimed throws of the house keys.

And there was Sudha, impressively fat and decidedly dowdy in her voluminous salwar-kameezes and 1990s'-era scrunchies, looking like some liquor baroness who had killed 325 with her spurious merchandise. Sudha teetered on that precipice of fury despite twice-weekly fasts to detoxify her body and daily

---

[41]Kaliyug: the final age of destruction, according to Hindu scriptures

meditation to cleanse her mind, but the inner rage seemed to galvanize her into action; it was she who stood over Mum and made her have her medicines and do her physiotherapy exercises, who monitored her diet and didn't allow her to overindulge, who played her bhajans to calm her fears and did pujas and practised reiki and wore an unsightly pendant with large coloured stones to aid Mum's recovery.

'You've got to hand it to her,' I told Mum. 'Nobody could have looked after you better.'

'I'll disinherit her and give you her share if you can make her stop,' said Mum, ungratefully.

I suppressed a smile. 'Maybe if you throw in Dad's love letters.'

'What?'

'You know, the ones you used to threaten him with when we were young. Surely, we're old enough now to be granted access?'

Her eyes darted away. 'I threw them away long ago.'

'Liar!'

'Really, I'm telling you.'

∽

Govind checked the reports with a few doctors in the States and confirmed the diagnosis. Ramu started Mum, without much hope, on medication that might correct the levels of chemicals in her brains and perhaps stem the damage, slow down the rot.

'Are all these medicines necessary?' Mum asked from time to time.

'Yes, Mum!' said Sudha. 'Would we be giving them to you if they weren't?'

'Don't worry, Aunty,' said Ramu, 'See, three of these are merely vitamins.'

'What about the others?' she asked.

'Some are your routine medicines—for your BP, to keep your heart strong. This one is to improve the levels of probiotic bacteria in your stomach, which gets affected by the other medicines you're taking. The other tablets contain chemicals to improve the levels of dopamine in your brain, which may slow down the degeneration.'

'May?'

'The science is not perfect yet,' he said.

'What if I don't have them?'

'You could get worse.'

'And could I get worse if I continue having them?'

'So many questions, Mum!' fumed Sudha. 'Don't you trust us?'

The falls continued, sporadically, unannounced, unpredictable. One moment Mum would be on her feet and the next she would be on the ground, face down, legs splayed, sari askew. Sometimes weeks, even months passed without a fall, and sometimes they were days apart. Once she crumpled as soon as she got up from her chair but the fall was broken by Clooney, who was lying at her feet and wasn't nimble enough to escape. Another time, in front of Preetha's classmates from medical college, all already certified doctors, who stood around gaping helplessly as she lay on the ground, until Prakash, hearing the crash, rushed over and heaved Mum up. At this point, one of the girls, a thin young thing with a tattoo of a dancing skeleton on her forearm, which Preetha thought was delightfully ironic, came over and offered Mum a tissue to staunch the blood from her grazed temple. 'Our health is in good hands,' said Mum, and the young thing beamed, oblivious to Mum's wry tone.

Despite her denials, I could see Mum's confidence waning with every fall, and she confined herself to the house, when once she had roamed with Dad or alone, taking buses to Nalli's to buy silks and autos to Marina beach for an evening walk. Now she restricted her walking to Sudha's driveway, leaning on a walking stick for support.

Ramu said it was important to keep her motor functions running, to shore up her weakening muscles. So Prakash's treadmill, which had become a hanger for clothes, handbags and other detritus, had been decluttered and placed in Mum's room. At least one thirty-minute session a day, Ramu prescribed, and Sudha would loom over Mum like a drill sergeant and ensure she did it, even when Mum complained that she didn't feel like it. 'All she needs is a cane,' Mum complained.

The degeneration was inexorable. Around the time the Budget for 2013–14 was being presented in Parliament, Mum couldn't always get her hands and legs to do as she commanded them. When she tried to change channels on the television, she found that her fingers wouldn't respond immediately. If she wanted to cross her legs, it sometimes took the better part of a morning to get her body to comply.

Ramu increased the dosage of her medicine. The treadmill sessions were increased to two forty-five-minute sessions a day; twice-weekly sessions of physiotherapy were started. Govind sent Ramu reams of research material on experimental treatments, colour-coded and neatly spiral-bound in plastic folders, and asked Sudha why we couldn't try something like deep brain stimulation for Mum.

'What is she, a lab rat?' Sudha asked me, furiously. 'Ramu says there's no evidence of its benefits for atypical Parkinson's!'

By June, as flash floods were inundating temple towns and sweeping away a gigantic statue of Shiva in Uttarakhand, Mum needed help getting out of bed. In Bangalore, Malini and I argued about whether Mum's speech had deteriorated further. Chand, all long arms and spindly legs decorated with temporary tattoos, took Malini's side—'I can't understand anything Achamma[42] says, Dad!'—and I snapped at her and told her not to interrupt when adults were talking, wondering idly when I had turned into this twenty-first-century version of my Dad—my pants hitched a couple of inches lower than where his used to be, my ₹20,000 progressive lenses standing in for his large square bifocals for which, he used to proudly declare, he had never paid more than ₹350, but him nonetheless. Tara looked up from playing Temple Run with smeary fingers on my brand-new iPad to laugh delightedly at her sister's comeuppance. Chand rolled her eyes and sauntered off to wreak her revenge by inciting me in another way, by playing *Badtameez Dil* at full blast for the two-hundred-and-fifty-fifth time, while watching herself cavort to the beats in the mirror.

In July, as the very last telegram in India was being sent out, Govind and Maggie came to see Mum—their first joint visit since the whole Matt incident. Maggie's chain of fitness centres was doing well, and she now sported a belly button ring and a tattoo of a butterfly (a real, permanent one, Chand observed admiringly) at the base of her spine. While Sudha looked at Maggie with simmering disapproval, the rest of us worked overtime to pretend nothing had ever been amiss. Riyaan was now sixteen and had hung back to be with his first girlfriend. It was a sign of the times that Mum didn't seem to be surprised that Riyaan had a girlfriend, and even thought she was very pretty. Maggie rattled on brightly about the trek that she and Govind were about to embark upon in the Himalayas, a rigorous weeklong affair that involved sleeping in tents and doing your business in a hole in the ground.

---

[42]Grandmother (father's mother)

'What?' asked Mum, horrified. 'Is that hygienic?'

'Oh, very, Aunty! You do your thing and then throw some sand over it? Like a cat, you know? You know how clean cats are?'

'So you have to ask somebody to dig a hole when you feel like going?'

'Do you have to specify size?' cackled Prakash. 'Tell them what you ate for dinner, perhaps?'

Maggie rolled her eyes. 'No, silly. It's one big hole for everyone?'

'Eeekss!' squealed Preetha. 'You have to do your business over someone else's business?'

'These are the times I am thankful I can't walk,' Mum told Sudha afterwards, which made Sudha abandon her air of self-important stressfulness and crack a smile. By now Mum's gait was so uncertain that Sudha had got her a wheelchair. Despite the wheelchair, Sudha still stood over Mum and made her do her sessions on the treadmill. Moreover, Ramu had arranged for a physiotherapist, a hefty Kashmiri girl called Fatima, to come home daily and stretch and pull and twist Mum's body despite her yelps and barely stifled curses.

'Have you tried homoeopathy?' asked Maggie, sending Sudha into a furious rant.

'Who made her the queen of therapies? She and her loony ideas!' At the same time, with no sense of irony, Sudha waxed lyrical about the reiki she was doing for Mum. 'I can see it is helping. Her speech is getting better, don't you think?'

'Mmm-hmm,' I said, non-committal.

On another day, she told Mum, 'You know, there's a temple festival held every year, not far from here. I'd like to take you. They do pujas there for good health—the goddess is supposed to be very powerful, many have had miraculous recoveries. The only thing is…'

'What?' Mum asked.

'Try to keep an open mind…'

'Hmmm. O-kaay…' Mum looked at her warily.

'The thing is, during the puja, they will smash a coconut on your head.'

'What?'

'People say it doesn't hurt…much.'

'Oh they do, do they?'

'See, that's the thing, you have to have an open mind…'

'An open skull, you mean!'

By the time Sudha was organizing a special function in the ashram for Navaratri, two of the fingers on Mum's left hand seemed to be in permanent rigor mortis. She now had to be lifted out of bed bodily, and although Mum was a featherweight, the dead weight of her body made it a task that could only be accomplished by Prakash—or when he was away, by Sudha with the help of the driver, a chap with a radiant white smile who favoured bright green pants and checked pink shirts and went by the name of Rose. 'Rose?' Sudha had asked him on first acquaintance. 'Short for…?' and he had looked confused and said that it was short for nothing, that that was the name his parents had blessed him with.

By now, Mum also needed help draping a sari around herself, her fingers struggling to accordion the pleats or tuck them in. 'Why do you need to wear a sari, Mum?' asked Sudha. 'Where are you going anyway? You're at home always, why don't you just wear a nightie like I do?' Mum was quietly horrified at the prospect; she had always loathed Sudha's default homewear of matronly nighties in indifferent colours and indeterminate patterns, all with a frill around the bosom. But by Diwali, Mum had abandoned vanity for practicality, and as she swirled a token sparkler from her wheelchair, she held it well away from the ballooning swathes of her frilly grey nightie. From then on, her starched cotton saris barely saw the light of day.

Despite Mum's physical decline, she seemed to be in fine fettle, due in no small part to the strong dose of antidepressants Ramu had added to the heap of tablets she was now taking. Sudha, on the other hand, was constantly on edge, swinging between bouts of crying over Mum's condition and impotent rage about the hopelessness of it all, rage that manifested as frequent minor explosions directed at a completely indifferent Prakash and Preetha, and a most un-indifferent maid. '*Why this Kolaveri, di*, Ma?' Prakash would chant at her, causing the maid to crack a gap-toothed smile.

'Here, take one of my antidepressants,' said Mum once, to diffuse a particularly violent eruption, but Sudha had seemed to have lost all signs of a sense of humour by then and didn't even pause mid-rant.

But between the bouts of anger and hopelessness, occasionally Sudha would make an attempt to console me, and herself.

'Even great spiritual masters—J. Krishnamurti, Ramana Maharshi—had to suffer pain and illness before they died, you know,' she said.

'Wasn't Krishnamurti ninety when he died?' I asked.

'Ya, so?' countered Sudha belligerently, and I sank into silence.

ა

After Diwali, Ramu suggested taking Mum to a hospital at Vellore for a special round of therapy, which would take a month. There would be a room with extra beds for the carers, and a kitchenette.

Mum would be taken through various physiotherapy sessions, sessions with a psychiatrist, counselling sessions to help her prepare for an even bleaker future, a future where she would not be able to speak or eat solid food. 'I think Sudha is the one who can do with a session with the psychiatrist,' Mum grumbled, but didn't dare argue with Sudha. 'What to do?' she told me. 'I am dependent on her. And let's admit it—I'm a terrible nuisance. She has enough on her plate already with the kids and the ashram and her health. So I've learnt to keep quiet—mouthshut.com.'

I laughed. 'Do you even know what MouthShut.com is, Mum?'

'I don't know, some website about vipassana?'

We drove down from Bangalore to Vellore armed with some packets of instant noodles for the kitchenette and some special deliveries for Mum: two block-printed nighties which Mum had surreptitiously asked Malini to buy ('Strictly no frill around the bosom!' she had instructed) and some chicken puffs, a large plum cake and a box of Dharwad peda. The medicines had now started to play havoc with Mum's digestion, so Sudha had switched her to an all-vegetarian, low-fat, no-sugar diet, and Mum had complained to me over the phone that if she didn't get some sugar or protein very soon, she might just assault somebody, autoimmune disease or not.

The hospital was in a distinguished stone building with neat gardens outside. Mum's room was at the end of a long corridor, where the relatives of other patients stood deep in discussion. We saw her from afar, sitting in her wheelchair. The top of her head was fully grey now, the bit tied up into the bun still black from the dye that she had stopped using many months ago—another vanity sacrificed at the altar of practicality. She was in a matronly nightie of a greenish-black hue with a lace ruffle around the chest.

Tara yelled and ran towards her. She turned and smiled just as Tara screeched to a halt in front of her.

'What are you doing in that?' I asked her, waving at the wheelchair. 'Get up, you old hypochondriac!'

Sudha looked at me as though I was wearing a suicide vest around my chest, but Mum dissolved into laughter.

Soon we were crowded into the little room—us and Sudha and Prakash, and Rose, who was iridescent in yellow jeans and a red floral shirt. By the time Mum had gobbled up one chicken puff, a slice of plum cake and half a Dharwad peda, despite Sudha's disapproving looks, a nurse arrived to take her for an art therapy session. Malini and I tagged along. 'You really don't have to,' said Mum.

'We want to,' I assured her.

Mum was wheeled into a large room where other patients had already gathered. In a corner, a young boy groaned intermittently with pain—he had broken his spine in an accident and was wheeled into the therapy room on what looked like a vegetable cart. Next to Mum was a bent-up woman who had been born with some terrible bone condition. I tried not to stare. 'See, look at them, cut down in the prime of life,' said Mum, characteristically finding the silver lining. 'I feel lucky when I see them. My time is over in any case. So what if I suffer for a little while?' Malini met my eye, and I could tell she was aghast.

A kind-looking nurse came around distributing crayons and pieces of paper bearing photocopied drawings to colour in. Mum's was a picture of a clown—a kindergarten-school picture, all simple lines and cartoon features. Mum looked at me, a little embarrassed. 'Like a little child, no? They say this will help my muscles,' she slurred.

The nurse wrapped Mum's fingers around the crayon. Then

Mum started to colour, slowly, deliberately, trying to keep within the lines. Often her hand shot out of the boundaries. 'Am I doing okay?' she asked me.

'Fine,' I said, 'very good,' wondering if she had had to lie to me like that when I was a child.

'I can colour better than that, Achamma!' It was Tara, who had managed to steal away from Chand's indifferent supervision. Malini fixed her with a glare which made her lips quiver.

By the end of the hour-long session, Mum had coloured in one-third of the clown in bright haphazard strokes—beads of sweat around her temples and mouth stood testament to the effort. I noticed that the lone grey hair on her chin that she used to tweeze off had grown long and curled along her neck like a spring. 'What, Amma, you can do better than that,' said the kind-faced nurse as she came around to collect the coloured-in sheets. Mum's face fell a little but she managed a tired smile.

Malini and I walked behind her as she was wheeled back to her room. When Rose and Prakash put her back in the bed, Mum fell asleep instantly.

'Don't let her sleep now, she won't sleep in the night,' said Sudha, and Prakash shook Mum awake. She got up with a snort and wiped the drool from her mouth. Chand and Tara broke into giggles.

Lunch was a rudimentary rice-and-sambar-affair, which Sudha had managed to whip up in the poorly equipped kitchenette. Mum ate slowly and painstakingly, occasionally spilling a spoonful on the floor. Even before we had time to wash the plates, Mum was being wheeled out again. 'Psychiatry session,' Mum said, over her shoulder. 'I am supposed to tell them my woes.'

'She's looking better, isn't she?' asked Sudha, when she had left. 'The treatment's helping, don't you think?'

'Sure,' I said, and Malini pretended to be riveted by the newspaper headlines.

'But she's getting very cranky, you know. Refuses to attend the bhajan sessions or satsangs at home, and last week she shooed away one of the ladies, just because she said she would do a puja for her.'

'Mmm-hmm,' I said.

Mum was wheeled back in an hour, and almost immediately, wheeled out again for a full-body physiotherapy session. When she was back, she was nodding off in the wheelchair.

'Hey, Ammamma, wake up!' said Prakash loudly, looking up from an article that was speculating about Deepika Padukone's latest relationship.

Mum started and looked at me sheepishly. 'All those exercises make me tired,' she said.

By the time it was time for us to drive back to Bangalore, she was being wheeled out once again, to have a session with a counsellor about the future that was in store for her. We walked her out. 'How long do I have to keep doing all these exercises, following all these restrictions?' she asked me, when Sudha was out of earshot. 'Will they help me in any way?'

'Keep your chin up,' I said, enveloping her in a hug. She smiled brightly but as Malini bent down to embrace her, for the first time I could see fear lurking behind Mum's eyes.

When I turned back to look, she was gazing after us, looking frail and tiny and helpless hunched up in the wheelchair. The relatives of other patients who were pacing the corridors all turned to stare at her as she was wheeled by. Then they rounded a corner and she was gone.

A month later, we visited her in Chennai. 'Did you get me some plum cake or Dharwad peda?' asked Mum in a low whisper, and I kicked myself for having forgotten. Fatima, the Kashmiri girl, had taken up where the physiotherapists at Vellore had left off, pushing and pulling and prodding Mum's increasingly resistant muscles. 'It's good for her, it has to be done,' Sudha told us as Mum squealed with pain and Malini looked horrified. After the physiotherapy session, Sudha roused Mum to exercise on the treadmill, refusing to listen even when Mum pleaded that she be allowed to skip the exercise just for a day, so that she could sit and chat with her son. 'Vivek can talk to you while you exercise,' she said, and so Malini and I tried to keep up a bright chatter as Mum self-consciously trudged on the treadmill in her nightie. Later, Sudha waved away Mum's objections and wheeled her out to a bhajan session in the living room, which Mum sat listening to grimly, while a lady with a bald patch and an overbite leaned into her face and said, 'What, Amma, so thin you've become. Do not worry, we are all praying for you.'

'I can't stand it!' Malini burst out on the train home, close to tears. 'The constant exercising, the physiotherapy sessions, those horrible sanctimonious women from the ashram, that disgusting slop that Sudha feeds her! Is all this treatment doing her any good? I know Sudha means well, but can't you see that Mum's exhausted? You have to do something, Vivek. Does she have to suffer more than necessary? Get her to Bangalore, do something.'

And that is how Mum came to my home to die.

18

Little Left Unsaid

'Do you ever sleep like that?' asked Mum. 'So soundly, so much at peace, free from dreams or emotions, and when you wake up and register the world around you, it's with a twinge of regret that you haven't actually left it all behind, that the feeling of peace that enveloped you just moments ago has slipped through your fingers?'

'Can't say I do, Mum.' My slumber might have been dreamless, but it was born of the exhaustion of twelve-hour workdays and two-hour commutes, the burden of mortgage payments and the worry of the burgeoning cost of support staff for Mum and medical bills piling high; and when I woke, it was with a weariness that suggested a disturbed night, and with an acute anxiety uncoiling in the pit of my stomach in anticipation of a stressful day.

'I imagine that death will be a version of that, you know, a sound, peaceful sleep, an afterlife suspended in time—weightless, emotionless, ego-free. Until it's time to wake again, in another body, another place, another time, another family.'

We talked about death a lot now, even more than we used to, with the detachment of people who know that when it comes, it will be a release.

'It's not death I'm afraid of, you know. It's the waking up, it's the repetition of the cycle. What if the deeds of this life haven't been enough to secure me a good rebirth?'

I wasn't sure what to say.

'You know, your Shivan Mama had a friend...he visited a medium to enquire about his deceased father, Motilal Mehra, a man who had been universally disliked when he was alive.'

'Mmm-hmm?' I wasn't sure where this story was leading, I was just happy she was feeling well enough that day to tell it, for there were good days and bad days. And very bad days.

'The medium closed his eyes, took a deep breath and pronounced, "Your father has been reborn as a pig in a farm off Bhayandar. He goes by the name of Motu."'

'Really, Mum...' I laughed.

'I'm not joking. Ask your Shivan Mama if you want to. Anyway, so the medium says Motilal Mehra's been reborn as a pig called Motu. "If you go there and call his name, he will come rushing to you. But hurry, for he is destined for the table."'

'Tch, tch!'

'Just listen! So the friend left, cursing the phoney medium, but guilt bedevilled him, so a few weeks later, he sought out the farm the medium had described in great detail, and like the medium had prescribed, he called out the pig's name, "Motu, Motuuu!"—diffidently at first, and when no pig appeared, with growing confidence.'

I was listening now, if a little sceptically.

'He scoffed at the medium's blather and was about to leave when he heard a horrible squealing. He turned around and there he was, a fat black pig, caked in mud, short squiggly tail wagging madly, dashing wildly towards him! It was Motilal Mehra, his father, now going by the name of Motu.'

'What rubbish, Mum,' I said, laughing helplessly.

'Really! Your father and I laughed at the story back then, all those years ago, just like you're laughing now, but these days, I wonder if a similar fate awaits me. Will I be reborn as a beast of burden? An ox perhaps, whipped to work the fields, one of those chickens reared en masse in those hatcheries, biding my life in a tiny cage, fattened with steroids and pumped with antibiotics, other chickens crowded around me?'

'Of course you won't,' I consoled, although I was still laughing.

'Or, far worse, a bride burnt for dowry, a man sold into labour?'

'Oh, don't be silly, Mum.'

'Well, I *have* chanted a lot of prayers and visited some temples and done a few good deeds, haven't I?'

'And drunk copious amounts of Champion oats in the name of fasting for the gods.'

She laughed. We sat in companionable silence, half-watching a *Koffee with Karan* rerun, Karan in a moss-green jacket. 'Ha! And you thought Govind's maroon jacket was bad,' said Mum. 'Anyway,' she continued, 'I suppose I'm paying off some of my sins in this life itself by virtue of my disease, aren't I?'

If I had rued that Dad's sudden demise had robbed me of the opportunity to unravel some of his memories, to preserve some of his experience, with Mum, there was little that was left unsaid. We had conversations longer than we had ever had, sitting in the sliver of garden at the back of my villa or at the dining table, and as her speech got increasingly slurred and difficult to understand, the more eager I became to hear what she had to say, to make her tell me everything before she no longer could. Gone was the impatience with which I used to listen to her rambling stories, gone was the eye-rolling and the urging to get on with it.

We discussed the early days, how she and Dad met; she told me about her parents, the younger brother she had lost at childbirth. I discovered she had learnt French as a young wife, never letting on when we siblings would talk to each other in our classroom French, under the impression that it was a code that our parents could not understand. She reminisced about how she and Dad had had to black out their windows during the 1971 war, how she was convinced that Govind's unusually quick heartbeat, which the doctors had all assured her was nothing to worry about, had been brought on by the trauma of the sirens sounding and fighter jets roaring overhead during the air raids. I heard of how they had stood in queues for bread and milk and baby food when we were children, because of the constant famines, food shortages and rationing measures by the government in those pre-liberalization times.

I learnt that when her slumber was not dreamless, it was usually Dad she dreamt of. 'Mostly he just sits there, watching me, head cocked, a slight smile on his face, as though he is going to mock me for snoring too loudly or sleeping too long. Sometimes we are back in Kerala, him reading his newspaper on the porch, or we are gossiping idly at the dining table about how Rajan is still going strong and Vimala will never be a merry widow. Sometimes I see him as the young man I had first met, or with you three children gathered around him—you with your arms around his shins, Govind draped around the back of his chair, Sudha perched on the arm. The dreams are so real that I can see things I thought I had forgotten—the hair on the tip of his earlobe, the moles on his neck, the birthmark on his leg. And sometimes when I have had a bad day, and I have allowed my mind to dwell on the future, I dream of him, and it is always the same dream, of him sitting by the side of the bed and stroking my head without a word. When I wake up, I am sad that it was just a dream, but the fears are gone, as though they've been caressed away in the throes of the night.'

The only thing I could never get her to reveal were the contents of Dad's letters from all those years ago. 'There were never any letters,' she blushed. 'I was just joking.'

ᴄᴏ

It had taken months of secret negotiations with Ramu, a lot of tact and some luck to get Sudha to agree to let Mum move to Bangalore.

I had approached Ramu first. 'Sudha has too many responsibilities,' I ventured. 'The kids, the ashram, the dog—let Mum come and stay with us for a while, give Sudha a break, you know?'

He had looked at me wide-eyed, unaccustomed as he was to being asked to take a decision on behalf of Sudha. 'I'll try,' he said uncertainly.

At first, Sudha had resisted. 'Why? What is she going to get in Bangalore that she won't get here?' she bristled. 'You think her daughter-in-law can look after her better than her daughter?' and Ramu had retreated, defeated.

Eventually, fate had intervened. Or Preetha did. Preetha had quietly completed her postgraduation in ophthalmology surgery, doing exceedingly well with very little fuss, and was now practising in a large hospital in Chennai while waiting to complete admission procedures to a super-speciality course in the UK. Sudha and Mum had been wringing their hands about her going abroad to study even more, to get even more qualified and skilled and experienced. 'Of course, we're proud of her accomplishments,' Sudha said, 'but qualifications and experience, not to mention her advancing age, effectively puts her out of the league of 70 per cent of eligible boys.'

And that's what was most important even now, one and a half decades into the new millennium, despite Happy to Bleed campaigns and shrill clamour about women being allowed into temples that had been male preserves once. Even in the most progressive of families, a girl was not considered settled until she was married.

'How can you be so regressive?' I chided Sudha. 'She can earn more than any boy her age, she's immensely capable, she'll be an asset to any hospital—why shouldn't she pursue her career? Why should she settle for marriage and kids?'

'Talk to me when Chand and Tara are that age,' said Sudha shortly.

But now, Preetha announced, she didn't want to super-specialize any more. And before Sudha could get all excited, she added, 'I want to work with Doctors without Borders.'

'What?' rumbled Sudha, like an earthquake measuring 9.2 on the Richter scale, causing worldwide tsunamis. 'My flesh and blood leaving a perfectly good job to go to some godforsaken war-torn place to be raped and killed? Over my dead body!'

'To serve, Mum! To heal those who need it the most!' said Preetha. 'How is this different from what you and Gurudev do?'

And Sudha got incoherent with indignation as she tried to explain just how different it was.

The debate raged like wildfire for several weeks. Sudha tried to rope in Gurudev to advise Preetha, who was getting increasingly adamant.

'But you must be proud, Akka,' Gurudev said. 'She wants to be of service. You should encourage her.' And Sudha looked at him with a dislike she had so far reserved for Ramu's mother and the weighing scale. Mum reported that there were daily explosions at home, Preetha stalking out and returning only after two days on one occasion. I took the opportunity to try again, this time taking a different tack.

'Can I take Mum just for some time? It will give you some time to sort out this thing with Preetha as well.'

Sudha hesitated, but I could see she was tempted. 'But how will Malini manage? Do you know how much work it is?'

'Ramu could organize some help for us, a nurse.'

'But still...'

Eventually Sudha capitulated, but insisted we take Rose with us. 'You'll need someone to help out, believe me,' she said.

So, as chief minister of Gujarat and BJP prime ministerial candidate Narendra Modi was being hologrammed to dumbfounded election crowds in remote villages on the eve of the general elections, Rose drove us back to Bangalore, Mum in her block-printed nightie at the back with Malini.

Bangalore was no longer the city I had first come to more than fifteen years back—the city of low-slung buildings and gentle weather and early-to-bedders. Now residential anthills mushroomed in what were once the outskirts; restaurants, breweries and branded stores elbowed each other where bungalows once stood; flyovers and expressways and a Metro line tried to cope with the burgeoning traffic; temperatures soared to almost 40°C in the summer, and the mild-mannered monsoons of old had given way to ferocious deluges and the occasional hailstorm.

By now we had moved into our villa in a gated community at the edge of town. Our water came in tankers, the nearest grocery store was a couple of kilometres away and we had to pay a small fortune to lure domestic help to commute all the way there. But it gave us the illusion of staying in an independent house, although we shared a wall with our neighbour, our back garden was a slice of land overlooked by a sixteen-storey monster that had come up on the adjacent plot and our family room was the ribbon of landing on the first floor. The idea had been that the kids could ride their bicycles on the tranquil inner avenues of the gated community without fear of being run down, but in reality we had to practically bribe them with promises of pizza or the use of our phones to play games so that they would reluctantly ride their bikes up and down the street before ducking back in at the earliest opportunity to slouch in front of the television.

It had been a few years since I had moved in, but Mum had never seen it, busy as she had been with Govind and Sudha and doctors and hospitals. Her eyes widened at the grand entrance, the guards at the gate, the clean paved internal roads, the neat uniform houses, the pool and the landscaped gardens, the badminton and tennis courts and the play area. I almost felt sorry for her that there was no Vimala Aunty to boast to about this.

For convenience, Mum had to be put in the downstairs bedroom, which Malini's father had been using till now. He was not pleased.

When he had first come to live with us, Malini's father had been a dear old man who barely caused a ripple in our lives, and never ever intruded. During the day he would take himself off to visit friends or to catch a morning show, or to his old institute, the National Bureau of Agriculturally Important Insects, where he'd sit reading journals in the library. In the evenings he would babysit the children, leaving us free to catch up on work or take off to the pub or just put our feet up in front of the television.

As the years went by, his friends passed on or moved away. The people he had known in the institute retired. And he became increasingly hard of hearing, making him more housebound. He spent his time tweeting indignant and mildly insulting comments to news anchors and politicians (and prompting Malini to worry if he would be taken away in handcuffs), playing Scrabble against the computer and swearing at it when it proffered words like Ya and Xi, and constantly asking Malini if it was time for lunch.

Despite his increasing eccentricities, he was a benign presence who floated around the periphery of our lives, never prying, seldom obtrusive. Until Mum got ill. At first, he had been equally concerned about her frequent falls, urging me to consult specialists and try new treatments. But as Mum declined and Malini and I got increasingly caught up in her health, a resentment seemed to have taken hold of this amiable old man. When the talk around the table turned to Mum's health, he pouted like a sulky child, increasing the volume on the television or changing the subject by talking loudly about the thrilling discovery of a new species of parasitic wasp. When I took his daughter away to spend weekends in Chennai, he moped, and often developed mysterious symptoms that had to be attended to urgently, making Malini drop out on more than one occasion. After our trip to Vellore, Malini had found him sitting on the stairs. 'What's up, Papa?' she had asked.

'I fell. I can't get up. I called and I called for you,' he said, accusingly. Frantic calls were made to the doctor, who couldn't locate so much as a bruise.

When Malini had informed him that Mum was moving to Bangalore, he had made a production of researching senior living facilities in the city. 'I don't want to get in your way,' he told me, and before I could protest, Malini pulled me away and warned me not to indulge him with the attention he was seeking. He even visited an old-age home, where he was chastised by an enormous lady with a big head and a humongous bindi: 'A daughter in the same city who you've been living with for years, and now you want to leave her house and move into an old-age home at this age? Stop this nonsense, sir, and learn to adjust!' He had quietly returned home and asked Malini what was for lunch.

Now he was not pleased with being shifted out of his room, and tried to convince Malini that he was in more urgent need of the downstairs bedroom.

'The heater in the upstairs bathroom is faulty,' he ventured.

'I'll have it repaired,' countered Malini.

'In the summers, it's very hot because of the heat from the terrace.'

'I'll put in an AC.'

'Air-conditioning aggravates my asthma.'

'What asthma?'

'You know, I didn't want to tell you, but I've been having breathing problems of late.'

'I'll get you an inhaler. And a nebulizer.'

'I can't hear anyone calling when I'm upstairs.'

'We'll come up to call you.'

Eventually he ran out of excuses, but he made it a point to hold his knees as he walked up to show how much he was being inconvenienced. 'Ignore him,' Malini said, shaking her head in exasperation.

∽

Inevitably, the days of companionable conversations were numbered, and in the time Mum was with us, her body failed her, one organ at a time. The fingers on her hands started seizing up, and even so, she insisted on eating by herself, painfully slowly, missing her own mouth at times, like a toddler learning to use a spoon. In time, she could not wrap her fingers around a fork and had to be fed.

Another World Cup came around, inciting once-in-four-years football fever in the neighbourhood kids. Even Tara and Chand took to kicking their throwball around, breaking a lamp and almost decimating my coveted sixty-inch smart TV. By now Mum could not summon the strength to walk even a few steps.

'Has she been doing her treadmill exercises?' asked Sudha. 'She shouldn't be deteriorating so quickly.'

'Yes,' I lied, for I had long stopped enforcing an exercise regimen on Mum. I even let her eat what she wanted, sweets and chocolates and all. Ramu agreed that all the physiotherapy, the diet, the large doses of medicine were probably not doing Mum much good; that rest and inertia would probably achieve the same results. 'But Sudha wanted to try everything,' he shrugged.

Then Mum's optical muscles began to betray her so that she could no longer focus on a page, no longer read the romance stories and biographies that had kept her mind occupied in Chennai. Malini made the children read out to her from her *Reader's Digest*s, although Mum protested that they didn't have to. Eventually, she couldn't even watch a television programme or a movie for any length of time.

Over the months, her diction became more and more slurred, until there came a time when even Malini and I found it difficult to understand her. Only Saraswati, the full-time help we had employed for her, seemed to be able to wring meaning from the garbled sentences Mum was trying to string together.

Saraswati had come recommended by a neighbour. 'A bit of a character,' we were told, 'but worth her weight in gold.'

She was. Apart from an unwelcome proclivity to call me 'uncle', despite her own greying hair and middle-aged flab, Saraswati was a sunny presence in the house, unflappable even on Mum's worst days. She was the epitome of efficiency, feeding and bathing and cleaning Mum with a speed and competence we had not expected, while keeping up a flow of conversation in far-from-perfect English that flowed from her tongue like the Cauvery river in spate. Every salacious bit of news that had appeared on regional television would be recounted to Mum as though it had happened in her very own neighbourhood. 'He kill lover and three small-small babies, Amma, and want to throw in drain, Amma. Paavam[43], that woman, I know ten years, Amma, next house my!'

'But the news said she has just come to Bangalore,' Malini would intervene after listening to such stories for a while, tight-lipped and disbelieving.

'No, no, Madam, I want to know she ten years!'

As Bangalore was officially being renamed Bengaluru, we were wringing our hands about Mum's speech, which had become so impaired that Saraswati had fashioned rudimentary charts for her so that she could point with her head to show what she needed—misshapen apples to indicate fruit, globules for medicines, tears to indicate pain, a glass to indicate water. A few months later, Mum couldn't even summon the coordination to point.

By the time 2015 came around, she was in adult diapers and we were pureeing her food. Malini insisted that she should eat whatever we did as long as she could—so sambar-rice was pureed and vegetables too, and sometimes even a tiny bit of fish and chicken.

I still remember the day it happened, when she first started having difficulty swallowing. Saraswati had tipped some lukewarm tea in her mouth and it had all come back out. Tara had started laughing and spitting out water from her own mouth, thrilled with

---

[43]Poor thing

this new occupation, her laughter dying out only as she looked around the table and saw our stricken faces, and Mum trying to fight back her tears. We all knew what the next stage was—her throat muscles seizing up so much that she wouldn't even be able to eat the pureed food; she would be fed through her nose.

By the time kurta-clad politicians were stiffly contorting themselves into asanas on the world's very first International Yoga Day, Mum was confined to her bed, her tongue still, her body dysfunctional for the most part, except for the heart that beat and the lungs that breathed. I read out to her a report about the politician who had fallen asleep during shavasana and had to be shaken awake, half-expecting her to break out into a chuckle, but, of course, she stared back at me, expressionless, mute.

What can I say about the indignities of the days that followed? As children we pray for our parents' long life, their immortality. As they age, and you mature, you realize that there are things worse than death, and you stop praying for their immortality and start wishing for their endless good health instead. You hope that they will never have to wrestle with pain or deal with a failing mind. You hope they will die in their sleep, unknowing, unharmed; that they will pass peacefully into a better world. As far as Mum was concerned, our prayers would not be answered.

People came to see her. Sudha, Ramu and Prakash came whenever they could, bringing along sacred threads, lucky rings, prasadam from some temple Sudha had done prayers for Mum in and, often, a letter from Preetha, who had eventually been convinced not to join Doctors without Borders but was reluctantly allowed to pursue a six-month stint in rural Tamil Nadu instead. Sudha would sit by Mum's bed and sing bhajans, say prayers, do reiki. When she couldn't come, she would send me sanctimonious messages from the scriptures:

The real cause of one's difficulties in the hard struggle of life may be found in one's forgetfulness of one's relationship with the Supreme Lord.—Bhagvad Gita

And when all else had been exhausted, motivational messages on Facebook and WhatsApp, whose authenticity might have been deemed slightly questionable:

'When Life Gives You a Hundred Reasons to Cry, Show Life That You Have a Thousand Reasons to Smile'—Kahlil Gibran, and *'In a Crisis, the Best of Us Can Come Out.'—Pablo Neruda*

It was then that I understood why Govind had blocked her missives so many years ago.

Govind promised to come—once Riyaan had finished his applications for college, once Riyaan had joined college, definitely during his Christmas vacations. But in the end, he never made it.

'I don't think he can bear to see Mum like this,' I told Malini.

'I think he's too self-absorbed to bother,' she replied. 'Shame on him, when it was she who single-handedly pulled him out of his self-pity all those years ago.'

In the early days, when Mum had still been able, they used to converse on Facetime, which had replaced 'the sky'—Maggie determinedly bright in the foreground; Riyaan, lounging with his shoes on the bed behind; Govind skulking somewhere just outside the frame; and Mum shouting as loudly as she could at the screen in the manner she used to employ at one time while talking on STD and international calls, as though distance could be bridged by decibel.

Shivan Mama, his walk slowed, his breathing now more audible, his chest caved in ever so slightly, came and stayed for a week, sitting by her bed most of the time, talking to her, occasionally humming her a tune from the past—*Mere Sapnon Ki Rani* from *Aradhana*, the very first movie they had watched together at the Strand back in Bombay after she had married Dad; *Teri Pyari Pyari Surat Ko*, which Dad always claimed Mum had serenaded him with the first time they had met. The muscles on her face did not twitch, but I liked to imagine that she heard, she knew, she remembered.

Vimala Aunty arrived, Rajan Uncle shuffling behind her with a cane. He was nearly ninety now and bent double, but he doggedly trailed Vimala Aunty everywhere, much to her irritation—he was chronically forgetful now and prone to say things to embarrass her, when all she wanted was the freedom to roam around and meddle in other people's business without Rajan Uncle cramping her style. Vimala Aunty sat mournfully looking at Mum lying stiff and wide-eyed, mouth fallen open, not even responding to the chatter around her that day.

'She was the best of us, you know,' Vimala Aunty said to my surprise, her eyes shining. 'She doesn't deserve this.' I didn't tell her that I agreed with her, that Sudha and I had discussed that of all the three siblings, it was Vimala Aunty who deserved suffering the most, even though we would not wish this kind of suffering on anyone, not even our worst enemies.

Rajan Uncle sat hunched over a pile of clothes in an armchair in the corner of the room, clearly trying to figure out who Mum was. 'What is that smell?' he asked after some deep contemplation, and Saraswati hurried over to change Mum's diaper. Vimala Aunty rushed Rajan Uncle out to the living room, where he cornered Malini's father and told him that he knew Mum from way back, when she had taught him Sanskrit in school. Malini's father dropped his pants and showed Rajan Uncle, apart from a loosely hanging pair of faded briefs, the invisible scar on his upper thigh. 'Fell heavily last month. Fourth time in a year. Hurt myself badly. Malini didn't even take me to the doctor,' he confided.

'I can't see anything,' said Rajan Uncle in a moment of clarity, shouting into Malini's father's hearing aid. 'Not one tiny thing!' Malini's father pulled up his pants and left the room in a huff.

Others came; to give their commiserations, to see her before she died, they said, to pay their respects while she was still alive; but really, to ogle, to come to check for themselves the extent of her misery and to be content in the knowledge that their lot was better than hers. As the word spread, cousins thrice removed, a friend who claimed to have been in touch with Mum before the illness but of whom I'd never heard, and Mrs Mathew, a neighbour from back in Kerala who had made surly cross-country calls to Mum and Dad when their house was being constructed to complain about the noise and the dust, and was therefore automatically persona non grata with Mum, despite Dad's irritating attempts to see the whole matter from Mrs Mathew's point of view at the time. And my own neighbours—the lady in 2B who sold cupcakes came offering her wares in a pretty pink cardboard box with her card Scotch-taped to the inside; Mr Fernandes arrived smelling of alcohol although it was not yet noon, and after making tutting noises in Mum's direction, sat cracking ribald jokes and singing increasingly off-key Goan folk songs.

Eventually, Malini deputed Saraswati to turn visitors away at the door. She handled it all astonishingly well, Malini did, the comings and goings of nurses and doctors, the smell of antiseptic and despair, the relapses, the breathing problems, the regurgitated food, the rushing to hospitals from time to time, the father who complained that she had forgotten to make payasam on his birthday. She seemed more equal to the task than I was, making phone calls to doctors and barking at nurses and smoothing her father's ruffled feathers by buying him his favourite pineapple cake from Sweet Chariot on her way home from office, which he gulped down quickly but ungratefully. And still she found time to like a photo of a friend in Number 63 of the #100sareepact, to let me know that Maggie had just posted a healthy recipe for millet crepes on her website, to ice cupcakes into the middle of the night for a school raffle that Tara remembered just as she was packing her school bag for the next day, to gush over the photo of a sonogram that a cousin had posted to announce her pregnancy.

'An uncanny resemblance,' I said, tetchily, looking at the bean-shaped blob.

Me, I took the coward's way out, lingering at work, willing time to stop, so that I didn't have to return to the reality of the monsters that had taken hold of my mother, the demons I could not fight, just hold at bay for a little while longer. I didn't mind any more when I was stuck in bumper-to-bumper traffic, my feet aching with the constant employment of the clutch, my temples throbbing with the effort of concentrating on the cars cutting across and tail-ending and grazing me from all sides, the headlights blinding me with their harsh glares. For when I was home, all I could do was watch helplessly as Mum lay there gazing into the distance, her optical muscles now so weak that it took effort for her to even focus on us moving around the room, an effort she was rarely able to summon; as Saraswati put up the apparatus to feed Mum through the nose, while she chatted cheerfully to her all the while about that bad lady Indrani who had strangled her own daughter with her own two hands ('What and all she did, Amma! My aunt's husband's cousin—neighbour of her driver, Amma, stays next door, Amma—he confess everything, God promise.'); as she was physically rolled over by Rose and Saraswati from side to side to prevent bedsores; as all the muscles in her body were massaged, even her tongue, to preserve whatever strength was left in them for even a little while.

There was no courage in this, I thought, this preservation of the body, when everything inside it had died. And I thought back to the conversation we had had so many months ago, when she had still been able.

'They're putting Clooney down,' I had told Mum. 'Water in the lungs, he can't even breathe.'

'Lucky thing!' she'd said. 'Maybe in my next life I will be born a dog!'

She had shown me a book she was reading—a love story between a terminally ill patient and his nurse. 'He is euthanized in the end,' she said wistfully. 'Some clinic in Switzerland, where it is legal. Is that true, that you can do that?'

I had no idea, but I said, 'Of course not.'

She looked at me disbelievingly. 'You don't have to lie to me to spare my feelings, you know. I'm ill, not a child. In any case, it's not something I can do, our scriptures forbid it.'

'Yes, Amma,' said Saraswati, eyes wide in alarm. 'If you suicide, you will not dead, not alive. You want to float around, ghost aaalways.'

'Yes, thank you, Saraswati,' I said, my tone astringent.

'No mention, uncle,' she replied, cheerful, oblivious.

'But don't hesitate to pull the plug if you're asked,' Mum had said.

Fortunately, I was not called on to make that decision. She passed on a wintry Sunday afternoon. The sun had just begun to peep out after a fortnight of unseasonal November rain that had chilled our bones and clogged our roads. It had been a tough week, with two visits to the hospital to clear the phlegm in Mum's chest too deep down for Saraswati to clear as she usually did, by putting a hand down her throat. There had seemed to be a slight recovery, Mum appearing to be more responsive in the ensuing days, following our movements around her room with her head, occasionally making attempts to speak, which came out only as sounds. But not agonized sounds, the kind she made when she had an itch somewhere or an unknown ache or a blocked nose that she wanted someone to take care of, but satisfied ones, like the gurgles of a well-fed and burped baby. We smiled, relieved, that she didn't appear to be uncomfortable, that as far as we knew, she wasn't in pain. For this was the best we could aspire to, this was our new normal, Malini observed.

'It little waarm today, no uncle?' Saraswati asked me. 'We take Amma out for walk?' Yes, I said, so Saraswati bundled Mum in some extra shawls, and pulled a monkey cap over her head, and she and Rose lifted Mum into the wheelchair and strapped her in. Then Saraswati 'walked' her in our sliver of garden, doing rounds of the little cobbled pathway around the tiny lawn, which was bald in patches and overgrown in others, Malini having had no time to tend to it for months.

Later, as we sat there in the garden, Malini and Mum and I, Chand and Tara practising how to forge our signatures—'Yours is so easy, Dad!'—and Saraswati massaging Mum's shoulders, Mum took a very long, very deep breath, and she died. We barely noticed, immersed as we were in a conversation about Malini's dad, who, miffed at the special treatment Mum had been getting in hospital, had taken to bed, claiming that he was feeling very ill. It was a conversation Malini and I were having in our tortured Malayalam, to thwart the flapping ears of Saraswati. It was only when Saraswati wailed, 'Something happen for Amma, uncle,' that we noticed that Mum had not just been sighing, but that her head had slumped forward and her eyes had closed.

In the end, it was a liberation, a collective family exhalation of breath at no longer having to see Mum suffer. We immersed her ashes and her room was cleaned—the wheelchair shifted to a corner of the garage, her clothes given away and the room scrubbed to get rid of the smells of Dettol over faeces and Amrutanjan and suffering. Malini's dad was offered the use of the room once again, but now he refused to move, saying that he couldn't summon up the strength to shift from the first to the ground floor.

Flotsam

How does one sort through the debris of a life? It is this I face today. So much has happened since Mum's passing: Brexit and demonetization, #MeToo and #Section377, Donald Trump and Meghan Markle, covfefe and the Kiki challenge. And yet some things are oddly déjà vu: the Babri Masjid/Ram Mandir issue of decades ago continues to dominate political rhetoric, another generation of the Gandhi family campaigns for elections, and Imran Khan is once again on television, albeit leading a country rather than a cricket team. I often find myself wondering what my parents would make of all this—I picture my father quite animated with indignation, my mother shaking her head at the ways of the world but always looking to find a silver lining.

The ancestral land is going up for sale and I have been deputed by my siblings to clear out the minutiae of my parents' lives. Shivan Mama is moving to a one-bedroom flat around the corner, which he says is way too large for his needs, and Vimala Aunty has convinced one of her sons to have her. For years now, Vimala Aunty has been dropping hints about that nice neighbour who has been looking after his parents for thirty years, and the evil acquaintance who left his parents' home to live independently with his wife and children, and every time her sons come to visit she subjects them to multiple viewings of *Baghban*, clicking her tongue at the heartlessness of the fictitious children and the selflessness of their parents. She has been so vociferous about the duties of children to their poor old parents that one of the daughters-in-law had eventually observed that, according to the scriptures, old parents had duties too, one of them being to renounce their worldly life and retire to the jungle, saying which she had casually tossed a map on the coffee table with the nearest forests marked out in red ink.

The sons have been putting up admirable resistance to Vimala Aunty's overtures for years; every time Vimala Aunty visits their homes, even for a few days, she manages to infuriate their wives and annoy their children, and the thought of her being foisted on them permanently makes them quail, Shankaran/Pete had confided to me. But a few months ago, there had been a rather frightening episode when Rajan Uncle had wandered off and gone missing for two days, only to be found sheltering at a nearby shop. When Vimala Aunty had tracked him down, Rajan Uncle had peered at her suspiciously at first, before the mists had cleared and he had declared, 'Ah, my mother has come to fetch me.'

I had found a note in the suitcase that was used to transport Mum's things from Kerala to Chennai and then from Chennai to Bangalore. It was a list of things to do, loose ends to tie up, something she had started writing when she still hoped that she would one day return to her home in Kerala. She had added to it over the months—I can tell by looking at the handwriting, which is progressively spidery and laboured, almost unrecognizable from the assured loopy scrawl I remember, the one that used to fill up the inland letters she sent me every week when we were separated by cities, words running into words as though impatient to reach their destination. There was a list of things she should destroy—useless trinkets, faded pictures and personal letters; a list of things she should bequeath—old Kanjeevarams which would fetch money for their zari borders, some furniture valuable for their vintage, a few pieces of silver and gold, although she had handed over most of it during her lifetime to Sudha and Malini and Maggie and the grandchildren. Later, when it had become apparent that she would never return to her home, she had added instructions for us—where the will was kept, and the nominations for the FDs and post-office savings and the senior citizens' scheme. She wrote that Sudha and I should reimburse ourselves for her medical expenses from whatever money was left before we divided it as per the provisions of the will. She had added that she would perhaps like to give some money from whatever was left to Rose but not Fatima, the Kashmiri girl, the last bit underlined twice. At the end, she had written, almost illegibly, 'and Saraswati'.

Sudha had already descended on the house some months ago to take care of Mum's wishes, to ferret out the pieces of gold and bits of silver that were hidden in aluminium tins of rice and behind books in the bookcase or in the folds of a particular petticoat in the back of the cupboard, to direct the full force of her will at the bankers and post-office staff, and she has already divided up our modest inheritance and sent us our individual demand drafts. It is she who has found a buyer for the land as well, a builder who is going to raze the three houses and build luxury condominiums called, he tells us grandly, Molu's Chalets. He pronounces this as Molu's Shallots.

Now it is time to sort through the flotsam, the knick-knacks of little value, the sunken treasure of submerged memories. Sudha says she cannot handle it; that I will be more detached, less sentimental.

Dad was the hoarder, and his possessions are still squirrelled away in the old wooden trunks in the garage, the battered suitcases in the upstairs room, the space under the landing. Old records, scratched beyond repair. Cans of paint, dried out from years of disuse. A length of clothing line. Bits and pieces of wood left over from various DIY projects. Cardboard boxes and pieces of thermocol from televisions and fridges that are long obsolete. A glass sheet. Some old textbooks, a diary from 1972 that's filled with the household expenses of 1987 written in Mum's expansive hand, with occasional diary entries like 'Vivek submitted his engineering admission forms today'.

Mum had tried to sort through the rubble after Dad's death, but the task had been so overwhelming that she had abandoned the project. 'It's as though I am throwing out a piece of him, you know,' she had said. 'I feel he must be up there, cringing, every time I toss something into the bin.' After a brief pause, she had added, 'Although, to be fair, it wasn't attachment that made your father hang on to things, it was prudence, it was thrift.' She had promised to return to the task when this unusual sentimentality in the wake of Dad's demise had subsided and her customary practicality had been restored, but it appeared she never had.

It is late afternoon before I sort through a bulk of the things. Most I have tossed into black plastic bags destined for the garbage dump; others—a neon-green alarm clock that may or may not work, with stubby legs, a big button on its head and a colourful cartoon of cows in a pasture on its round face, a gramophone that lets out a garbled song, an Eagle flask, a film camera, an HMT watch—I have piled into a cardboard box for Manikandan. Just a handful of items I have retained—our school report cards and certificates, the long-forgotten satin-encased jewellery box that Dad had made for Mum which I think I will hand over to either Sudha or Malini, a notebook that perhaps Prakash would like to have, with recipes for chocolate fudge and American chopsuey in

Mum's hand, some of the pages splashed with mysterious stains like some modern-day culinary scratch 'n' sniff catalogue.

It is the grumbling of my tummy that alerts me to the fact that it is late afternoon, for the sky is overcast and the usually sunlit house is dingy; it is a clammy day here in Kerala, a day that portends rain. I contemplate lunch, but then decide that I will skip it in favour of completing the task, for I have a return flight to Bangalore booked for tomorrow. A bunch of young associates have left our firm to launch their own start-up on the eve of an important presentation, and I have to sweep up the pieces left in their wake. When I see their puppy-like enthusiasm for the mobile app they are developing to aggregate food deliveries, I am alternately envious and cynical—green-eyed at their unsullied innocence that has long passed me by, and yet dubious, almost certain of the pitfalls life is likely to throw in their path.

Only the photographs are left. Dozens of loose ones dumped into plastic packets, old albums of sepia-tinted photographs pasted on black pages and separated by wax paper, more modern albums with the developer's logo emblazoned on the front, where the plastic sleeves have stuck to the photos and have to be peeled away, leaving tell-tale splotches.

I almost miss it, tucked as it is into a fraying A4 brown-paper envelope in which some letter from Govind had been air-mailed home many years ago. I think it must be more loose photographs, and I almost cast them aside, but something makes me look inside. It is a bunch of letters written on blue inland paper, and when I open one, I read, in Dad's handwriting, 'My darling Latha', and I know what it is—those almost mythical love letters that Dad had written to Mum so many years ago. I seesaw between reading further and putting it back in the envelope, and I choose the latter. For safekeeping, I tell myself, against prying eyes. Perhaps

I'll toss it into my office shredder.

As I leaf through the photographs, two fall out from a bunch of others from an ancient plastic bag which says 'Dinesh Stores'— it must have carried home notebooks or a pencil box from Flo-Jo's shop. One photograph is of us in front of our villa, which was still unfinished at that time. Tara is in my arms and Chand is draped around Malini's legs. My hair is still mostly black, Malini still has a bit of baby weight around her.

The other is one of those black-and-white miniatures, two inches by three inches, which suggests that it was perhaps taken in the late Seventies. It is a rare family photo taken on Marine Drive, us leaning against the apple-green Ambassador with the sweep of the Queen's Necklace behind us. We are staring impassively at the lens—no radiant smiles or ironic pouts of this selfie era but that self-conscious stance and the slightly suspicious squint at the camera which said, 'Okay, let's get this over with, quick!' Dad is handsome in his wide-collared bush-shirt, Mum's plait is plump and long, and we are skinny-armed in our matching ill-fitting clothes made from a single bolt of cloth.

It is a photo of such innocence, such youth, such unfulfilled promise. That's what we are, I think—made of different coloured threads and woven by life into different patterns, but part of the same weft and warp, the same tapestry, cut from the same bolt of cloth. It was all those years ago, before life started changing in ways we couldn't imagine, before the well-plotted script of our middle-class lives began to unravel. Who was to know what was to come?

I look back at the photo of my own family in my sliver of garden and wonder: Do Mum and Dad, suspended somewhere in the afterlife, know what awaits us—who Chand will marry, when I will die, how many grandchildren we will have? What's around the corner—death, disease, disappointment? Do they know the answers to those big questions—what is the meaning of life? Where do we go after we die? Does anyone ever buy anything from a telecaller?

I am suddenly exhausted. I decide to keep all the photographs, even the formal portraits of unknown relatives, thinking that one day, perhaps, somebody in the family may want to piece together our story. I drop them into the 'retain' pile and move the garbage bags and the box for Manikandan on to the porch, from where he is to collect them. I take one last look at the house—it looks a bit derelict. The facade is streaked with rainwater, the garden is overgrown, an upstairs window is broken. And it has not heard the sound of chatter, the echo of laughter, the pitter-patter of footsteps in a while.

As I lock up the house, I see that the rain that has been threatening all morning has not yet fallen and, although it is overcast, the sky is beginning to lighten. And as I stand there, jingling the house keys in my pocket and scanning the skies, I see, just beyond the mango tree in the garden and the scaffolding of the building that is coming up at the corner where the grocery store used to be, the one in which Dad had had his last drink of coconut water, that the sun is just beginning to peep out over a sullen rain cloud, lighting up its edges with silver. It makes me smile, this gentle celestial sign, and as I let the gate swing shut behind me, a whistle is just beginning to pucker my weary lips.

Acknowledgements

My sincere thanks to:

Kapish Mehra, Amrita Mukerji, Elina Majumdar and Shambhu Sahu for their faith in the book, Rudra Narayan Sharma for continuing to champion its cause, Ujjaini Dasgupta for meticulous copy-editing, Sourish Mitra, Amrita Chakravorty and Mugdha Sadhwani for the cover design, Raj Kumari for elegant typesetting, Vasundhara Raj Baigra for marketing support, and all the unnamed heroes at Rupa Publications who have helped deliver this obdurate child to the world.

The effervescent Shinie Anthony, selfless mentor to writers new and established, for unstinting advice and guidance, but most of all, for a million laughs.

Dear friend Shubhra Raizada, for throwing light on the workings of the hotel industry—'Prakash' and I thank you for that, and much more.

So many friends in the writing and publishing community who I've been fortunate to meet, for being generous with advice and a helping hand at various points in my writing journey.

To all my readers—your feedback, reviews and messages have kept me going on that long, lonely writing road.

To my husband Raghu and my parents—long-suffering first readers, fact-checkers, cheerleaders, sweepers-up of debris left in the wake of occasional writing funks, and only occasional eye-rollers.

To my sister, Raghu's family, our extended families and friends who are family—for buying my books and attending readings, for 'candied' feedback and spreading the word.

And, not least, to William Shakespeare, whose 'The Seven Ages of Man' from *As You Like It* has lent itself to the titles of the sub-sections in this novel.